INDO

INDO

— ❖ —

Emily Hahn

DOUBLEDAY & COMPANY, INC.

GARDEN CITY, NEW YORK

1963

Library of Congress Catalog Card Number 63–19027
Copyright © 1963 by Emily Hahn Boxer
All Rights Reserved
Printed in the United States of America
First Edition

INDO

CHAPTER ONE

I was waking up but fighting against it every step of the way, with eyes and teeth clenched shut. The thought of Michelle sound asleep in the upper berth kept me from groaning as I would have liked, for things were even worse than usual, and I'm always bad-tempered at first. That was the champagne, I remembered gloomily. Why do people take it for granted that a woman who is practically a non-drinker can nevertheless swallow glass after glass of that? Though they wouldn't have cared what it did to me: they were celebrating because the voyage was almost over, and I had to celebrate getting to Batavia too, willy-nilly, even though I was not at all happy. I'd enjoyed the trip. It was all new and lovely. I'd learned to appreciate the easy life aboard that liner, and I'd met Phil Brewer, who'd been a charming companion. Arrival would mean the end of both, luxury and Phil's company. Certainly neither was a heartbreaking loss (I was feeling better now), but I wasn't glad about it. As for Phil, I'd have it out with him before we disembarked. He'd been less than open with me. I'd have to scold him before parting. To have heard it from Mrs. Vanderlip, of all people on board. That was the worst of it.

"It's such a tragic situation about Mr. Brewer's wife, isn't it?"

She'd said it in the Ladies' off the saloon, while I was brushing my hair. I could see her little eyes in the mirror, aiming at me like twin stilettos while she talked, and I wondered why fat women are always supposed to be good-natured. Mrs. Vanderlip was not good-natured at all; she'd had it in for me all the way from Rotterdam, though she dissembled. She had to hide it because her husband liked me so much. But I could dissemble, too, and now I pretended to be indifferent as I combed and combed my hair. I said:

"I don't really know much about it, I'm afraid. He doesn't like to talk about it."

Not much? I didn't know a thing, not a thing. Phil had behaved like a free man from the very beginning, when he started talking to me on deck the first morning out. He'd been so open about it, in spite of being acquainted with more than half the passenger list, that it simply never crossed my mind he'd had something to hide. But I realized now that it was from me, not his older friends, that he'd concealed whatever it was. Well, what was so surprising about that? It was the old story, I told myself as I pinned back my hair in the smooth curve I always used. The world was in league against me, against all young women alone, and I would do well to remember it. Keeping it in mind, I would always be able to fight back. I shouldn't have let Phil persuade me to forget. I turned and looked Mrs. Vanderlip straight in the eye, and said:

"All right, let's have it."

She looked as startled as if a rabbit had suddenly snarled at her, but the chance was too good to miss, and soon I had it all. Part of it I knew already—how Phil, an American, was a long-time resident in the Indies, where he worked for one of the big oil firms. The part that was news concerned his wife Lily. Mrs. Vanderlip claimed to know Lily, though she hadn't met her for eight years, the American woman having spent most of that time in a nursing home somewhere in the Middle West.

"Breakdown. You know," said Mrs. Vanderlip, and tapped her temple meaningly. "So many of those American girls go off balance, don't you think? Lily Brewer was always too intense. Clubs and good works and card-playing, and so thin, you know; you could have broken her in two." She glanced down complacently at her own pillowed body. "You're another," she put in irrelevantly, "though it's not so bad with you, being short. Lily was a tall girl. And no children, which worried her. Well, there it is, and we're all sorry for Mr. Brewer, because he's a good man. Everybody likes Philip Brewer." Her eyes threatened me again. "We always make allowances," she said, "for a lonely man. We're not narrow-minded in Batavia."

So that was it: I was one of the allowances they were willing to make for poor old Phil. She couldn't have said anything more deadly. I could well imagine what went unsaid: "Pretty little thing. They always are, you know; funny thing how race-mixing always produces pretty girls and weedy men. Of course they do age early . . . I don't care what they may say, I'm on Phil Brewer's side, a lonely man like that, where's the harm in it? It can't make any difference to his wife, that's what I always say."

I had smiled at Mrs. Vanderlip, though I was boiling. We went back together to the men and had more champagne. Yes, of course; that's why I'd had it, one glass after another, as fast as silly old Vanderlip poured it out, until I forgot the conversation altogether, forgot I was furious with Phil, and that I hated old Vanderlip fussing around me. Let him fuss. No matter how much I drank, I still resented his wife. So here I was in the morning with a splitting headache and a bit of unfinished business on my mind, to give Phil Brewer his *congé*. Somehow, though, I wasn't so angry any more. I'd still have to get rid of him, of course, but I wasn't angry. Come to think of it, he wasn't so bad; he hadn't behaved as some men would in the same situation and compromised me. It was only Mrs. Vanderlip's malice that made her behave as she did. Nobody aboard ship could claim to know, without any doubt, that Phil and I had slept together. We'd been careful. *He'd* been careful—a lot depends on the man in cases like this—and I was grateful for that discretion. I hadn't blemished my record, which was a good thing, since

9

today my new life was to start. It was nice to know the slate was clean. Eyes still closed, I stretched out comfortably and my bare leg touched a warm, bare flank.

My God! I jerked the leg back. In spite of the close warmth of the cabin I lay rigid and wrathfully cold. This had never happened before. We'd taken a few risks, but we'd never waked up in the morning in bed together. This was sheer calamity. It was extraordinary that everything else was normal. The shadow swaying back and forth, pendulum-like, across my closed eyes was the same shadow that bothered me every morning, and was cast by the curtain across the crack where our door was propped open for air. I heard a patter of feet on the deck above, and a sailor's shout. All was commonplace, all was at the same time nightmarish. Worst of all was Michelle's regular, ladylike snore, and cold sweat broke out on my face when I thought of what it meant. Michelle was up there where she belonged, and Phil Brewer was down here where he didn't, with me. Horror grew by the second, and my brain kept ticking over. I couldn't imagine how it had happened. I could have sworn I'd gone to bed alone. I'd always slept alone during the last part of the night at least, because of Michelle and because Phil had a single-berth cabin anyway. I'd always, always come back alone. Until last night, of course. . . .

The special shrinking shame that only a hangover evokes was washing over me. I was drowning. I had sinned and hell yawned for me, but I'd done worse than that: I'd let myself be caught. At any moment the steward would bring in morning tea for his two missies, and the secret would be out. Even as I thought of this, Michelle stirred. A rustle of bed-clothes, a tiny "twing" in the mattress like a ghostly harp-string, a cessation of snores. She cheeped like a waking bird. How was I going to fix things with Michelle? We weren't intimate friends; we'd never even met before the voyage, and somehow there had never been time for long cozy chats. Michelle was a good, conventional girl as far as I knew, and I'd been careful in front of her. More chill entered my bones as I thought of what she may have heard in the night, but surely, surely she'd have objected if she'd heard anything? Of course she would. She couldn't have heard, then. I must be *mad.* . . .

The steward's tap sounded at the edge of the open door and Michelle, in a sleep-clogged voice, called, "Come in."

Now for it, I thought. Let Phil cope with the situation, because I can't. I'm paralyzed. Eyes squeezed shut, I waited and cowered and heard the chink of the tea things. I seemed to wait a long time, but nothing happened. No gasp, no apology, just silence. I thought that the stewards aboard the liner were pretty cool, to say the least: of course one takes into account that they must see a lot of funny business. Still— curiosity pried my eyes open at last, but they immediately closed again as I lay back in sick relief. I was alone in the bed. What my leg had found was a fat, sun-warmed bolster, the sort called in Asia a Dutch wife.

"Julie? What are you giggling about down there?" asked Michelle.

Phil leaned against the rail and looked down at me, shaking his head indulgently. He'd laughed, but he was a little shocked too by my laughter. He had strange ideas about women: he felt they should not be humorous about lovemaking. He said:

"You're a bad girl sometimes. But what a story!"

"It was just as much your fault as mine."

"Only in your filthy little mind," he said fondly, and we turned together to see how the ship was progressing toward shore. Java was still some distance away, but she could be seen; a shadow that had been blue and was now growing more and more green. "Tanjong Priok," Phil said, pointing. "That's the harbor for Batavia." The scented wind in my hair I accepted as a prophecy of some undefined happiness. That wind had tinged the salty atmosphere several days before we sighted any of the islands, and now it was quite strong. I thought I could even separate the ingredients of the smell. I said:

"Listen, Phil, and see if I have it right—the smell of Java, I mean. Sniff it. Lemon blossom, cough medicine, cooking spices?"

"That's not bad for a beginner. You've left out the durian, though."

"No I haven't. There wouldn't be any durian at this season."

"What a girl. You know such a lot, don't you? You talk like an old-timer." He paused and looked at me speculatively, teasingly. "You still maintain none of your family was ever out here?"

I said tersely, "Absolutely." The strain in my voice could not be helped, and he noticed it and was surprised. Regretting it, I could not stop; I followed it up with more mistakes. I said defiantly, "I knew about durians from the school geography book. Everybody knows about durians—any schoolteacher, at any rate." When he remained silent I actually stamped my foot. "I've never been in Java before!" I said shrilly. "Never, do you hear?"

"Steady, steady." Phil took my arm in his firm hand and held on though I tried to pull away. "I'm sorry, baby; it was only a joke. Don't get so excited. Seriously, Julie—don't you think it's silly to go on fighting against this? It's no secret, is it? Not really. Anybody could see, who looks at you."

"See what?" I hung my head and watched the toe of my shoe, drawing small circles on the deck. My few seconds of unreasoning panic had subsided: he'd misunderstood, and everything was all right. But I wouldn't make it easy for him. Impatiently he shook the imprisoned arm.

"That you're an Indo," he snapped. "What's wrong with that, anyway?"

"Nothing, I suppose." I made my voice sulky, not that I really cared whether or not he spoke of it.

"It's written all over your face," said Phil. "All over, and

12

very nice too. Those big brown eyes, that little nose"—he dropped my arm and tapped the end of my nose softly, as if caressing it—"and the sweet little chin; darling, if you ever had any wild idea you could keep it secret out here, it's time you gave it up. These islands are full of Indos." He waited for a reply, but I had nothing to say. "Damn it," he said, "I never meant to hurt any feelings: I had no idea you'd be sensitive about it. People aren't usually. Come on, stop pouting, won't you?"

I smiled at him, blinking as if my eyes were wet. "I'm sorry I was foolish, and I'm not sensitive about it, really I'm not. I suppose I behaved that way because—oh well, you know. Growing up as I did in an orphan's home—"

"Sure, I understand." He didn't, however. I went on:

"It just reminded me, that's all, when you teased me. I wouldn't be so touchy if I knew more about where I come from, but I don't even know who my father was, do you see?"

"Oh Lord, of course I do. Julie, I'm sorrier than I can say. If I'd had the slightest idea—"

"As for being a Eurasian, well, of course I know I must be: everybody thinks the same. The girls used to mention it, but they were orphans too, we were all in the same boat and I didn't mind with them."

Phil said uneasily, "You don't need to say another word, baby."

"No, I want to now. My mother was—was in domestic service, and she wasn't married that we know of, and she died when I was a baby, and there you are. Now you know everything."

Our colloquy was so absorbing that we failed to notice we were being nearly swamped by an eruption of passengers, rushing to the rail to see the rapidly clearing coast. At that moment I felt friendlier toward Phil than I had ever done since I'd met him, and I had liked him from the beginning. He was gentle, he was intelligent, he was reasonably unselfish—it was a pity that we were about to say goodbye. I suddenly remembered that he didn't know that as yet.

13

I looked up to tell him, and saw his forehead creased in a worried expression. Obviously his confession was on the way.

"Darling," he said, "there isn't much time, and I've got something I ought to have told you long ago. I'm wondering how to put it."

I spoke quickly, and as coolly as I could manage. "If you're talking about your wife Lily, don't bother." He started and began to turn red. "I heard about it last night, *all* about it," I hurried on. "I didn't want to say anything until you did, but of course it means we can't go on seeing each other."

"I had an idea you'd feel that way," he muttered.

"Of course I feel that way. Goodbye, Phil. Don't come to see me, please, and don't ring up."

"Oh, hell," said Phil. "It's so— Well, never mind. I see your point."

He turned away, but not very far: at that moment we were attacked and overwhelmed by the Vanderlips. Mr. Vanderlip bellowed genially: "The little missie! And Mr. Brewer close at hand, as always. Are we interrupting a fond farewell? Good! You can't expect to keep her all to yourself. We too want to say goodbye." There were handshakes all round, and then Phil escaped: a moment later Mrs. Vanderlip took her noisy husband away and I was left alone in the current of hurrying people. The engines ceased abruptly and the deck no longer throbbed underfoot. A moment later the current was dammed by a new crowd of relatives and friends swarming aboard, carrying flowers that were squashed in embraces, shoving toys and sweets at puzzled small children, squealing and even crying. Adults wept, Javanese servants wept, children wept in fright and discomfort—never in my life had I seen so much display of sentiment. The sun seemed to elicit it even from members of a cold Northern race, I reflected, and my detachment wouldn't long be proof against this infection, so I went below, where it was quiet, to pick up handbag and coat. I hardly recognized the cabin. Michelle had taken her things and gone. The beds were stripped. There were no flowers left. All was empty, and I suddenly thought of another empty, bare little room, the one I occupied at the home. I've never said I was violently unhappy there, but I didn't particularly want to be reminded of it on that day of all days, so I went back to the deck.

It was not so crowded now. A long serpent of passengers moved slowly down the gangplank, quickening pace when they came to the bottom, and scattering into the customs shed. They seemed to take with them all the fun and color of the voyage. It happened that I saw no familiar faces among them, and I had a fancy that the whole thing—the quick little friendships, the parties and laughter—had been a dream. No doubt Phil was gone with the others; no doubt someone he knew had come to meet him, and he'd left me to take up my old life, my single, third-class passage. . . . Catching myself back from the brink of self-pity, I hurried to join the serpent and disembark. I hoped Mrs. Vanderlip was gone. I didn't want her to see me moving off the ship all dismal-looking and alone. Creeping along gave me time for day-dreaming, and I filled it with an imaginary dialogue between Mrs. Vanderlip and me. I imagined her calling me a poor little thing, and saw myself retorting, crushingly, "I'm quite all right, you silly woman; my mother is looking after me." It was just as well the exchange wasn't real. I decided then. She would think me a lunatic if I really said that, which was bad enough, or a religious mystic, which was worse. At the orphans' home we didn't hold with religious mysticism.

I can't say with assurance just when I decided that I knew who my mother was. Naturally I heard of her, though not as my mother. Even we orphans heard about Holland's most famous, villainous spy. In a perverse way, a lot of quiet, law-abiding people were probably proud of her because she was Dutch. The name of Mata Hari had become part of the language, and it would be credible if I'd adopted her without any true claim to relationship. Children do such things, especially when they are children without settled relatives of their own. One orphan in our dormitory used to insist she was a royal princess, heir to the throne, and nobody objected or disputed her word; why shouldn't she inherit the throne if that's what she wanted? The only reason I didn't make equally extravagant claims was that I had a faint, glimmering memory that somehow got in the way. I knew I hadn't made up what I remembered, and I also realized it was too fragmentary to talk about, just a scene or two floating in darkness, of a beautiful woman with heavy dark hair and a warm flushed face, laughing down at me where I lay in a low bed. I rather think I was crying at the time, because she was coaxing me in a loving way, but that bit of the vision isn't clear.

It was a sweet fragment and I treasured it, but it wouldn't have sounded like much next to the Lost Princess's story or the others one heard at the orphanage, so I never talked about my mother until one day a long time afterwards. By that time all the others had forgotten the old game of pretending, but to me, with my private store unexpended, my mother was as real as ever. In fact she had become more real. I must have thought of her as non-orphans thought of their parents, as something alive, reliable, and protective. That must be why I invoked her name on the morning an assistant matron boxed my ears for some deed I hadn't committed. It seemed perfectly natural to shout at her:

"I'll show you! I'll tell my mother on you!"

This is one threat never heard in an orphanage, and the matron laughed. It wasn't a kind laugh, but she was not cruel either, and wouldn't have said what she did if she'd thought I could understand it. I didn't, not really, but I kept it in mind: "Your mother! That's good, that is. Why, your mother learned how to behave from the devil himself." She paused, and added in a quieter tone that meant she was talking to herself, "Never mind her; she's where she can't do any more harm."

As a child does, I soon forgot to be angry any more. I might have forgotten more than anger, given time enough, but that afternoon when I was playing alone near the kitchen, bouncing a ball on the packed dirt that surrounded this part of the house, I heard the matron's voice again. She was chatting with the cook and the baker's boy, whose bicycle I saw propped against the wall outside. First I couldn't make out any words; my eavesdropping was idle, for want of something more interesting to do. The matron said something that made the cook laugh in a startled, shocked way. Then she said something about somebody named "Mata Hari," which sounded strange and pretty, and went on, ". . . shocking when you think she came from this very district, and we're left with the pieces to pick up, as it were."

"That poor little thing." That was the cook, in a protesting tone.

A short silence followed, and then the matron resumed: "She went to school to the devil himself."

Again the cook made a protesting sound, but it was the baker's boy who spoke. "Oh well, it's all over now and she can't do any more harm where she is." Two pious murmurs applauded him. "It seems a waste," he added quietly. "She was beautiful, beautiful."

"Talking about my mother," I thought, and calmly went on bouncing my ball.

Would I have been different, I wonder, if I'd never overheard this gossip and put it together to satisfy myself? I don't think so. I agree with the Javanese idea that whatever we do, whatever happens to us, is a detail of a larger pattern. We may think we hold our fate in our own hands, but we don't. For some time my only reaction to this incident was spite against the assistant matron. In every way a child can I took revenge; little ways, stealing her pencil or mislaying her letters when I got the chance. In time I forgot exactly why she was my enemy, but the one-sided feud lent sauce to an otherwise dull existence until that, too, lost its savor. I was growing up.

If the experts are right and security is all a young creature needs, we orphans were well taken care of. Nothing altered around us, with the exception of the staff. The solid redbrick house, smelling indoors of cooking and soap; the cut and color of our uniforms, the severe Sunday ritual remained unshaken. We were the changing element. Girls flourished or languished, though they were for the most part healthy. Girls caught whooping cough and measles and chicken pox. New little girls arrived, and grown-up girls departed, in such ceaseless rotation that the aging of our guardians was almost imperceptible in comparison. Still, they did age. My enemy the matron was replaced, and so was the Head herself, but these were landmarks, not part of the routine. It was by routine that I matured, passing through the regulation fat stage and the thin. Routine took me into the awkward age when I was too big for my clothes, for my bed, for the whole orphanage, and then, mercifully, routine brought me out. Suddenly I was small again, a thin little maiden for whom surroundings had changed in the oddest fashion. Now men looked at me, made way for me in crowded streets, carried my basket, and seized chances to talk with me. I did not reject their help, but I liked them no better for giving it. We of the orphans' home didn't care for men, knowing as we did how many of us owed our presence there to men who had ducked their responsibilities. Even our legitimately born girls, who had been orphaned by death and not neglect, took on the bitter philosophy of the others, summed up in one short sentence: "You can't trust them."

We knew too much. We knew that the same thing might happen again to one of us; any of us, if unguarded, might produce an orphan of her own. Oh, decidedly one was better off without men, and if I spared my own father, whoever he was, from this condemnation, it was only that I preferred not to consider my mother a victim of anyone. *My* mother was a conqueror, not a victim.

When I was seventeen and had more freedom, I fulfilled an ambition I'd cherished for several years. I went alone to the city, to the library, where the public had access to newspaper files. I could scarcely believe I'd accomplished it at last when the attendant brought out the old copies I asked for, and there was danger that I might tear the yellow, brittle pages, my hands shook so. I sat back and waited a minute until I was calm, then got to work. After all that, success was no surprise. There she was. Whether I really did recognize her I can't honestly swear, but I thought I did: I was convinced that my mother and I, in the musty air of the reading room, were looking at each other again after many years. Yes, I knew those searching eyes and that heavy dark cloud of hair. Of course I knew them.

The text accompanying the photographs was of secondary importance, but I read it, I took it in, and felt no shame. Whatever she had done was right. The important thing was that I had certainty. I wasn't alone any more.

It had been a fancy of this wicked woman, said the article, to claim Javanese ancestry, but the writer scouted this claim as an outright lie. He said she had built up the legend quite cynically, to enhance her stage personality. She performed in European night clubs and at recitals as a native dancer from the East Indies, and in her adopted guise she had more success than an ordinary Dutchwoman would have gained; it was a less sophisticated age than ours. Scoffingly he added that this Eastern stuff was all based on the few years Mata Hari had actually spent, or misspent, in Java.

"Her infatuation with the Orient, however, was genuine in one respect," he commented. "It was common knowledge that the lady didn't scruple to take native lovers, in the Indies, and, later, in Europe."

Chiming bells reminded me that the library would soon close, and I would be expected at the home. They supposed me to be reading for a term paper and I would have to fake the material I hadn't collected, but I was equal to the task. I was a quick student, and in the past year I had become the prize senior pupil, recommended for a scholarship at the Teachers' Training College. Altogether I was a privileged inmate. Without panic I strolled to the station and found the train, settled down in it, and gave myself again to thoughts of the last newspaper story I had read. I resented it more than all the others. I said to myself:

"If that reporter knew as much about her as he pretended, it's strange he didn't know more. For all his digging he didn't find *me*." Probably he'd made up a lot of the material, I decided. But what was the use of wasting feeling on him? It was a long time ago, and he was only one of the whole crowd of vultures who had pecked at the scandal. I turned to thoughts of my own small world, at the Home: they knew about me, but did any of them give thought to it now? The Head, with her unsmiling face, was equally cold to all of us: one couldn't tell what she was thinking. As for the teachers who petted and were proud of me, hardly any of them had been there when I arrived. Still, they must know. Scandals lose their freshness, but they aren't forgotten altogether.

An old man climbed awkwardly into the coach and limped, using his stick, to the seat opposite. He had a yellowish mustache and wore thick-lensed spectacles, through which he looked at me. Paternally, he smiled. I made a frightful grimace in reply and returned to my thoughts. In less than a year I would be leaving the home, scholarship or no scholarship. What should I do if I failed to get it? But I was fairly confident I would, and I thought comfortably that teaching was far more to my taste than stenography, or selling things in a shop. Yes, I liked teaching. Several times I'd been sent into our primary classroom to practice. The teacher would hand it all over to me and leave the room, and it went pretty well. I really enjoyed it. I knew I found pleasure in getting inside a young mind, persuading the child to figure out problems. There was satisfaction in knowing I mattered to someone. And the child profited too; if a child doesn't have affection for you, dependence, he won't learn from you. I reflected that I would never take the same pride in teaching older students.

At the station before mine, the old man stood up to go. It may not have been his destination: possibly he just wanted to get out of the coach. His cheeks were still flushed from the snub. He kept his face averted as he clambered out, but I was waiting, maliciously. Catching his glance as the window glided past him where he hobbled along on the platform, I made a worse face than before. "Dirty old man," I said to myself as I sat back in triumph. "Serve him right." It seemed impossible that I should ever care for one of those creatures. I think of him now and then, and I'm sorry. I'm sorry.

I was eighteen and had won my scholarship. We, the departing senior class, went through the customary ceremonies. In Sunday white with blue pinafores we met in the chapel and sang and said prayers. One of my more idiotic colleagues actually cried and wiped her eyes. I couldn't understand her. What did it all mean but moving from one institution to another? What I did wait for with impatience was next morning, when, before we took our bags and left, we met with the Head, each of us alone, in her office. It was her custom to do this, to hold one last interview with her charges, and though in many cases it was the first interview as well, she took her duty seriously. "Just a little general talk," was how she described it, but I knew better: the Head discussed very personal matters indeed—one's past and one's future. What was she going to bring out of the hat when she talked to me?

Like people outside a dentist's office the departing class waited, nervous and fidgeting. One by one, as our names were called, we went in. A girl named Lilianne, who was pretty and silly, came out from her share of the Head's time in a pink, giggling state. Her hand cupped around her mouth, she whispered to me on her way to the passage, "You'll never guess what *I* got. Advice on the facts of life!" As she vanished, the others crowded around to get the news from me. "Oh no!" they cried, and "Incredible!" There was so much giggling that the secretary had to rap her desk loud to attract our obedient attention.

"Julie, if you *don't* mind. You're wanted; Julia de Jong. Please, young ladies."

Inside the Head's office I lost all desire to laugh. I stood solemnly in the middle of the floor, noticing in spite of my tension that the room bore evidence of weaknesses I wouldn't have expected in that awesome woman: curtains of a sentimental rosebud pattern and any number of family photographs, including babies. She let me go on standing for a while, because she was—rather ostentatiously—absorbed in the study of a large book lying on the desk. Seen upside down from my point of view it looked like a hotel ledger, with marked-off spaces that were lined and interlined with entries of writing in different hands and different inks.

"Sit down, Julia," she said at last, her eyes still on the ledger. I felt impatient. Why should she make such a show of reading that record when she must have been familiar with everything in it? Then I realized that she, too, was wondering what she was going to say to me, and my heart beat faster.

Sighing, she began to read out loud, indicating the portion of squeezed-in script with her finger. "Julia de Jong," she said impressively, as if in quotation marks. Dropping into a normal tone she continued, "I'm reading your official record, Julie. Your mother's name is"—a pretense of reading—"de Jong, Margrethe. Unmarried." Afraid of a pause at this point she went too fast, continuing. "Occupation, housemaid. Age twenty-nine . . . That's all it says here."

The decision, then, had been made and I was to be told nothing. I couldn't accept it; I couldn't leave it at that. Yet the only protest I could make, in my position, was a feeble-sounding question: "Really is that all? What about my father?"

"Your father's identity appears to be unknown. That is what they've written here—'Father's name unknown.'"

I stared at her, but my defiance melted when I saw that the redoubtable woman was confused. If it hadn't been the Head I might even have thought her afraid. She said, gently:

"I'm sorry, Julia. Do you know, this is the hardest thing about my job, the very hardest. It might help if you'll remember that none of this is your fault. Nobody worth your friendship is going to care how your parents behaved.

Whatever the Scriptures may say about the sins of the fathers. . . .

The woman had depths I had never suspected, but at the moment her character meant nothing to me: I was furiously angry at her lies and her pity. For there was no doubt she pitied me, and I considered it an impertinence. I was no pitiable object. I was enviable. The Head thought I didn't know about my fascinating mother; she wanted to pull me down to her own level, but I was too wise for that. I would be even wiser; I would conceal my knowledge. So I asked with quiet self-control:

"Then she didn't tell anyone at all about my father? It doesn't seem natural, in a—a housemaid, does it?"

The Head looked down at the desk, at her fingers, busy lining and realigning pencils. "When I say she didn't speak or confide in anyone, I mean, of course, that she divulged none of this to persons in authority. Her friends knew, no doubt, but in many of these cases the officials don't know a girl's friends. Even today with the almoner system it's not easy, if a girl in trouble is determined to keep her secret." Her smooth voice carried persuasion that almost hypnotized me. I could see and believe in that wretched, scared housemaid, Margrethe, big face blotched with tears, stout country-girl's body that had lost whatever waistline it possessed, and a shabby black suitcase waiting on the matting as she answered the official questions in a sulky voice. Yes, a girl like that wouldn't be likely to make new friends easily, or trust the women she'd turned to for help when there was nowhere else to go. Somewhere in the background, without doubt, was a peasant who would be furious with his sinful daughter if he knew the facts. . . .

I jerked myself out of the unpleasant daydream. Margrethe de Jong had never existed. She was a figment, a myth, an invention of the Head's predecessor, and I blessed my luck that this was so. I would have hated to own Margrethe as a mother.

The Head was going on with her explanation, her words

23

softly pushing me toward acceptance. It was no use, but I
didn't say so. "You can be sure the authorities did what they
could, and made a record of everything they knew. It was
in their own interest as well as yours. If a claim can be
made for maintenance, you see . . . Look, Julia, I'm going to
give you every scrap of what we have here, though I'm not
required to. According to the record your mother brought
you to the home when you were not quite three years old,
saying she could no longer manage to support a child, at
least not for a while. She declared that she was going to,
well, to Amsterdam, to take a job there. She would try to
get a place that would furnish accommodation for you as
well."

"Yes. I suppose she was never heard of again." This feck-
lessness seemed in character for Margrethe, I reflected, but
the Head said:

"Oh yes, she did try. She wrote to the people here quite
regularly. It lasted about a year—no, fourteen months—before she dropped out of sight." Though I kept my eyes down,
I felt her keen gaze. "Almost certainly, Julia, she died without telling anyone in Amsterdam that she had a child. It
would be the natural thing to do, if she wasn't aware she
was dying. If you had seen as many of these cases as I have—"

I didn't want to hear the word "case" again, even applied
to an imaginary mother. Quickly I stood up. "I'm very grateful to you for telling me all this . . . You're absolutely certain
there's nothing anywhere in that book indicating who my
father might have been?"

She shook her head implacably, giving me at the same
time a bright flashing look as if she could have said something but wouldn't. I had an idea what the unspoken remark
was: "Whoever he was, he couldn't have been a European."
Something like that. She needn't have felt qualms about saying it. My companions in the orphanage had never felt the
slightest delicacy, and we laughed about it together. Still, it
was written in the ledger, "Unknown," and Unknown he must
remain. By law.

Some of the young women who were at college with me still talk as if those days were wonderfully happy. Given the chance they would do it all again, which is an attitude I don't share. There is little about my life in Holland that I would want to repeat in any case. My college days weren't bad, but they weren't good either: I didn't ask myself if I was happy, because happiness was not the point of a training college. One trained. One heard a stated number of lectures and wrote examinations and read and worked; at the end of this program one started out in the business of living, and that end couldn't come too soon to suit me. I looked with wonder and hidden contempt at the girls who were all too glad to stop working in favor of flirting and serious love affairs. They weren't types like those I had known at the orphanage. Their frivolity puzzled me, and they were equally puzzled by my lack of it. I shared a room with a lively girl, Ellie, who tried harder than any of the others to bring me around to what she considered a normal state. I remained stubborn until one evening when she lost her temper.

"What *is* the matter with you, Julie? Just grinding on, day after day; it doesn't make sense."

I said, "I don't want to go to the party, that's all. For one thing I haven't a dress fit for it."

"Yes you have. Your blue one's quite all right, and you know it. You always give some excuse. Sometimes I wonder if you're human."

I admit I enjoyed holding off like this. It gave me a queer little sensation of superiority. I raised my eyebrows and went on studying, or at least gave the appearance of studying. As Ellie said no more but continued to get ready as noisily as possible, I added, "It's just that I wouldn't enjoy dancing with a lot of pimply boys. I really haven't any use for boys."

"They're not pimply, but I begin to believe you. I think you're fundamentally cold, even though you don't look it, and it's a wicked waste having so much magnetism when you don't get any fun out of it." Ellie rubbed indignantly at her nose with a piece of paper guaranteed to remove the shine.

"Magnetism?" I said inquiringly.

"Or galvanism, or whatever you call it. Sex appeal anyway. You're full of it; Professor Muller can't keep his hands off you. It's a regular joke among us. The way men turn around and look again when you go past them—we've noticed that, too. One woman can't tell about another, but we can see how the men react."

"Nonsense. I'm no beauty."

Ellie agreed with unflattering swiftness, but added that it made no difference. "Look at Berta. She's a genuine beauty, she's taken prizes for it, but you'll notice Professor Muller never pats *her* hair."

"He couldn't reach up that far," I retorted absently. Ellie laughed and dribbled cologne water on her arms. It smelled of lilies of the valley. At the same moment a mild spring breeze blew through the window and stirred the hair on my forehead, and suddenly I felt such a rush of undirected longing that I couldn't bear it. Fierce and sweet and inexplicable, it shook me. The room was a prison. I threw down my pen.

"Ellie," I said, "may I change my mind and come?"

And so I met Martin. This late in the day I can't explain why it should have happened as it did; why my careful little program should have been turned topsy-turvy by a rather stupid young man. I might blame Ellie's cologne scent, but I don't blame anything or anyone, and I don't repine. Sooner or later someone like Martin had to happen to me. Sometimes I visit the memory as if to see if it hurts any more, as you might poke your tongue into a tooth that used to ache. The only thought that makes me wince today is that he wasn't worth all that emotion. If he hadn't been quite so obvious a seducer, if only I'd held him off a little longer . . . But why need we treat the great battles like child's games, to be played according to certain rules? I didn't lose and Martin didn't win, not by my philosophy, though I daresay he keeps somewhere in his brain a scoreboard with girls' names on it. If so, mine is written there with a very few points in my favor against many in his. No matter, I wasn't playing

26

for points: it was no game as far as I was concerned. It never was, from the minute I saw him at the dance, ruddy and handsome and sure of himself. I was knocked out. I can well understand why the French call such a moment a lightning-stroke, how can I describe it better? His particular voice, his eyes, the smell of him when we danced close together—words are no good: I was struck by lightning and that's it. Of course after that it made no difference how much Ellie warned me. I didn't listen. Everyone in the world could have told me the truth about Martin—that he was spoiled because his father was rich, that he was the dream of all the little shop-girls, that he was lazy and thoroughly selfish—but I wouldn't have listened, because I knew more important truths about him. I couldn't hear: I was unable to hear anything but celestial music.

I won't dwell on the story because it doesn't amount to more than an incident, and was brutally short. Martin made love to me and I was more than ready to be made love to. The word "seduction" scarcely applies. It must have been this readiness of mine that surprised and shocked him, and caused him to turn away so soon. My technique was wrong, as Ellie often told me later. A girl who goes headlong into an affair as I did is bound to lose.

"Lose what?" I demanded, the first time she used the expression. "Do you mean this was a sort of contest?"

"Yes," said Ellie. I turned away wearily.

"I don't know. I don't know what to think any more . . . Yes, I do. I've been stupid and loving and passionate—"

"Please don't talk like that," Ellie begged me. "You make me feel it's my fault. It was that party I dragged you to that started it all."

"If a person's a fool, she doesn't need help to act like one," I pointed out. "I've been luckier than I deserve. I might very well have gone and got pregnant in the bargain."

And then in the stress of the moment I did something I had never in my life done before. I told Ellie who my mother was. She was so shocked that she began to cry . . .

27

But none of this is important and I'm never going to chew it over again. It was finished long ago. Before Ellie completed the second year of the course she was married, and by this time must have forgotten all about me. Martin too married, the daughter of a factory owner in the South, and their first child was two months early. I went back to work and got first place in the finals. It wasn't hard because I had a goal to lure me on, though the principal wasn't pleased when she heard what the goal was.

"The colonies? Why in the world? You'll be wasted out there. Of course it sounds very glamorous, but those places are backwaters really; it's my opinion the government uses the East Indies as a dumping ground for all their incompetents. Why not stay here, Julia? You'd do well in this profession. I wouldn't say so if I didn't mean it."

Respecting the principal as I did, I wanted to give her a straight answer, but it wasn't all that clear even to me, so I stammered a bit. The name of Java had a strong pull. It had, probably, ever since I read that nasty newspaper story in the library. Only Martin had put it out of my head, and then for merely a short time. My mother had loved Java, and if the appearance of her child meant anything at all, she had loved a Javanese. I felt that I must see the island for myself. Since it was impossible to say anything of this to the principal, I muttered something instead about personal reasons.

"Yes, yes, of course, I understand perfectly," she said, at once fluttered and appeased. "How stupid of me not to have realized! You have relatives there, no doubt?"

"No doubt," I said agreeably. She made no more objections.

Because, as I have said, I respected the principal, I took her advice and did not hurry with my application to go abroad. She wanted me to have experience at home for two years, and I complied. It was valuable training. A teacher of children gets a peculiarly intimate view of their homes; more than doctors and hospital nurses, teachers are involved in the everyday lives and backgrounds of children. These contacts wouldn't have added much to the knowledge of a person raised like most other people, with parents and a private family life, but to me all that had been a closed world. If I hadn't seen it while I was still young enough to be impressed, I might have gone on thinking with yearning sentimentality of all I have missed. Many of the orphans thought the existence of non-orphans was like the domestic scene familiar to us only on Christmas cards and storybook illustrations: Papa and Mamma surrounded by loving children, or loving children playing together agreeably, perhaps with a baby to fill out the circle. Closeness, clannishness, coziness were what we had never possessed and bitterly missed. We thought people who live together in families must of course be happy the day long, and dreamed away our frustrations in thoughts of how safe and comfortable we would be cuddled in Mamma's or Papa's arms. A lot of orphans grew up with these dreams unchanged. When, in a hurry to achieve this paradise for themselves, they married, reality must have come as a shock. I was spared all that. I saw family life at close quarters, and rapidly shed childish regrets.

More and more I admired my mother—or rather the idea I had built up about her—for having scorned the false safety of domesticity. She had gone out into the unwalled world, beautiful and wild as a leopard, and taken what she wanted. . . . I saw marriages with love and those without, and there was not as much difference as I had been taught. I saw husbands and wives telling lies to each other, and men and women struggling against each other for power. Often one would manage to ignore the existence of the other by wrapping him in habit, like a silkworm in a cocoon, so that no sharp corners were left. In these households of self-absorbed parents, children went their own way as children do, along the same path we orphans had traveled. They, too, quarreled and defended themselves, but there was one difference: a child in a private home occasionally trotted back to its mother, like a lamb in the field, to make sure she was there and the world was still the same. When I saw this happen I did feel a little envy, but not of the child.

The months went by. I did my work conscientiously, and saved my money, and had a lover—or two—perhaps even three: it didn't matter. None were like Martin, and I was glad of it; it was good to know that nobody ever again would be like Martin. I was free of love. With this assurance I found it possible for the first time to like men, to grow fond of them as I grew fond of Phil Brewer. I was free, too, to forget them as I now forgot him, stepping ashore into a warm spicy fragrance, the new world of Java. I moved slowly toward the customs house, while the sun beat down on my head. The small barefoot men hurrying back and forth were like old friends. I saw a bit of the coastline beyond the dock buildings, and it should have been riotous with color—yellow, green, blue—but the sun's immoderation took away ferocity from everything else. Java was vivid but tender. I said softly:

"Mother, here I am."

CHAPTER TWO

Within the rim of the great earthen pot, mosquitoes stood motionless on the surface of the water until they were disturbed by the dipping tin, then rose in an angry swarm, fleeing in all directions. I stood naked and shivering on the tiled floor and splashed myself, trying to wake up. The water always felt icy at that time of morning, but mosquitoes no longer worried me as they had done, and though it was chilly in the damp little bathroom I knew it would soon be warm— all too soon. A few minutes later, clothed, I called the servant who was sitting on his heels outside the bedroom door, and he appeared promptly as a genie. He walked as servants did in Java, bent over at the waist as if in expectation of a beating.

"*Tabe, njonja.*"

For a week or so after I arrived, the servility of Javanese domestics had startled and outraged me, but that too had passed, like the sensitivity to mosquito bites. After all, as my colleague Agatha pointed out in her commonsensical manner, it wasn't as if these people were like the Siamese, who actually got down on their knees and bumped the floor with their heads.

"It's merely a convention, and means no more than other conventions," said Agatha. So now, completely accustomed to so much respect, I gave directions to the *djongos* like a haughty Roman matron. Such habits had grown on me, as had the whole color of life; visiting the club late in the day as everybody in my circle did; swimming there in the pool, sitting at bright little tables for drinks, dancing every Saturday night; these activities were made not only possible but delightful by the scores of servants everywhere. They kept the pool sweet and clean, they polished the tables and floors, they brought the drinks, and—what was most important of all—they were simply there, to emphasize our height by their lowliness. The ambience of it went to the head like brandy, until, without being aware of the addiction, you had to have it. But I would have been shocked if anyone had told me this.

"This is for the wash, *djongos*," I said.

"Yes, *njonja*."

"Tell Bibi to mend that tear very carefully, you hear?"

"Yes, *njonja*."

"The white shoes for this evening."

"*Njonja* . . ."

The poor working girl's day, Batavia style, had begun.

In the hostel dining room where I went for morning coffee I took for granted, as I took the servants, the airy place shining with cleanliness and fragrant with new-gathered flowers and hot fresh bread. Several other women were there ahead of me. We said good morning, but chatter did not prevail at that early hour. Phil would never believe it, I reflected: he was firmly of the opinion that women gathered together always talked their heads off.

"That must be the worst of your setup there, Julie. The Virgins' Retreat! I don't know how you can stand it," he'd said the evening before when we were driving back after dinner.

"It's not bad."

"It must be bad. It must be awful. Nothing but feminine chat about clothes and men, isn't it? You must get bored to the teeth with all that female business, because even if you don't look it, inside that pretty head is a pretty good brain."

32

I rose to the bait, as he'd wanted me to: "They all have good brains, Phil, or they wouldn't hold the jobs they do." Phil's laugh kept me going, more sharply: "I know what you really don't like about the hostel: it's a place I can find refuge in."

He grunted, and I settled back proudly, having drawn blood. My choice of living quarters was the main source of friction between us. Though I'd surrendered and thrown away my shipboard resolution about never seeing him again—for, to be frank, those first empty days in a strange city had worn me down so that I was delighted to hear his voice on the telephone—I wasn't exactly easygoing any more. Our friendship was nothing like the carefree, intimate relationship of the voyage. Our love-making was held down—by me—to a strict minimum of occasions. I hedged the meetings with a lot of demands for secrecy; whenever he protested, I reminded him that a girl in my position must be careful. More than once we quarreled over this and Phil sometimes walked out on me in a rage. But he always came back.

After a pause he reverted to good-humored teasing, no doubt thinking it the best way to handle me. "You'll be telling me next that you all conduct intellectual debates there, at the Retreat," he said.

"As a matter of fact, we do. We had a lecture the other night, while you were away in Surabaya. A journalist from home gave us a talk on the political situation, and we had questions afterwards and a discussion. Do you know, it's really hard to keep all those funny associations and movements separated."

Phil nodded. "I've found the same thing myself, but you needn't spread that around; I'm supposed to be the expert in the office, and write reports on it. So don't let the boys know how dumb Brewer is. What did your journalist say about things? How do they look to him?"

"He didn't give an opinion about that. We were talking about past history. Anyway, nothing's going on just now, is it? Everything's quiet."

"Oh, is that what he said?" His tone was so sardonic that I answered it rather than the question.

"I'm sure it's been quiet enough since I got here, Phil. What do you mean?"

"Oh, I grant you Batavia's quiet enough. Why shouldn't it be, with all those islands outside where the police can pack off the troublemakers? Yes, I guess you could call it quiet."

The intricacies of Indies politics seemed very remote. I tried to think of the *djongos* in revolutionary mood, and found I couldn't do it. It was hard to believe in those dissentients Phil was referring to—Hatta, Sukarno, and the others with outlandish names—being a threat to security, being taken out of town for disturbing the peace. Still, it happened.

"Phil, have you ever seen any riots yourself?"

"No, not to say serious outbreaks, though we had some strikes over in Sumatra at the refinery while I was training. It was a long time ago."

"Was it scary?"

"No-o, hardly scary. Lily got a bit upset, but nothing happened. They're pretty tractable people when you treat them right." He had lost interest in the subject; his hand was creeping up my leg, patting and exploring. I shoved it away vigorously.

"You pay attention to your driving, and don't start that, because there's nothing we can do about it."

"Why can't we?" He slowed down and swung the car over to the side of the road, where he stopped the engine. "Who says we can't? Come on, Julie; let's go up to the house. Please."

"No." Again I pushed away the questing hand.

"Why not?"

"You know why not—it's not your servants' night off. Take me home, Phil; I don't want to fight."

He'd brought me home then, and driven off in an ugly temper. It worried me not at all, because he always came back.

34

Agatha and I left the breakfast table together. I had hit it off from the beginning with this big, cheerful, rosy girl, perhaps because we were so opposite in most things. She taught at the same school I did, and was out in the East because she'd been bored at home and thought it would be fun to travel.

"My family are darlings," she had said. "They're the salt of the earth, I think—one always does think that way; I'm sure you're the same about your people. But I must admit they're dull. You have no idea how dull they are. I *had* to get away."

She owned a little sports car, and usually I rode with her to work. The *djongos* stood at the front door with our book bags as we went out, bestowing them on us with the humble flourish of a medieval armorer presenting swords to a pair of knights. As she unlocked the car door Agatha looked at the sky and said:

"Overcast. Probably the rains will start in earnest soon."

"I hope they do. We need some moisture," I said. "My skin's cracking."

Early as it was, we were not alone in the open air. The gardener was already squatting on his hunkers on the lawn, busy at some mysterious task, involved with the roots of an ornamental shrub. Like most Europeans coming out to Java I had expected to find myself all but smothered in jungle growth, but this garden, like all the others in the neighborhood, was only sparsely green, and such vegetation as it had survived thanks to unremitting irrigation and work. Gardening was quite a game of skill among Batavians, and enthusiasts talked endlessly on such topics as good carpeting plants to be used in lieu of the honest European grass that refused to grow in this alien climate. They could have had splendid gardens of local vines and shrubs, but most Dutch gardening enthusiasts liked it better the hard way. It was a triumph to produce the home blooms of roses and pinks and such tame flowers, and orchids, being easy, were considered a trifle vulgar.

We drove past houses that would have looked in place in Rotterdam or Groningen, the neat pavements running between disciplined beds of European flowers. But sometimes the road changed abruptly, carrying us into and out of those surprising little settlements that were like foreign bodies in the city—groups of toylike houses standing high on stilts, built of thatch or wooden slats around a bare plot of earth, with fruit trees scattered behind. Other breaks in the Dutch landscape were the native eating houses like sheds with three walls, the roof affording scanty shelter for one long table. These variations, even if it had not been for the people, showed that Batavia could never quite win the battle between Asia and Europe. The street was well-paved and broad, but it was an insane jumble of bicycles, children, coolies, carts, market women, and food vendors with portable kitchens. Every so often Agatha switched quickly to avoid something or someone—an unusually long shoulder pole, perhaps, on which a full pail of cakes or a load of bamboo dangled. None of us, car-drivers or pedestrians or cyclists or ricksha coolies or oxen, had much space for maneuver, since down the center of the road ran the notorious sewer canal that provided native Batavia with water for all purposes, from drinking to sanitary flushing. Occidentals in Southeast Asia were always horrified by our sewer system, and for all the adaptations I had made, it was the one thing I could not seem to get used to. This morning, however, I wasted no thought on it. The sight of some Javanese children carrying school satchels reminded me of a topic more important.

"I wish I had those in my class," I said, indicating them as we rode past.

"Javanese kids? Why?" asked Agatha.

"Wouldn't you like it yourself, Agatha? It's a pity, as I'm here in Java, that I don't have more to do with the people; at any rate why shouldn't they share our schools? If they were in Europe—"

"Oh, that! Yes, newcomers always talk that way." Agatha sighed. "It's different in Europe, Julie. It wouldn't work here;

36

though actually we do have a few Javanese pupils. I've got one myself, but I'm not so keen on it as you seem to be. We can't very well refuse some children, when they come from important families, but we couldn't possibly take in everybody without letting down our Dutch standards. And then where would our own children be when they go home?"

I thought that over. "But if this is a part of the Netherlands, as everybody claims it is, why aren't they entitled to the same schooling?"

"Oh, really, Julia! The economics of it alone . . . You must have been talking to Jan Vries."

Jan Vries was the school eccentric. I hadn't been talking to him, not on this subject at least, but there were topics that only led to endless argument between Agatha and me, and this was evidently one of them. I let it drop without more dispute, and chose something safer.

"The reason I was late for tea yesterday was that I paid a duty call. That Dekker child was absent again—four times since the first of the month that makes, and never any adequate excuse. So before I came home I went to see her mother." I paused to lend emphasis to my next statement. "The woman was drunk."

Agatha merely nodded without surprise. "Yes, I expect she was. I know Mrs. Dekker."

"Don't you think it's pretty bad?"

"Well . . . yes." Agatha's severity was, I felt, inadequate. She went on, "She's an unhappy woman, you see. I do think it's sad when a woman takes to doing it all by herself like that."

A trickle of sweat ran down her neck. I felt warm myself, which no doubt was why I replied with so much emotional heat. "I don't agree at all. Drunks aren't necessarily unhappier than anybody else; if you ask me, it's a lot of sentimental nonsense." Arguments were apt to spring up in the same senseless way over anything, just before the rains. It was not that I really cared about Mrs. Dekker's private life, but I went on nevertheless: "Everybody talks like that over

37

scandals in this place. Everything that goes wrong, from hang-nails to arson, is blamed on the climate and the easy life. In another minute you'll be saying Mrs. Dekker makes a pig of herself because when she got out here she found herself at loose ends with nothing to do all day but play cards and drink coffee, poor girl. I've heard it so many times, the same excuse—boredom, too many servants, seeing too little of her husband . . . I know it by heart."

By this time I was really angry. Not with Agatha or even Mrs. Dekker; just angry. Understanding this, Agatha was silent as she drove into the school yard and placed her car. "It's the truth," she said equably as she got out, "so why shouldn't one say it over and over?"

"Because it's too easy to explain wrongdoing that way," I snapped. The screened door swung shut behind us and we went down a shady passage toward the classrooms. In the coolness, I speedily simmered down. Still, I had to finish. "If the climate's so fatal, why don't the other Europeans go under? Most don't. Most people can take that dreadful shock of release from chores without being knocked silly. Think, Agatha, of the European women you know who *don't* drink. There's altogether too much talk about the debilitation of the tropics, and all that mysterious East nonsense. I've even heard the climate blamed for a woman's going completely off her head. Yet she must have been unbalanced to begin with."

"Oh no. From what I've heard, Lily Brewer was quite a balanced woman when she first got here." Agatha's calm, cool voice stopped me short. Having made her point, how-ever, she turned into her room and left me to walk on alone. I was blushing. That should be a warning to me, I re-flected, to make no more generalizations based on private grudges.

A stampless envelope lay on my desk with the message "By hand" written on it, and the letterhead of Phil's company on the flap. It was probably an apology, I thought; unneces-sary, as we'd had far worse quarrels in the past. The clock said I had several minutes before the bell, so I ignored the interested gaze of my children, and opened it.

"Darling Annoying Julie: I'm afraid you'll have to look around for a better date on Saturday, as I'm going to a conference in Palembang. By the time you get this I'll be on the way. See you next week. Take care of yourself, don't forget your quinine, and go to church, but watch that conscience, will you? Anyway I kiss the tip of your nose. I'll kiss more than that when I get back—I hope?"

As the bell rang I assumed a severe expression and faced the class. Books banged and paper rustled; desks squeaked.

We always made a long morning and finished the working day early in our afternoon, so that lunch and the nap followed late. The children needed a break in the middle of the morning and so did we. That day, as it wasn't my turn to superintend their milk-drinking and cookie-eating, I went straight to the common room, where I found Agatha standing at the bulletin board, reading something with an interest surpassing any she would have shown over a tennis schedule or appeal for funds.

"Julie," she said, "look at this. We're entertaining a guest, it seems. Willy-nilly."

I read it: "To the staff. Ahmet, a lively young member of a leading political group, is coming in this morning for coffee. (Signed) J. Vries."

Agatha looked at me with raised eyebrows, and I looked back. I said, "Javanese, I presume."

"Oh, obviously, from the name: he must be a Nationalist if he clings to the old style. That's just like Jan Vries, isn't it—asking someone without making sure first if we'd like it."

"Well, he *is* interested in the Javanese," I said, as if in apology. The fact was, Vries hardly needed an apologist, and if he did there was our *doyenne*, Miss Scheffer. She usually agreed with him, and always supported him anyway. Where most of us tacitly admitted that the training of young children did not necessarily call for creative brainwork in any other field, Vries felt that a teacher was entitled to a dignified place in society. He looked the part of an intellectual: anyone who saw his tossing hair, horn-rimmed spectacles, and sallow, bony face knew immediately that Vries was of a different stamp from the comfortable young men of Batavia's business firms. He was the eager sort who is always starting things. Drama clubs, painting exhibitions, evening classes in the arts and crafts of Java—Vries harassed us and demanded that we all participate, and though we grumbled, we participated. We gave him credit for zeal, and in an exasperated fashion were proud of him.

"A Nationalist. I mean to say, what next?" This was Agatha, but we were no longer alone. Mina said hotly:

"I think it's splendid to have a Nationalist here."

Mina was our games teacher, in love with Vries—an inexplicable thing, since she had never willingly read a book in her life, and Vries hated games and all exercise for its own sake. Stammering with earnestness, Mina told us we should be ashamed of ourselves for being narrow-minded and snobbish. More and more of our staff entered the room, but Mina did not stop talking; some encouraged her, and everyone listened, much amused. For herself, she said, she welcomed the chance of enlarging her horizon by meeting a Javanese Nationalist. She ended triumphantly:

"Some of you forget that even natives are people."

A burst of clapping came from the open door, and Vries walked in with a stranger. It was the stranger who had applauded: when Mina saw him she turned bright pink. Vries avoided her eyes. I had to stand on tiptoe to see the other man, the Javanese. Dropping back, I said in low tones to Agatha:

"Why, he's rather attractive, actually."

She said, "Not bad for a Communist. The clothes help of course—he's dressy, isn't he?"

Ahmet *was* dressy, though, as I reflected, it was rash to call him a Communist with no evidence. He wore Javanese costume, which was unusual in Batavia except for regents or other aristocrats: the smaller fry adopted foreign-style shirts and trousers. Ahmet seemed to be insisting on the validity of his national style, and I had to admit it suited him. Though he was fairly tall for a Javanese, he seemed smaller because of his slight build. Jacket and sarong were white, turban a mixture of brown and beige—and he was barefoot. Surrounded as he was in that common room by Dutchmen and Dutchwomen built, most of them, on Agatha's lines and towering over him, Ahmet with his bright dark eyes reminded me of a wild, wary animal. He also gave the impression—as many animals do—of being cleaner, glossier and better formed than the domesticated creatures around him. I tried to trace in his eyes a glimmer of amusement at least. After all, he had mocked Mina, and he must be laughing at us, but the eyes showed nothing; they were almost opaque. I had a better look when Jan Vries introduced him. When my name was pronounced, Ahmet's glance flicked my face before moving on. Irrationally I thought, "That man doesn't like me."

Vries as host fussed around nervously, but his guest was at ease. He accepted chair and cup of coffee, as composedly as if he always dropped in at schools like this. He took a cookie and tasted it and said it was good. All the time he smiled politely. There was a stir as the rest of us found our seats. Jan had probably intended an informal, jolly, friendly gathering, but it didn't work out that way, at least at first. It was stiff. Ahmet was tacitly accepted as the center around which the others placed their chairs in crescent formation, as if he were conducting lessons. I didn't try to get close, but sat near the door. Miss Scheffer started proceedings by addressing a question to the guest in a loud, clear voice.

"You are a politician, a Nationalist, aren't you, Mr.—er— Ahmet?"

Ahmet made a deprecating little gesture. "I suppose everyone in the Indies is a politician, in a way." His Dutch was perfect.

Vries said, "Oh no, I wouldn't have said that. Do you

41

really think the uneducated masses of your people have any understanding of the principles involved, Ahmet?"

Ahmet indicated that he did, but added, "However, it is only my opinion, and I'm not an authority. In fact, *njonja*," he added, to Miss Scheffer, "I'm afraid my friend Jan has romanticized me a little. I am not a politician, merely a teacher. Like yourselves."

"Oh, how interesting," said Miss Scheffer. She meant well, but she irritated me by speaking with a sort of kindly majesty, as if Ahmet were a particularly bright pupil in one of her classes. "Which school is it?" she asked, and Ahmet gave some reply that I couldn't catch, a native name and unfamiliar to me. The girl sitting in front of me turned to say that it was probably a wild school. Wild schools was the name for the institutions set up by native societies and supported by them without any government funds to help. The Dutch vernacular schools, which the government did support, weren't big enough or numerous enough for the demand; that was why I'd spoken to Agatha about schooling for Javanese. It seemed a strange coincidence that Ahmet should have turned up so soon after our conversation; Agatha and I might have gone for years without speaking about such a topic, and here it was, occurring twice in a day.

"It's very odd," I thought, "that there are so many children in this city who study their lessons in a language I don't understand, and worship in a religion that means nothing to me, and read books I wouldn't be able to read."

The world was much bigger, in fact, than I realized most of the time, and I felt small in it. To quell my discomfort I lit a cigarette and began shuffling through one of my notebooks, as if the party didn't interest me.

Certainly Ahmet wasn't putting himself out to be interesting. He parried questions or let them drop with a short reply, and conversation kept coming to a dead end. This was apparently pure shyness, because as other people took the ball from Miss Scheffer and talked with genuine warmth, he became more communicative and began to talk louder, too.

42

Inevitably, the cause of nationalism came up. Agatha asked him if he was in favor of complete self-rule for the islands, and Ahmet said yes, without elaboration.

"But do you really believe," Agatha persisted, "that after four centuries of protective government of the sort we've had in the colony here, the natives would be ready to run their own affairs? Surely it's an art, or a trade, that needs practice."

"That is true, but how does any nation get its start? Holland had to work her way up, didn't she?" asked Ahmet. "Of course there will be difficulties, and we must overcome them. We have added disadvantages; after those four centuries you've mentioned, our culture patterns are distorted. We'll have to set them right again."

"Oh, come." This was Miss Scheffer. "I don't know what you mean by distortion. It's well known that whatever mistakes our administrators have made in the past—and I admit there have been mistakes—they've tried very conscientiously to respect your customs, your *adat*. We've not behaved like the British or French. Everybody knows we've been careful not to interfere with native traditions and religious observances. Why, you've even kept your native rulers."

He had begun to smile before she finished, and leaped to talk as soon as she came to a halt. "I have heard the theory expounded many times, *njonja*, and it is a praiseworthy one, I grant you that, but I'm afraid it hasn't worked out according to plan. You speak, for example, of the nobles, the *priyayi*."

"I do." Miss Scheffer's deep voice throbbed.

"Before the Dutch came we could manage these people," he said. "They had their place and they kept it; it worked. Afterwards, under the foreign regime, they were able to take advantage."

At this even Jan Vries protested. "Your own nobles!" he said.

"Why, yes, our own. I'm sorry my vocabulary isn't good enough to explain, but . . . Let me say it this way. We hold no grudge against the Dutch as Dutch, only as colonizers, since no matter how benevolent colonialists may be, injustice creeps in. It comes in even through our own people. I am not proud of this, but it is true. Colonialists must have tools, and when they have selected and trained these tools—their henchmen, or go-betweens, whatever you call them—these persons form a new elite. Because they are protected by the overlord they do as they like, and the overlord does not see this because he's a stranger, whereas the henchman is in his own country and knows how to conceal what he's doing. How do you think the little man feels, the one on the bottom? He isn't going to love a petty tyrant any the better for being of his own race. He must always submit: to the Dutch, to the Javanese, to the Chinese who make up their own elite of usurers. And he also hasn't much love for his half-brother the Eurasian, who betrays his native blood"—here the dark eyes again flicked my face—"by supporting the Dutch."

Not everybody thought immediately of me, but enough did to cast a pall of shocked silence over the party. It lasted only a few seconds before Jan asked another question, and a babble covered the awkwardness altogether. I sat rigid, fists clenched on my open notebook, torn between the desire to say something crushing and another desire to rush from the room, through the door that was so temptingly close. I did neither.

A bell shrilled, tearing the air, to tell us the coffee break was over. Chairs scraped and people stood up to go, saying goodbye to Ahmet in polite little phrases, "Such a pleasure," "So interesting," "I do hope we meet again." I thought of dashing out before everyone else, but it would have been conspicuous, and after they started moving into the passage I lingered, not wishing to accept sympathy just then. Thus there were only two or three people left when Ahmet, talking to Vries, saw me across his companion's shoulder as I was at last moving toward the door. He surprised me; he walked over and held out his hand. Slow-witted, I didn't snub him, but took it. He said:

"Have we met before today?"

44

"No," I said. "I haven't been here very long." Then I spoke with emphasis. "You couldn't be expected to know, but I was born and brought up in Europe."

"Not Batavian?" he repeated with mild surprise.

"Not Batavian. Not of the elite." I bowed my head coldly and left the room. In the passage Agatha was waiting, and pounced.

"Julie! What a dreadful little native: why didn't you slap him? None of us would have blamed you."

"Oh, don't think about it. Who cares what he says—a little show-off like that?"

I was lying in my teeth, of course: I cared a lot. By whatever blunder or ignorance, the little show-off had *broken through*. I was invaded. I hadn't cared as much about things since Martin. It made it all the worse that I'd been full of good, eager thoughts of the Javanese people, wanting to be fair to them and let them into our schools. . . . And now, this. Ahmet was one Javanese I'd have liked to grind down in good old colonial fashion.

Agatha and I linked arms and walked away.

The Palmers, Chick and Marge, were having a small party. They were American friends of Phil, inevitably, as Chick, too, was in the oil business. He was even rather like Phil in type, rugged and forthright in his manner, but perhaps most Americans look like that. Both he and his wife Marge were nice to me and I liked them, but we weren't enough of the same age to have been particularly friendly unless there'd been Phil. They loved bridge and I didn't: I loved dancing and they didn't. Still, we got on well enough.

It was a pretty party, out on the Palmers' lawn, with a long buffet table lit with candles in silver holders and two gasoline lamps in addition; in Batavia there was always a night wind and candles were uncertain. The moon was full, and when my nose was not filled with the fumes of mosquito incense, burning away in plates at our feet, I could smell flowers. I stayed away from the main party as long as I was

45

allowed, because the noise deafened me; the guests' glasses were kept brimming and everything was getting a bit raucous. It was often like that. Americans were blamed by the Dutch for drinking too much, but I could never see that one nation outdid the other on it, and the Palmers' party was mixed, nationally speaking. I sat by a bush where I wasn't easy to see, looking at the stars, so much bigger than they are in Holland, reflecting with gentle content that one can spend a whole lifetime in North Europe without seeing the skies of the ancients. Then Marge, on a hostess's errand, came from the house and spotted me.

"How's your drink, Julie? Are you sure?" She sat down. "You look like a little ghost tucked away here in the moon shadow; what a pretty dress, what color is it? It looks white."

"Yes, it's white." I smoothed my lap.

"What do you do for clothes, Julie? Or are you still living on what you brought out? I find it awfully difficult here; what do you do?"

I said, "It isn't easy. If I could make my own—but sewing bores me, ever since I had to do it as a child."

"Me too. Besides, there just isn't the time. But you're so little, you shouldn't have any trouble out here where they cater for midgets like you. You know Yvonne's? That's a little shop on your block, near the main road, just where the street turns off. Try her. I never can find anything there myself because I'm not a midget, but she has cute little ideas. Oh, Chick! Chick, Julie's nursing an empty glass. Do your stuff."

She went off to superintend the waiters who were bringing out hot food. It was *rijstaffel*, which meant that we would have a ritual. The Dutch in Java had created quite a theatrical business of serving *rijstaffel*. One man carried the great rice container, and after him marched a whole lot of waiters, single-file, with dishes of the food that was to be taken in little dabs on the rice, no two of them alike, until the table stood triumphant, like some great altar laden with bowls and dishes. We guests then made a procession of our own to ladle out the food. When I'd collected mine, Chick made me join Phil on another part of the lawn, and the men resumed talking where they had been interrupted. Phil was reporting on his visit to Palembang.

"Then you'd say the situation isn't too healthy," said Chick.

Phil shook his head. "I'm not going to stick my neck out prophesying a major strike. Not yet. Just the same—"

After a long pause Chick prompted him. "Just the same, you were saying."

"I didn't like the pattern," said Phil. "Little flare-ups neatly spotted, here one day and there the next, as if somebody was working it from a map. I never bank much on coincidence around here; I'm damn well sure somebody *was* working with a map."

"Yeah, I see." Chick puffed at a cheroot and looked at the stars. "You contemplating any action at your place?"

"I don't know what it would be if we did. We wouldn't go so far as to call it an emergency, as I said, but Washington's been asking the home office a lot of questions, and they passed the buck to me, so I'm taking off a little earlier than I'd planned. It looks as if I'll be getting home leave halfway through the tour this time."

"Some people have the luck. How do you like that, Julie? This man works things so he can get away every year, practically, instead of sweating it out like us ordinary mortals. He's got it down to a fine art, hasn't he? A couple of scary cables, and wham! back he goes for another high-level consultation. Why wasn't I born with brains?"

"I don't know," I said. "I don't know anything. I didn't even know he was going to America."

"Oh-oh, somebody's in trouble now." Chick laughed loudly, and went off to talk to other guests. After a minute Phil said:

"The only reason I didn't tell you anything is that I wasn't sure until this evening, honey."

"Oh, that's all right . . . Phil, are things really so bad? I didn't know the Communists were that strong around here."

47

"Who said Communists? No, I think our trouble just now is Japan."

"Oh, that."

People were always talking about the Japanese threat, but I didn't take it seriously. There were quite a few Japanese in Batavia and the ones I knew, those who had shops, I rather liked. There was a man who mended shoes, and another one who sold fruit; they were nice, hard-working people who showed up well in comparison with the Javanese who did the same sort of work. I said, curiously, "What can they do to you, anyway?"

"Plenty. They've got their eye on these islands, you can bet your life; they keep after the natives here with talk about how they're being exploited by the wicked white man. The idea seems to be that if you're going to be exploited, better have it done by somebody the same color as yourself. The trouble with that is, our people listen. They think a lot of the Japs. They respect them. It's old history to us, but the little brown brothers around here haven't forgotten how the Japs beat the Russians. Moreover, the Jap militarists keep on and on about how they've been robbed, and need more room to move around in. That's no lie, either—you ought to see the streetcars in Tokyo. Just look what they're doing in China. No, I don't like it."

Somewhere I'd got the idea that women ought to soothe their men, so I spoke soothingly. "Oh well, I wouldn't worry about the natives, anyway. They're such quiet, gentle people— like children, really."

"Yes, you Dutch always say that. I wish I could believe it."

"Wish you could believe what?" demanded Marge, looming up in the moonlight. She dropped into the chair her husband had vacated and kicked off her shoes, sighing with relief. "Oh, how wonderful! I think I've earned a rest. *Djongos!* Bring me a brandy-soda, please. Are you kids enjoying yourselves?"

"It's a swell party," said Phil.

"Go on, you're just *saying* that. Phil, you rat, what's this I hear about you going home so soon?"

They went over it all again. I didn't pay much attention until I heard Marge say, "I guess you'll be stopping off in Michigan, won't you?"

"If the doctors think it would be a good thing," Phil replied. I pricked up my ears: so Lily's nursing home was in Michigan, was it? Marge, serious for once, put her hand over Phil's and said:

"I know you wouldn't fool me. Is it getting tricky? Do you think I ought to go on back before we get caught out here?"

"Why, Marge, you mustn't jump to conclusions. It isn't one hundred per cent certain that nothing will happen here, but it's nothing like Europe and the situation there. I'd a hell of a lot rather be here than in France, or Holland, right now."

"Sure?"

"Dead sure. Now shut up before you scare Julie."

We all laughed at that. It *was* a good party. Afterwards I went home with Phil. After all he was going away, and for once he'd had the forethought to send the servants out.

I knew from a glance at Agatha's pale, shocked face when she came into my room that something really wrong had happened.

"I came to tell you as fast as I could," she said. "Terrible news. The Germans have attacked everybody, everywhere, all at once. They're all over the place: Belgium, home—I can't believe it."

"But how could they? So quickly? No, it's not possible."

"They've done it all on motorbikes. It must be all over by this time—they may even have got to England." Agatha's knees gave way and she sat down on my bed, her face hidden in her hands. Later we rejoined the other hostel girls and talked it over.

It was hell, but I would be lying if I said I suffered like Agatha and the rest. After all it wasn't the same for me;

49

nothing that mattered was still in the Netherlands; nobody I loved was in danger. Even Phil, who in a way I loved, was safe in America. For all the difference it made I might as well have been a foreigner with no connections in Holland; yet I regretted my luck. It reminded me of certain childhood grievances. Again I was being left out. Enviously I saw how the very comprehensiveness of the blow gave comfort to ordinary people. They had each other. Not many of our girls hid in their rooms to weep.

Despair didn't last very long: soon we were picking up the pieces and resuming our old routine, as people do. Children had to be looked after, catastrophe or no, and that meant school as usual. After a little while it was almost as if nothing had happened on the other side of the world, and to make it more bearable still, better news began to trickle through. One morning Agatha, reading a letter, gasped and jumped up, and pulled me to my feet to dance a few steps. The letter was from a favorite cousin, a boy who had escaped to England and was writing to tell her that her parents were all right. I think life at that moment must have been better for Agatha than it ever was before the war. Other people got letters too, and some spirits rose like the wave that comes in after a particularly deep depression in the surf. Not that we had anything particular to be jubilant about; but the Batavia broadcasting station chattered away with little items about the escape of the royal family, the British fighting and holding on, the remnant of Free Europe still trying, and it added up to hope of a sort. In spite of the other side of the story and the accounts of refugees moving by the thousand, and prison camps, there was hope. Now with Free Dutch refugees to work for, the colonials threw themselves into the job of collecting money.

This was hardly a new pastime. Ever since my arrival there had been collections and benefits on all sides, but until now they'd always been for the Chinese of the Indies, the "overseas people" as they called themselves. Some Chinese families had lived in the islands for generations, for more than a century. There were stories of ancestors who came over in the sixteen hundreds, and still their descendants refused to give up their national identity, though they had never seen China. They *wanted* to be alien. Stubbornly they clung to their Chinese customs, wearing Chinese clothes and eating their own kind of food. Jan Vries was talking about them:

"It isn't exactly reasonable. A lot of them aren't even pure Chinese. There were intermarriages with the native women in all these generations, but Chinese don't count that sort of blood transfusion important. It's more vital, in their minds, to be faithful to the traditional culture."

"For my part," said Miss Scheffer, who was listening to the little lecture, "I consider that sentiment admirable."

"Possibly it is, but the people here resent them and I can understand it," said Jan. "If a man settles in a country and makes his living out of it, he ought to give it his first loyalty." In the wrangle that followed, Jan and the little lesson were forgotten, but I had been growing impatient with Vries and his tutoring anyway: I was restive, and wanted to find out about the country more directly than through another foreigner. If Vries could know Chinese people, why shouldn't I? It was in part a kind of turning away from the Javanese, I suppose, but one day I came home in triumph with a book of tickets to a charity benefit dance, which I had promised to sell on behalf of an aid-to-China Fund.

"Where did you get that?" asked Agatha.

"The Chinese girl who washes my hair at the Clover Blossom asked me to help. It's to buy an airplane for Generalissimo Chiang."

Agatha scoffed at me. "What did Generalissimo Chiang ever do for you? I don't think you'll manage to sell one ticket. Nobody here cares whether or not they've got another ambulance in China."

"Plane, not ambulance. You're going to buy a couple yourself and make Pieter take you."

Of course in the end she gave in, and so did most of the others I tackled. It gave me something to do, but still I fidgeted. I missed Phil. He didn't write often, not being that kind of man, and when he did the letters said little. He gave no date and no hint of when he might be returning, nor was Michigan ever mentioned. Once Chick asked me for news, but I had to confess I had none.

"Well, that's what I'd expect," he said. "Once they've got him there in Washington they're bound to hold on for a little, to pick his brains. They need somebody who knows what's really going on."

When I came home that day, Agatha asked me if I'd collected a date myself for the charity ball, and I said I hadn't bothered.

"There's nobody I'm particularly eager to go with," I said.

"I know what's the matter with you; you're moping for your big American. Poor girl!" She laughed.

I said, "I'm not denying it. Phil's nice. I *like* a big man with a deep voice. Though he's no beauty, he's nice."

"He's no beauty," Agatha repeated. "That's true. Do you know, I think he's your substitute father, Julie."

"Rubbish!" I was really annoyed. "I'll find somebody for the party in good time, but I haven't a thing to wear for it. Do you want to come out with me now, to shop?"

Agatha shook her head, and patted a heap of notebooks that lay on the desk. "I'm a day behind with my grading," she said. "I daren't go out. If you really haven't got a special date in mind, I'll ask Pieter to bring a friend for the party. The town's swarming with extra men. All those Free Dutch uniforms!"

"All right," I said indifferently, and went out to get my dress.

Ever since the Palmer party, I'd kept Marge's suggestion in mind. Today I looked for the shop she had described, Yvonne's, and soon found it. It was a very little place of the sort one only finds in the East, where the owner can make a modest success as designer, manufacturer, and retailer in one. Indoors, through the bead curtain that kept the flies out, the whole space, about the size of an ordinary sitting room, was redolent of beeswax, and was cut in two by skimpy hangings across the middle. Behind these I heard the sound of a sewing machine, and a woman scolding some other woman in the Indonesian Malay. Nobody had heard me; the scolding went on and on, until I called out, "Anybody here?"

A girl stepped out, saying "Sorry!" This was Yvonne. Round-faced and dark, plump with small bones, she looked too good-natured to be capable of the tongue-lashing I had heard. Somebody still behind the curtain was giggling now, and I decided that Yvonne's bark was deceptive. I said I wanted a dance dress, and that Mrs. Palmer had sent me.

"Palmer? Oh, the gray-haired American, yes." She pulled a tape measure from where it hung around her neck and began to measure me. "But you're not American," she went on. "Do you come from somewhere around here?" Then she changed over from Dutch to the vernacular. I shook my head.

"I don't speak the language very well yet," I said. "But I'm learning. Actually, I'm from Holland."

Ahmet was not the only one who leaped to conclusions: it was always happening, and when it wasn't Ahmet, with his accusations, I didn't mind. I didn't mind Yvonne at all.

"Let's see," she said, and pulled a dress out. "Try this. You *look* like one of the local girls."

"I know I do. I just happen to have been born abroad, though. . . . Have you got something not quite so bright?"

She was a likable girl. So were her two little seamstresses likable; by the time I had tried on half the stock and made a choice, we were friendly. I went back home carrying a parcel and feeling better about things.

CHAPTER THREE

When violent thunderstorms broke close, I felt like the hub of some infernal wheel surrounded by whirling plum-colored clouds, or like one of those many-armed Hindu gods wreathed with fire. Oftener, however, the storms of the rainy season originated just off stage, beyond the flat dark shadows of the horizon; I say off stage with purpose; such weather belonged rather to the regions of drama than to reality. The thunder and flashes were bigger than life, and the sight of a jagged streak of green-white light traveling up the sky from that unseen source reminded me of stage managers, not angry gods. All this explains why we dealt with the threat of war—war, that is, in the East, around us—with such a light hand: it seemed much the same sort of thing as the latent storm, permanently threatening, but permanently a bit outside our vision. Radio news and government pronouncements growled like the sound effects of stage thunder, and in time had no more effect than surf at the seaside.

Still, we did change. Habits altered and one's little circle was pulled out to a larger size. Because of the off-stage war, for example, I met Ming. It was during a course in so-called volunteer nursing. I'd been directed by the higher authorities to take it, and so, in spite of her husband's money and influence, had Ming. Perhaps she didn't attempt to dodge the duty: perhaps she was bored, and welcomed the course as diversion. However it was, we were partners in First Aid, and from the beginning I was charmed with her. She bandaged my ankle in a practice exercise, and she made—in spite of jangling gold bracelets and long, lacquered fingernails—a surprisingly good job of it. My efforts in return, though my hands are supposed to be practical, were awkward and fumbling to an unbelievable degree. I started wrapping the wrong way: I caught a nail in the mesh: I failed miserably. There was silence until, under my breath, I cursed. Ming laughed, I laughed, and we were friends. After that we sat next to each other at lectures, and when class was over we usually went off together for coffee.

I learned very soon, though not from her, that Ming was a famous figure in Batavia; she was the favorite wife of Mr. Djung, one of the most powerful of our local Chinese millionaires. Even Agatha was impressed by our friendship. Certainly, going out with Ming was something new in my experience. We would step into the shiny black limousine that waited for her outside the lecture hall, the driver in his peaked cap standing at attention beside the door until we'd settled in. One afternoon as the car purred past the entrance to the Hotel des Indes, Ming leaned over and tapped him on the shoulder, saying:

"We will have our coffee here today."

The car halted at the great entrance, and more lackeys rushed out to escort us in. I had learned to expect the little stir that Ming always caused—the first glance that people gave her, quickly followed by a second, longer look and perhaps a whispered remark to a companion. It wasn't only her sharp, polished beauty that set up the flurry: it was because she was Mrs. Djung, whose husband very probably held financial control over a lot of the people in the room. That day it was the same. We found that the tables were all occupied, but the headwaiter hurried over to assure Ming that he'd bring out another table just for her, and all would be ready in a minute. It was always like that when I was with her: my trumpery superiority as a European dwindled to nothing. Perhaps it was pique that made me bring up an old grievance:

55

"You ought to be my guest today, Ming. It's weeks since I stood treat."

"But Julie, how many times must I tell you that I don't like your hostel?" Ming was always frank. "It's too much like a government dormitory. I don't see why you live there when no law compels it."

"Just the same, I'd like to—"

"Nonsense. We know each other too well for such empty gestures, dear Julie."

She was right, of course, and I subsided. Bracelets jingling and jade earrings swinging, Ming took the seat the head-waiter held for her, and when I too had been handed into place like a lady in waiting, she gave me the menu card. We always chose one cake apiece. Her fingernails today were lacquered in gold. I'd heard envious women say of Ming that she looked like a singsong girl, and sometimes they went further, declaring that she'd actually been one, if not something worse, before Mr. Djung made her his third wife—or was it his fourth? This annoyed me when I heard it, and I hotly disputed it until people learned not to say it, at least in my presence. Really, there was not a word of truth in the story. Chinese girls like Ming simply did dress that way. They liked to be pretty. Ming had grown up quite respectably in Canton, paying occasional visits with her mother and aunts to the bright lights of Shanghai, where they caught up with the new fashions. She'd been what is called a home girl, without even a career, until she married.

"My husband Mr. Djung," she had explained—she always referred to him in that style—"my husband is a sort of distant cousin to my mother. I believe in Dutch you haven't enough words for all our different relationships, so I must say 'cousin.' The families have not kept in touch between Java and China, but Mr. Djung came back to look up his relatives, and during the tour he visited Canton. There he met me and decided to marry me."

I smiled. "And you decided to marry him as well, did you?"

"Why, of course. It was a good idea. Everyone else thought so, and I did too."

By the time we held this conversation I knew her well enough to say what was in my mind on the subject. "But he has other wives, and he's much older than you. I can't help being surprised that a girl like you, well-educated and beautiful, and with modern ideas, shouldn't have wanted to select your own husband."

"But I have just told you, I did select him," said Ming. "I selected Mr. Djung, for excellent reasons. Why should I not have married him? I *like* Mr. Djung. And I was right, for he is an excellent father."

"All right, but—the other wives?"

Ming, about to speak, broke off and shook her head hopelessly. It was no use, that shake implied. We were too far apart and she could never explain. "Shanghai girls feel as you do," she assured me at last, "but I come from an old-fashioned family and I was brought up to accept it. It is all in how one is brought up. . . . Besides, he pays them no attention since he married me. I see to that. If he went back to them I would leave him."

I loved her for that burst of nature, and let the rest of the discussion drop.

In the hotel lobby, eating our cakes and drinking coffee, we were comfortably silent until Ming said, "Do you realize Friday will be our last lesson?"

"Yes, I thought of that. It doesn't seem so long ago that we started."

"We were so busy. Busy days are only half as long." For Ming, I thought, such days were also unusual, but they weren't for me. She was preoccupied with other thoughts, and suddenly brought them out in the open. "What are you going to do with your spare time now, Julie?"

"Well, I've never had a lot of that," I pointed out. "It's no real problem. I'll go back to my ordinary routine."

"What do they pay you at that school?"

I had learned that Chinese speak openly of money, so I

told her readily. Ming wrinkled her nose. "And you live on it?" she asked. "It's true I had far less in my pocket in the old days when I was a girl, but I'm spoiled now. Your salary sounds too small, Julie." I said lightly that I'd have to be satisfied, but she went on, "There is one way you might add to your earnings: let me tell you. Our children are not getting as much instruction as we would like them to have at that school of theirs, and Mr. Djung is displeased with their progress, especially in the Western languages. And I agree with him. Couldn't you come to our house once or twice a week in the late afternoon, and give lessons to them?"

I hesitated. "It seems awfully hard on a child to give it so much extra work."

"But they are really getting lazy. I worked far harder when I was a child, and it never harmed me. They would have to work harder in China, I can tell you that."

It did not need much persuasion, once my conscience was soothed. The thought of being an intimate in the Djung house intrigued me. I consented, and after that, twice a week after the heat of the day I went to the Djungs', up the long path that led through their garden to the door. I must admit it was a hideous garden. Part of it was laid out formally in the Dutch way, and the rest was a Chinese nightmare with an artificial mountain made of concrete, and honeycombed with walks, hidden caves, and vistas. Here and there were stuck brilliantly painted statues, also cement, of birds and animals. The Djungs seemed never to use the garden and I couldn't blame them. Indoors was quite different, plain and lovely in a sparse way. In a room almost bare of furniture the seven small Djungs—only the two youngest were Ming's—sat with me around a circular table, perched on high-backed chairs, to do their lessons. Servants constantly passed around us from one door to another, looking at us with indulgent approval. Once or twice the great Mr. Djung himself, a small gentleman with a sensitive face, dropped in and stood there to listen, but this made me nervous and I was glad he didn't come often. Otherwise it was nice. Everyone in the house was careful of me, and polite. Indeed, I had never in my life been so well-treated. The Chinese respect teachers, and I found it a tradition much to my taste.

After the lesson hour when the children had been claimed by the servants who looked after them, I would have tea with Ming, Mr. Djung joining us when he was not too busy. I soon understood what she had meant when she said she'd selected him deliberately. Mr. Djung never talked down to her or to me; he did not behave at all like my idea of a polygamist. In spite of Ming's beauty, he discussed the affairs of his business with her as if her were Phil talking to Chick— man to man. Listening to them together, I learned much of what was going on in circles I would otherwise never enter. Mr. Djung always seemed to know more than the newspaper reporters, and from a different angle. The trouble with this was that my ignorance often surprised them, even shocked them. Once when Ming mentioned the word I cut in with a question that obviously startled them:

"Just what is the Volksraad?"

Ming was incredulous: did I really not know? I said, "It's a government body of some sort, I know that much. The papers report what goes on at the meetings. There are Indonesians in it, aren't there?" I refused to apologize for my ignorance, but in my heart I felt, guiltily, that I was an unworthy daughter. My mother would surely have known all about the Volksraad. At that moment I vowed that I would try to stop being an ignoramus.

Mr. Djung was a literal-minded man; when a question was asked, he thought it his duty to reply fully, and now he set out to answer mine, and generally to explain what the main quarrel in the islands was about. It was lucky for me that I learned in that way, since he was neither white nor Javanese; he regarded the affair with less passion than a Dutchman would have, and I wasn't on good enough terms with any Javanese who could have talked about it. Mr. Djung explained that the Volksraad, the only institution in the government where natives were represented, had very little real authority. When it was formed the natives had expected that there would be a period of tutelage for themselves, and that as time went on they would have more responsibility, until little by little they arrived at self-government. Probably the Dutch had thought so too, said Mr. Djung, at the beginning. But the official policy had changed as the years went on, and while the government was still at The Hague just as the war began, they'd seemed determined on keeping things in the islands as they were, indefinitely.

But the Indonesians were getting restive, thinking with more and more impatience about independence. It happened to be just before the blitz in Europe that the Volksraad sent to The Hague a resolution demanding something concrete in the way of progress along lines they laid down: they wanted the Volksraad enlarged so that more native members might be accommodated, and suggested that some of the Governor General's powers and authority should pass into their hands. They argued as if it were understood that the ultimate goal of the colonies was independence. Since many people at The Hague had permitted themselves to forget the old promises, Mr. Djung said, the resolution came to them as an unpleasant shock. The Volksraad requests were doomed to refusal from the start, and most of the Indonesian members must have known this.

Then there was the Atlantic Charter, signed at that point by the Dutch in company with their Western allies. In a second letter the Volksraad reminded The Hague that one of the charter clauses declared that all nations had a right to independence. What then of the Indonesian nation? Having sent off this second message, the writers waited for a reply. They waited a long, long time. The delay was unavoidable, they told each other after a bit, because the government had been temporarily scattered and disorganized by the German attack. They must be given time to settle down in exile before being pressed for a reply. However, even with all allowances being made, the silence from Europe stretched out beyond reasonable limits, and when at last the reply arrived, its bluntness was that much more offensive. It stated that Her Majesty's government in exile refused to consider any changes whatever in the *status quo* because of the circumstances then obtaining. Nothing could be done at this time; everything would have to wait. The charter's clause, in any case, did not apply to the Netherlands East Indies, for the islands were not a nation, but a part of the Netherlands; they were a domestic affair.

"Well, really," I said, after a pause. The bare bones of it gave me a feeling of sympathy for Ahmet that I had not felt before. It was hard to tell what Mr. Djung's opinion was. He took off his spectacles and wiped them, and Ming regarded me bright-eyed, her face as impassive as his, waiting for comment. I said tentatively:

"I can see the point the Dutch make about waiting until the war's over, I suppose."

"But of course one sees the point," said Mr. Djung, settling his glasses on his nose again. "I'm an interested party, you understand. My well-being depends on stability in this country. I have every reason to want things kept as they are, except—*can* they be kept so? It is a mistake to ignore portents because one doesn't care for what they portend. It is careless to treat people in too highhanded a manner. All this has been harmful to Dutch influence."

"Yes, it does seem unjust."

He shot a keen glance at me. "Just or unjust is not the question. It's bad strategy."

I was still floundering. This was not the sort of talk one got in the common room. I said, "There's nothing to worry about, is there? These people are so gentle and childish. They wouldn't make trouble, would they?—except perhaps a few insurgents from Sumatra."

"Oh, Julie!" cried Ming in scornful tones, and her husband said, "Never make that mistake, young lady; it's due to the biggest blind spot you people have. Quite a few Javanese are not childish at all. As for the rest, who *are* docile to a point, they may accept that they'll always be mastered by someone,

61

but if they decide they'd rather have some master other than the Dutch government, you're in for just as much trouble as if you had a nation of strong-minded rebels, aren't you?" He lifted his tea glass and took a long, hissing sip.

"The other masters," I said. "You mean Japan."

Mr. Djung raised his eyebrows in cautious assent, and Ming said, "We'll be in the soup too, you know, if that happens. Mr. Djung sends *plenty* of money to Chungking."

I went home more depressed than I had been for a long time, and that night I wrote at length to Phil, though it had been several weeks since I'd heard from him, even by the scrappiest short letter. I asked him questions about the future which, as I read the letter over, sounded just like the questions Marge had asked at her party. And probably I would get no more satisfaction than she did, I thought as I stamped it.

As things turned out, that was a wasted stamp. In the morning Agatha spoke to me before the time we usually had much to say: she looked embarrassed, and came straight to the point.

"Your friend Phil Brewer—have you heard from him lately?"

"No, not lately. I've been wondering why. Do you know anything?"

She took hold of my arm affectionately and said, "Yes, I've heard a piece of gossip, and I've decided to tell it to you before some cat tries to get at you. Some other cat . . . Lily Brewer, you know, his wife—she's better. They've let her out of the asylum or whatever it's called; she's joined up with Phil again for a trial period. Now, Julie, it may not be the actual truth, but if they're saying it at all you may as well know." She stopped and looked searchingly at me. "Look, are you all right?"

I was. I was quite all right, if angry. Phil might have told me, I thought; he should have told me first. It fitted into a pattern, of course: it was the way men behaved, and I had a disgusted sense of recognition rather than surprise, but there was anger too. Anyway I told Agatha I was quite all right, and thanked her for a friendly act, and raced to the front hall to reclaim the letter that still waited there to be posted. Several girls saw me pick it up, and I hated that. I knew there would be whispering and giggling in the bedrooms. Suddenly I was filled with hatred for the hostel, and for the first time I said to myself:

"I've got to get out of here. I'll move."

It was the custom to have a Christmas party at the hostel, and we didn't let the situation make any difference this year. For the sake of those girls who had dates, everything was done early. We sang a carol that we had ourselves translated into the local Malay called Bahasa Indonesia, giving our performance for the benefit of the staff, and they obligingly went into giggling hysterics. After the party had dispersed I sought out Agatha, knitting in her room. There were photographs all over the place of her Pieter—Pieter in uniform, Pieter showing a fish he had caught, and Pieter as a little boy. I sat down on a footstool, hugged my knees, and said,

"Agatha, wouldn't you like to move? I've been thinking how nice it would be if we had our own place."

She peered at me, and let the jersey drop to her lap, saying, "Oh no, I don't think so, dear. I quite like this place; at least there's no fatigue over housekeeping."

"That's one of my points, Agatha. Don't we *need* a few responsibilities? It wouldn't kill us to go out and buy our own food. Besides, I'm sick of all the same faces around the table every day." Phil would have laughed if he had heard me, I thought. But Agatha picked up her work again, shaking her head, and started knitting a new row.

"I'm sorry if you've set your mind on it, Julie, but really I'd rather not. The main thing is, it's bound to run to more money than this arrangement costs me, and I'm saving as much as I can against a real home of my own."

"Oh, has it gone so far?" I asked, and she nodded happily. I said, "Well then, let me be the first to wish you joy and to say I could see it coming, and all that." We laughed together.

"So you see it's quite out of the question," said Agatha, "though I *am* sorry. Isn't there some other girl you could ask? There must be, if we think it over."

"Sorry, I couldn't stand anybody but you. Anyone else would give me the horrors." I jumped up. "Don't fret about it, Agatha; it was only a thought."

Irritably I reflected that I should have realized how the land lay with Agatha without being told. Really I had grown lamentably self-centered lately, but the thought did not prevent my having a number of self-centered regrets for my hopes of an apartment.

Soon afterwards I was in Yvonne's shop, wasting time in a mildly pleasant manner by pawing over her stock of pins and ribbons and such small articles. These, and buttons, were disappearing from the market. The natives had never manufactured them, presumably because they never needed such things, and now that European imports had dried up, one noticed the lack. I grumbled as I sorted out a few rolls of tape:

"Yvonne, can't you even get Japanese stuff these days? There used to be too much of it. Could you spare this bit of tape?"

Yvonne was sewing behind the curtain. She said, "If it's the narrow kind, take it. I have plenty. It's a mystery about the Japanese stuff, now you mention it. The shops were choked with things from Japan not so long ago, but it does seem to have disappeared. Probably it's because of the shipping shortage. What else are you stealing out there?"

"Some of your discontinued pearl buttons, and some pins. Many thanks: how's everyone at home?"

Yvonne came out to wrap my purchases in a twist of paper. She said, "They're much as usual. Mamma was asking yesterday when you can come in again and have dinner. I don't suppose you know somebody who needs a room, do you? We've lost our lodger, and she feels very poor: he went back to Malaya where his people are. He's a nervous type—thinks the Japanese are planning something funny. I must say, war's unsettling for the old folks."

That was the way we always talked about the situation and I paid no attention. I was thinking. I said, "Why shouldn't I come and live with you? I'd like that." And so I would, I realized. Occupying a room in the Dutoit house was not just what I'd planned, but at least it meant escaping from the Virgins' Retreat, and Yvonne's pleasure was reassuring. She said:

"Oh, that would be nice! It would bring some excitement into life around there."

"I don't live in a social whirl, exactly," I warned her, but Yvonne refused to listen. Evidently she thought of me as a glamorous figure, mainly because I had the entree to the club, and I realized that all her customers had that same glamour. It was why she enjoyed her shop. Nothing would satisfy her but taking off her work smock and coming with me at that very moment to consult her mother.

I knew the house well, but now I'd come to a decision I had some misgivings when I entered the living room. Might it not be too cozy in the evenings, after all? Mr. Dutoit would be home, and I thought without rapture of long hours in the bosom of the Dutoit family. Like most of the other Eurasians in Batavia they lived according to Dutch standards, though none of them had ever seen Holland: there were rugs on the floor and overstuffed chairs and a sofa, and European ornaments. It was the ornaments that showed how much the Dutoits overshot the mark. They would never have given house room to Javanese carving or Balinese masks, though most white Europeans collected these things. The Dutoits saw no beauty in such familiar objects. It was rather surprising that Yvonne had developed the sense to use native-style textiles in her shop.

Mrs. Dutoit was very like Yvonne grown older and fatter, with the same round dark face and beautiful eyes, and almost the same vivacity, and Mr. Dutoit, who worked as clerk in an import house, made little difference to the family life because he was such a silent man. At that time of day he wasn't at home. The servant was busy on the veranda where bedroom doors all stood open to air the chair cushions and bedding, with particular zeal since one inmate had gone for good.

"He was in a tearing hurry," Mrs. Dutoit said about the lodger. "He said he'd had a dream of the dreadful things that would happen if he didn't get home immediately, and off he went; I never heard of such a thing, did you?—without notice to speak of, and after staying here for two years at that. I told him; I said, 'It's all very well and I can understand about the dream, I'd feel the same way in your place, but it would have been more convenient to have a chance to advertise.' Still, Julie, if you want to come, nothing could be better, and things are working out all right, after all. We've been sweeping the place, as you can see for yourself, so you can move in whenever you like. Better just take a look in advance. Come on."

The Dutoit house was a bungalow that spread out a fairly long way to the rear, as one-story houses do. It was with satisfaction that I found my room some distance from the family apartments, in a little private wing that corresponded to the servants' quarters and kitchen at the other side. We three women straggled along for a dutiful glance at it, Mrs. Dutoit chattering as we went:

"Just watch that step down, dear. If you'd care to have the furniture moved or anything like that, you've only got to—"

Waved to the head of the party, I walked through the open door and stopped short, so that Yvonne behind me stumbled on my heels. I stood staring at the clean floor matting, at a man who sat there, cross-legged and comfortable in the empty room. He had been reading; the book lay open in front of him, but now he stared back in equal surprise. It was Ahmet.

"What's the matter here?" demanded Mrs. Dutoit, bustling in. Yvonne answered:

"Only Ahmet, Mamma. Gracious, Ahmet, why don't you give a person warning? You've scared poor Julie. Julie, this is Ahmet. We didn't know he was here."

"He's a bad boy," added Mrs. Dutoit playfully. Showing confusion, Ahmet rose to his feet. He said:

"Miss de Jong and I know each other. How do you do?"

If it hadn't been for all my researches with the Djungs I might have frozen Ahmet and washed the Dutoits out of my life then and there. But my grudge had melted a little. I understood him better: I was willing to call a truce. So I agreed politely that we'd met before, and stood there in neutral silence while the women exclaimed and twittered, and explanations filled the air. It appeared that Ahmet was some sort of kinsman of the Dutoits, which was after all not surprising—what did surprise me, though, was that they should be on such easy terms that he came and went in the house in the easy Javanese fashion, using it almost as his own. Javanese families did behave in that way, I knew; what I hadn't suspected was that people like the Dutoits, who had ostensibly moved such a long way from native habits, should still cling to even a shred of traditional custom. In fact, I learned later, Ahmet was the moving spirit in this arrangement: for purposes of his own he maintained the tie.

As Yvonne and I walked down the street on our way back to the center of town, I said what was on my mind. "This relative of yours, this Ahmet; doesn't he want to live in that room? I'd hate to think I was keeping him out, and if your parents prefer to let him have it—"

"Oh no, the question doesn't arise." Yvonne spoke quickly. "There's never been any suggestion . . . We couldn't afford to keep it just for him, and he's always slept wherever there's room, that is, when he comes. He doesn't *live* with us, you know; he's not even in Batavia very often."

This surprised me. "I thought he taught school in town? I'm almost sure somebody said he did."

"His school's outside, quite a long distance I believe. Something like fifty kilometers," said Yvonne.

"They must keep very odd hours. Ahmet told your mother he intended to spend the night here."

Yvonne was not interested in Ahmet's working habits. She shrugged, and began talking instead about the details of my removal: after all it was not her line of country. But the little mystery stuck in my mind, and next day I took advantage of a free period to drop in at Jan Vries's office. I said:

"You know that Javanese you brought in for coffee that day—Ahmet. I wanted to talk about him."

Jan looked up at me, alarm showing in his spectacled eyes. "Why, is he in trouble? Sit down, Julie."

"Why?" I asked in my turn. "Ought he to be in trouble?"

"It's no joke, this sort of thing," said Vries irritably. "Speak up if you know anything; you didn't come in here without some kind of news, Julie. What's going on with Ahmet?"

"I'm sorry if I've hit you in a tender place. Nothing's going on with him that I know about, but I happened to run into him yesterday and it all just doesn't hang together. He's not a genuine schoolteacher, Jan, you know that. What's it about?" As he hesitated I probed further: "Are *you* in on some conspiracy, yourself?"

"Really, Julie! You should curb your imagination." Jan's ease was convincing. "It's only that I take an interest in people like Ahmet; I think they've got a good deal to be said for their cause. These young men—they're very courageous in their way. Our government's cracking down on them and they have to take chances, even comparatively obscure people like him; every so often one hears about another one nabbed and sent off to exile, and Ahmet's one of the best of the lot, I'd hate to have him removed. He's loyal and he doesn't lose sight of what he wants. I don't know how you feel about the political atmosphere around here, but I tell you frankly, it stinks in my nostrils. These fools around the Governor General—it wasn't always like this in the colonies."

"I suppose it's the war," I said vaguely.

"The war gives them their excuse, certainly. Ahmet, you know, is passionately devoted to Sukarno. He maintains that there's no excuse now for keeping Sukarno or the others mewed up, and sometimes he says so rather too loudly for his own good. Have you ever heard him making a speech?"

"Good Lord, no. I hardly know the man; I've seen him only twice, after all . . ."

"Well, he's good. If I'd realized you were interested in these matters—"

"What are you two cooking up in here?" Mina stuck her head in at the door and smiled at us, but her eyes were coldly suspicious. She resented any other woman's talking to Jan, even the elderly Miss Scheffer, but Jan went on talking as if she wasn't there: "I could take you around to one of the meetings, perhaps. It's a bit risky, but—"

"I simply must know what this is all about," said Mina. She came in and sat down on the desk, imperiling an inkwell. Jan moved it to a safe spot and said to me:

"The chief threat to our friend as I see it is in his own circle. They're not all as steady as he is, and one of them may take it into his head one of these days, out of jealousy or some other cause—they're so volatile, these people—to report him to the Special Branch; you know, lay false information or something like that: it's one of the hazards of life as she's lived in this tropical paradise. What I think—"

"The bell just rang," said Mina. "Come on, we must go."

Jan said, "The devil," in an impersonal way, and stood up. As a matter of fact the bell had not rung, but I took my leave. Enough is enough. On Saturday I took my things over to the Dutoits' and moved in. Ahmet had left, Yvonne told me.

Ellie, my roommate at college, though a likable girl, had never said anything particularly memorable the whole time I knew her, but one phrase she often used haunts me for some reason, cliché though it is. "It's only human, after all," she would say consolingly when I agonized, as I sometimes did, over sins I had committed. When I used bad language and then repented, or forgot to return small sums of money

69

I'd borrowed; even when I'd misbehaved with Martin and confessed to her, "It's only human, dear," Ellie would say. Her lightly comforting voice came back to me now, at odd moments, especially in the long drowsy hours of the afternoon. I was seeking reassurance, but for what? I didn't know. The house dozed and everything was still. Even the leaves on the tree that shaded my veranda hung motionless and rigid, as if made of green metal: only I lay awake, gripped by mysterious excitement. If a bird, investigating flowers in the tree, stirred a clump of leaves; if a twig fell on the ground, I started up on my bed, tingling and eager. It was only after I dreamed one afternoon, in an uneasy nap, of Ahmet walking in through the veranda door that I faced the fact. It was shameful. I wanted Ahmet. I wanted that rude little Javanese.

"It's only human, after all," tinkled in my ears idiotically, but it wasn't human, I protested silently: even Ellie couldn't have forgiven me this aberration. Why Ahmet, by all that was unreasonable? He wasn't at all my type. He resembled in no particular my kind of man: he hadn't Martin's good looks or Phil's dependability. No, I *couldn't* be attracted by Ahmet.

Then a new, insinuating voice whispered, "Why not?" and I remembered my mother, who had herself loved a Javanese and could never have been as silly and shrinking and commonplace as I. For the first time, I rebelled against the urge to follow her example. It was different, I protested. Ahmet was simply not my kind of man. I liked men like Phil or Chick or Mr. Djung, men who knew how to acquire power. Ahmet was a boy. To mother children was one thing; to mother a lover was something else, and the thought offended me. I wanted someone who would be a father to me.

As the afternoon waned I woke up and bathed in cold water, and sanity took over again. All those distressed thoughts had been merely the unhealthy musings of a hot day. I put on my clothes and went over to the hostel—inconsistently, now that I was no longer living there I spent a good deal of time chatting with Agatha in her room. That afternoon especially, I felt that I wanted to see her. Agatha was Europe, and I realized that I didn't want to cut myself off from Europe because it was familiar and reassuring. I could not face the thought of losing Europe—losing Agatha.

"Oh, it's Julie." She seemed really glad to see me. "I've been moping, I'm afraid," she said. "Come in and cheer me up."

"You too?"

"Don't tell me you're in the dumps, Julie. You've no cause to be. Pieter's gone, you know; he's been sent to Singapore on maneuvers, and one begins to think . . . Let's talk about other matters."

I stayed with her for the whole evening; we dined with the other girls and joined them in the dubious pleasure of listening to the news on the radio.

Several times I surprised on Yvonne's face as she regarded me a puzzled, wistful expression. I knew what was going on in her mind; she was disappointed in me because I did not behave as she'd expected. Life wasn't a gay round of parties for me, after all. Ridiculously, I felt that I owed Yvonne more than she was getting. For her sake I began on the old round once more, going out and dancing with one or another of the young men in uniform who swarmed over the city nowadays. It placated Yvonne to make me dress up and use her lipstick; she stood at the door waving to me when I set out on one of these expeditions, and I knew she was mollified, but I found it desperately dull work, and after a few experiments of the sort I gave it up again. It was far better to sit at home and wait.

I waited for what seemed like weeks, and then at last he came. It was at night, just as I'd pictured it, when I heard a soft noise, like a cough, outside my veranda door. I knew it wasn't the servant. I knew who it was.

"Come in," I called softly, and as he appeared I added, "You've been a long time."

"I know," replied Ahmet, "but there was so much to do. I simply couldn't come before."

It was like that, simple and direct. A good deal didn't have to be said. We had done our thinking apart, both tending a plant that was now tall and flourishing.

He came in and sat on the floor at my feet, and we talked.

CHAPTER FOUR

For a few moments I stood with Ahmet at the edge of the highway, watching the bus out of sight. It was the only vehicle visible on the road in that quiet stretch, and I felt as if we were penetrating unknown territory. Around us on our side of the paved highway was thick growth of pale, feathery-green bush and trees: across on the other side the land fell away to a deep valley, beyond which was open countryside planted with rice, the paddy incredibly regular with its rows of light and shade, like wide, wide steps covered with yellow-green carpet, mounting to an unseen landing among the trees along the top of the hill range. Too far away to be seen plainly, a row of kerchiefed women stooped to their work on the rice. They always toiled together, bowing and rising, lined up like puppets being worked on a common system of strings.

I said, "Why didn't you tell me you were going into the forest?"

"Forest?" repeated Ahmet, perplexed. "We aren't." Then he laughed at me in genuine mirth that I had not seen him show before, with eyes nearly shut. "Come and follow me into this forest," he said, and turned to march into the greenery. I found myself on a path that was slippery under my high-heeled shoes, so that it was hard to remain upright, and I was nervous: what if we were to get lost? Ahmet, brushing aside a hanging banana frond, walked across a makeshift bridge of damp wood and continued to lead me until we came out into bright sunlight once more.

"Where's the forest now?" he asked.

I blinked, then joined him in laughing at myself. The trees and bushes had been only a thick hedge, and now we were in a village where little houses of bleached wood stood on slightly raised foundations, all around a large clear rectangular space. The whole thing was a few meters from the road. Up at the other end of the clearing was a large tree of unusual shape, the waringin that sends its branches over and down into the ground where they take root again. Javanese set great store by waringins; I had seen them planted like guardians at the doors of important buildings. This was a fine big specimen.

It was a very quiet place, but there were people about. Babies played near the houses and glanced at us without interest; older children, who were collecting sticks or carrying pots, interrupted these tasks to stop short and stare at us curiously. Here and there a woman appeared at the dark door of her cottage. A group of men, lounging near the tree, turned their heads toward us. Everyone was motionless for a minute, as if caught by a camera to put on a tourist's postcard. Then a dog barked and the photo broke up. The whole village recognized Ahmet: suddenly everybody was coming toward us smiling, holding out their hands and calling him by name. The men came first; women and girls loitered behind them, giggling shyly until he had finished greeting the men and turned to them. He knew them all. I loitered just as they did, standing in Ahmet's shadow until he remembered to explain my presence as Miss de Jong—a teacher in Batavia who wanted to see a genuine Javanese kampong, and so on and so on. Everyone beamed to think that theirs was a genuine kampong, worthy of being exhibited to a teacher. Finally we were wafted in the crowd to one of the houses, which belonged to the oldest man in the community. A few of his cronies were invited to come in with us and the others politely took their leave.

Ahmet said to me, like a Cook's tour guide, "Here you have a typical house. You can see how plain it is."

Our host must have been able to understand Dutch, but he showed no resentment: why should he? Facts are facts and the house *was* simple, to the ultimate degree—two rooms, very sparsely furnished and with a raised platform for a bed, made up the whole. In the back room where we gathered there was only one article that could be described as an ornament—a low platform supporting a glass case. When I went over to look closely at this, I saw inside the case a dagger with wavy edge and inlaid hilt, or *kris*, supported on a sort of cushion of green satin. I turned to ask what it was, but Ahmet shook his head. Our host's wife was far younger than himself, a small, plump, quick-moving woman, her face broad with high cheekbones, and her skin dark. She wore a headkerchief folded in a way that reminded me of a Dutch cap, and her smile too could have been a Dutch peasant's. She hurried to set a little table with glasses that had been jam jars, and bottles of bright pink mineral water, and a plate of those sugary white confections like petrified knots of tape that are a favorite cookie for the sweet-toothed Indonesians. Then she went out of the house, rather to my dismay, for it left me nothing to do and no one to talk to. At the same time there was something bothering my mind, something I couldn't place, as one can't quite locate a new rattle in one's car. The men, sipping and nibbling, talked in Javanese. They looked wise and absorbed, smiling in the mechanical manner all the natives had, but I couldn't follow what was being said, so I felt out of place, and cramped, and bored. Flies buzzed around us; the heat strengthened; before I knew it I was nodding. Ahmet's voice waked me:

"*Njonja* you need not stay here with nothing to do. Why not go out and look around until we've finished our business?"

Njonja? It was a peculiar way for Ahmet to address me, opening as it did the chasm that separates white colonial from native, but before I spoke about it and laughed at him

75

I realized that he had done it deliberately. It was what the villagers expected; what they believed was our relationship. Perhaps they were right, too; if that wasn't our relationship then how could it have been described? The thought added to the troublesome unlocated rattle in my mind, and I made an escape gratefully. Outside I found my hostess openly waiting to take me under her protection. Followed by a train of children and a few girls and women, we made the rounds. We called on my hostess's best friend, or perhaps it was a sister, in another house, where we drank more pink mineral water. We looked at gardens and fruit trees and fowls and babies, and I conversed with the ladies in halting Bahasa, about families and illnesses. We moved always in that particular glow of courtesy and friendliness that Javanese create by smiling and talking in their pleasant soft voices. Surely the alarmists were wrong, I thought: to suspect people like this of being angry and rebellious was like suspecting sedition in a nursery school.

It was when I paused to look through the shade of the waringin, and saw little figures propped in the foliage like dolls on a Christmas tree, and realized that people prayed to these dolls as no doubt they prayed to the waringin itself, that I understood my trouble. A very pretty young woman happened to be standing beside me, looking at my clothes and my face with a frank appraisal that could not possibly be offensive, and suddenly I found myself looking back at her in the same way and wondering if she had ever made love with Ahmet. The thought was so painful that I caught my breath. God knows why I entertained it at that moment, about that particular girl. It could not have been intuition, and nothing came of it: I never saw the woman again or heard of her, either. I never even knew her name. But there she was like a symbol, a threat; she was a pretty young woman who admired Ahmet, she was a Javanese like Ahmet; she possessed much in common with him. In all these respects she had the advantage of me, and she was only one of a great number. He may not have made love with her, but there must be others. I hated them all. I deplored the existence of Javanese women. I was jealous of the whole unknown. Besides, I now knew what was the matter with me.

"So that's that," said Ahmet on the homeward bus. "I hope you haven't been disappointed. You wanted to see a village, and you did, but as I said before it's nothing much."

I replied exactly as a young lady teacher would have replied to an interesting young native who had done her a favor. "I found it very interesting. It was nice of you to take me." But one couldn't keep it up forever, and I added, less formally, "Now perhaps you can tell me what the idea was of the *kris* in the old man's house, in the glass case. Was it a souvenir of some battle, or what?"

Ahmet seemed embarrassed, and hesitated before speaking. "I thought you might have heard already about that old custom. White people call it superstition, and they're right about that, of course. It's nothing much, only that some old-timers believe that their family spirit, which is a sort of collective thing in each clan, lives in the *kris*. It's always an old weapon that's been handed down from generation to generation. That old man who entertained us would certainly pray to his *kris* when he needs guidance, and the family sacrifices to it. It's supposed to protect the house. . . . It sounds foolish when one says it."

"Oh, I don't know. Prayer is prayer," I said. After a pause I added, "I saw some idols or something, propped up in that waringin. I'm not sure I understand all this. I thought the Javanese were Muslims."

They were, said Ahmet. Almost every Javanese was Muslim, hadn't I learned that? I said that of course I had learned it, but how did that square with prayers to daggers and trees? Ahmet then gave a little lecture about remnants of older beliefs, and the power of custom—the body of ancient rules called *adat*—over uneducated people. "Though I admit it isn't only uneducated villagers who do it," he ended. "I've known quite sophisticated people who stick to the old ways."

"What about you?" I asked.

Ahmet said that he didn't pray to a *kris*, nor even to trees. I asked even more boldly, "What about the rest of it? Are *you* a good Muslim?"

"Next you'll be asking the question foreigners always ask: how many wives I have," said Ahmet. "No, *njonja*, I am not a Muslim, at least not a faithful one. I don't hold with any religion."

"But you haven't answered the other question. How many wives have you?"

It came as a surprise when he replied quite simply, "One. Only one."

The road we followed had become busier. From tributaries the flood kept coming—rickshas, carts, and cars. We had picked up a number of passengers too, and though none of them were foreign, I felt self-conscious about talking in such a personal way. My next attempt was in a softer tone: Where had he gone to school? It was like pulling teeth to get that sort of information out of Ahmet, but at last I learned that his native village was near Jogjakarta on the slopes of a volcano, and that he had first attended a school supported by a nearby mosque. I said:

"Then surely you started out as a Muslim, no matter what's happened since."

"Oh yes, of course," said Ahmet. "They were good teachers too, within their limitations, and very good to me. Because they thought I showed promise, funds were found to keep me going even after I'd passed the age when most of my friends dropped out. We villagers have a community system, you know; everyone contributes if a clever child ought to have an education and his people can't pay for it. That's the way it was with me. I was trained to go into teaching. But as I got older, a good deal of it went against the grain with me. I quarreled with my masters, one thing led to another, and in the end I left them. . . . This is very boring for a young lady from Holland."

I protested, and kept him on the track. Never mind the

people sitting around us: it had taken a long time to coax Ahmet into a revelatory mood, and I didn't want to stop the flow.

"By that time I was ready to leave home," he continued, "and so I did, to take up a position here, but it meant a considerable struggle with my family. There was the question of my wife. They thought that if I insisted on going, she should accompany me—my parents are upset because the only child is a girl; they want us to try again. I said no."

"Why did you?" I had made up my mind not to speak about his marriage, but I couldn't stick to my resolution.

"Of course I refused. I'd been against marrying her—marrying anyone, if it comes to that—from the beginning, but they'd insisted. You see, it is the custom among us to marry very young, and I've nothing to say against custom in the ordinary case. For me, however, it was different. I felt that I had work to do in the world, that I should not be held back by personal responsibilities. At the time of the marriage I was a child with no voice to raise in behalf of myself. Very well, it was done and I had no reason to undo it, but to go on building up obstacles! . . . No, I would not do it. I feel stronger now. In time I'll take more definite steps. I am a grown man and know my own mind."

He looked stern; at that moment he did not at all resemble the popular idea of a Javanese. But I was shocked. He had a child, a little girl, so how could he talk so coldly about her? He seemed to think that his wife had no personality of her own; that she had been born and brought up merely to hang around his neck, a burden he'd never bargained for. It was hard to tell which thought distressed me more: Ahmet's being married and unattainable for me, or sympathy for that unfortunate woman. I preferred to concentrate on the sympathy, which gave an excuse for questions.

"Where is she?" I asked. He was talking and didn't hear.

"On the whole I think it's a part of the custom we'll have to throw away when we reform *adat*. Our young people are in revolt against it, though the whole subject needs further thought."

"What's she like?"

"One doesn't wish to imply that Western ways are invariably correct and the East is always wrong. Some of our leaders approve of the marriage customs we have, just as they are, but I don't. A man doesn't have to support foreign culture to see faults in—"

"Ahmet," I said, putting my hand on his arm, "where does your wife live if she isn't with you?"

"Heh?" He broke off, and looked at me as if he'd forgotten I was there. "My wife?" Clearly it was an effort to bring his thoughts back to the particular and personal. "Oh, she's at home in the village with my family. Where else would she be?"

"Is she pretty?"

"I don't know. I suppose she might be called pretty. The subject doesn't interest me and I try to forget the relationship altogether. As long as the child is well I'm satisfied. Must we go on discussing this? I find it a waste of time."

"But don't you ever think that it's an injustice to a woman to leave her like that? There the poor thing is with her child and no husband. The village must look down on her if she can't keep you at home. And you're traveling around just as it suits you."

"I do *not* travel around merely because it suits me." For a minute he sounded quite angry. Then he broke off and laughed. "So, even though you're a Westerner you're preoccupied like any woman here with personal matters! It's interesting." Now it was my complacency that had been pricked, and I began to boil, but Ahmet hadn't finished. "Never mind. At least you have other interests as well. If I ever thought it would fit into the scheme, though it won't, I should marry again. And it would have to be a European wife, or a woman trained in the Western way."

My anger dissolved. Ahmet relaxed on the seat, his arms folded, and seemed willing to ride for the rest of the way in silence. I was quite ready to fall in with his mood, since there was a lot to think about, but after another pause at a station he said:

"Now let's talk about *your* ideas, *your* experience, or you will think that all Indonesian men are spoiled by their women and think themselves gods. You've told me that you come from the Netherlands, but you look so much like a Javanese that I made an embarrassing mistake that day we first met. How does it happen that you weren't born here, where you obviously belong?"

"You needn't look at me so accusingly," I said. "I couldn't help it."

"Still, in the end you made amends: you came out to the islands. I suppose that was because you were in search of an easy life in the tropics, with plenty of cheap labor and a lot of leisure, wasn't it?"

"Oh yes," I said cheerfully. "That's why I came to Java." It was not easy to know when Ahmet was serious: he nearly always looked just the same. But when he nodded and said: "That's just as I thought," I decided that this time he was being playful, and I felt as triumphant as if I had persuaded a lion to disport with a ball of string. There was also satisfaction and escape in having turned the conversation away from my past. I had no desire to talk to him about my mother, though I continued to speculate, wondering if my father could have been anything like this rather ponderous but attractive Ahmet. All in all, it was a successful afternoon. I was happy about it.

When Ahmet went away again, letting drop a vague hint that his absence would be a long one, I was inclined to mope. School holidays were coming on and I had looked forward to spending far more time exploring Java with him. What was all this tiresome political activity that kept him away so much? If it hadn't been for the uncertainty of everything, I thought, I would have gone off myself on a journey, to Hongkong or Japan, where I might meet a man more to my taste than Ahmet. But there seemed to be nowhere to go, until the morning I met Marge Palmer near her house, looking through the shops for a suitcase.

She greeted me with a cordial cry, and though I knew it was not true that she'd been intending to call me up as she said, I was pleased to see her. I was more pleased when she said, "Julie, you've got to come with me. I want to go to Bali. Do come, it'll be only for a week, and I can't persuade Chick to leave that old office. My dear, I've been trying for years to make Chick take me to Bali, and he always puts it off, and before you know it we'll be home and he'll retire and I'll never have another chance. Won't you come?"

Of course I did. If I'd thought that the journey would work a change in me, however, I was mistaken. Through all the time we spent on the beautiful little island, I was either dreaming or fretting, and could not forget Ahmet for more than a few minutes at a time. At first Marge was an amusing companion. She chattered and made me laugh, telling about her life as a girl in the Middle West of America, where she had "gone steady," as she called it, with Chick from the day they first met at high school. American women were surprising, I thought: they never seemed to grow any older. Marge paid as much attention to her clothes and her hair as any young girl, though she must have been middle-aged. She drank a good deal, growing even more talkative and gay as the day went on. It wasn't long before I began to feel like a chaperon, when Marge made friends with an American tourist traveling on his own. I can't remember much about him; he was just a man. But Marge got on well with him, and because it left me more time in which to think my own thoughts, I was glad of him.

We three oddly assorted companions had the world nearly to ourselves. Bali had been a magnet for German tourists before the war, but now of course they had disappeared and only a few optimistic travelers like Marge's friend shared the customary pleasures of the place with us. I sat on the beach or watched dances or visited beauty spots, saying very little and thinking of Ahmet. Some of the dances were private performances given only for our trio; Marge complained that gamelan music bored her because it was always the same, an endless tinkle, but I found it insidious and Marge wrong. When I listened to it and watched some young girl dance, her supple body and painted, expressionless face, with the twining music and the smell of frangipani blossom woven in her hair, made me want to weep. I scarcely saw the American's hand gripping Marge's; I paid no attention to the fact that she was laughing more nervously now, and drinking more, or that sometimes she stayed away at night until I fell asleep, giving no explanation in the morning. Anyway, if she had explained I wouldn't have heard her. Marge didn't matter. I wanted to get back to Java: Bali was much too far away. The week seemed endless.

But at last it was finished and I could say goodbye to Marge, scarcely noticing her red-rimmed eyes and absent-mindedness after we left the American man. It was wonderful to get back to the Dutoit house. I knew Ahmet would not be there, but it was his place and he would come back. In the meantime, there was only Mrs. Dutoit, superintending the preparation of my room. She greeted me rather quietly. Merely because I wanted to use his name, I said:

"I don't suppose Ahmet's been here since I left, has he, Mrs. Dutoit?"

She gave me an unfriendly glance that cut sharply through my dreams. "No, he hasn't," she said, "but no doubt he'll come walking in as soon as he knows you're back."

I watched her stalk out, head in air, and felt worried. Other people had not until then made themselves evident in the world I saw myself inhabiting with Ahmet, and though my conscience ought to have been clear, this seemed a threatening development. Women like Mrs. Dutoit had been part of the landscape in the old days I preferred to forget. The Mrs. Dutoits of the world were one's natural enemy, but a good deal in the future might depend on keeping Mrs. Dutoit's good will. I had no definite plans, but I knew I had to stay in that house. It was with trepidation that I spoke to

Yvonne about the matter as soon as she came home from work. Much to my relief she took it calmly.

"Oh, that? Yes, I knew: Mamma's been getting sour about your thing with Ahmet for some time now. I should think you'd have noticed before. I'm not asking any questions, but you must have a lot on your mind not to have seen it." She looked at me archly. "Don't worry," she added. "I'll handle Mamma. You just leave it to me."

So Yvonne already knew how I felt. I should not have had to be told this; she was a clever girl and I had questioned her closely about Ahmet far too often for discretion, but I did feel surprised. It was a long time since I'd given any thought to other people and their awareness of me.

"Yvonne, you must believe me. There's nothing wrong going on," I assured her, and she laughed.

"Don't worry, Julie, I know. But you'll have to excuse Mamma. Look at it from her point of view if you can. Suppose Ahmet gets seriously involved with you—yes, I believe you if you say he isn't, but who knows how much gossip there'll be, sooner or later? He did take you out into the country and that's going to cause talk in itself. Now, I happen to know he isn't getting on with his wife, and so does Mamma know it. Ahmet's family might say it's all your fault."

"He'd never even met me when he—"

"I'm only telling you what *they* might think, not what I do. They could blame her for his meeting you in this house, and that would mean trouble in the family; quarrels. People have awful quarrels around here, Julie; you've no idea. Myself I think they enjoy it . . . Mind you, I don't think it would happen in this case. They realize Ahmet's marriage is a lost cause. It's an old story. I'm just telling you what goes on in Mamma's mind, but you must leave her to me; I'll talk her round."

Whatever Yvonne said to Mrs. Dutoit, it was effective. Peace returned to our house, but the incident made me do some hard thinking. The facts were clear: I'd fallen in love

84

with a Javanese, a Communist at that. At least there was every indication of it. I'd never expected to be mixed up with a Communist, of all people. In Holland the leftist students had bored me stiff, they were so serious and self-important, and later when Russia and Germany made their pact I'd been disgusted. The fact that Russia had been betrayed by Germany into falling on our side of the fence didn't make the country or the creed any more attractive. Still . . . no doubt it was different for Ahmet or any other Indonesian. Jan Vries once said that communism was bound to attract the natives in colonies. When I thought it over, I could see what he meant. For all the talk you heard from the Dutch about the Indies being a part of the Netherlands, it wasn't true. A Dutchman wasn't looked after and controlled by foreigners: it was *his* government he lived under, made up of people like himself. And now, in the war, our Army and Navy and Air Force—what there was of them—were made up of Dutch people; we didn't have many Indonesians in uniform. In fact, there were hardly any. The whole concept was false. I knew the communist concept was false too, but the Indonesians didn't. Besides, communism didn't ask them to make a break with their masters. Vries said:

"The policy right now is, Not yet: Get rid of the fascists first. You don't have to worry about the Reds in this part of the world, Julie, if that's what you're thinking: it's never amounted to much. I'm not sure the so-called Commie riots in '26 were anything but a fluke. They were more pathetic than dangerous, and the few Reds who had guts are following Sukarno now—keeping quiet, playing safe, not even yelling for independence. Not yet."

But Ahmet was yelling for independence, I reflected. I'd have to make him confide in me. I wanted to hear what he thought about all this—about Russia, for example. He'd studied there. He was maddeningly close-mouthed about Russia. If it came to that, he was close-mouthed about everything.

The holidays were over. We had a very long spell of particularly hot weather. I woke too early one morning and found the room so hot and humid that there was no question of going back to sleep, so I got up and went out on the veranda in a blind search for fresher air. I had been in Batavia long enough to know better; outside was just as close as inside, but still I hoped, and then, leaning on the porch rail, I was glad in any case that I had come out. The sun was not yet up, and I heard a bird talking softly as it woke. Dawn was just over the edge of the world, and things were taking shape: I could make out a tree at the edge of the garden, all silvery like a ghostly little fountain. My body, loosely covered with a sarong, was silvery too, and though there was no breeze I felt cooler because of that. I stood motionless until the moment vanished; then, turning to go in, I found another figure standing close behind me—Ahmet, naked save for a loincloth. At that moment the sun came up, and all the silver turned to gold.

We looked into each other's eyes. Then he raised his hand in a gesture that might have been greeting or warning, and slipped away, into the door next to mine. I watched him as he disappeared, brown and warm and living, and he seemed to take with him a little of the new sun. Still, everything remained flooded with brilliance. The bird was fully awake, and sang with all its heart.

I was impatient with my lesson at the Djung house that afternoon, and wished for the first time that I need not stay on for my usual visit with Ming. She may have noticed it; for a girl who seemed completely self-centered she was very intuitive. At any rate she suddenly asked:

"Julie, what are you going to do with yourself?" I was not quite sure what she meant, so she went on, "When all this is over—this war. Haven't you any plans? You know, it's time you were settled in life."

"Oh, nonsense!" I answered immediately and roughly, but there was something about the room, with Ming in it so sure of herself and comfortable as she lit a cigarette with a gold lighter, that struck me: I was bitterly aware of my lot. It was all very well for Ming to ask.

She spread out her bright fingernails and studied them. "It's no use shouting at me, my dear, you're no different from the rest of us, you know. You, too, will get older, and then you might wish you'd been more practical at the right time. It's fine while you're still young and pretty and can pick companions as you wish, but what would it be like as an aging spinster? You'll get old and queer."

I muttered, "I don't see the good of rubbing it in. Who is there in this place? You answer me that."

"Really, Julie—in a city this size, simply overflowing with men! You must play your cards better."

"Not all women think along those lines. Not all of us think of marriage as business."

Her laugh was without rancor. "And I suppose I'm no better than a rubber broker, watching the market! Always balancing accounts, is that what you mean? It may be true; if so, I'm not ashamed of it. But what are these superior ideals you cherish so carefully, Julie? What are you after that's so much better than marriage and security?"

I could feel my face getting red. One couldn't possibly talk to Ming about my mother's attitude toward life, even in roundabout terms. You might as well expect a pampered pedigreed cat to understand the fascination of a tigress's existence. I said:

"All right, Ming, you win the argument. I haven't any better aim than yours. I suppose I've got what are called ideals, the usual sort. I believe in honesty, and being kind, and going to church now and then, and—No, part of it is missing: I'm not patriotic. When the Germans came in at home, and people walked around this town weeping, and weren't ashamed of it—"

She nodded. "They weren't all Europeans, either. I remember."

"There you are. I wasn't one of them," I said. "You weren't

87

really talking about that, I know, but you asked what I'm after, and it's easier to say what I'm *not* after."

She tapped out the cigarette thoughtfully. "I wouldn't worry too much about that blank spot, Julie. You're bound to be a bit mixed up, being half-and-half. Let's get back to the real question. Why don't you marry? An unmarried woman is a wasted person. You don't see many of them in the East."

"Thanks to polygamy." It was out before I thought, and I was covered with shame as I remembered too late about the other Djung wives, but Ming only said composedly:

"Certainly, and from my point of view it's the best argument you could advance for polygamy. I've always thought China made a mistake when she outlawed it after the revolution in 1911."

"Was it outlawed?" I asked in surprise. "Then—Mr. Djung—"

She lowered her eyelashes. "Mr. Djung followed custom, not law. He wasn't muddled by all that stupid Christianity that's done so much harm to China. I'm sorry to say rude things about your church, Julie, but it isn't Western Christianity I'm talking about—only converts here. I'm sure Christianity's all right in Europe."

"And, of course, if Mr. Djung ever really did attempt polygamy, you'd be on the spot with your little hatchet, wouldn't you?"

"Oh yes," said Ming. "But that too is custom."

"Ming . . ."

"Yes?"

"Just now you said something about me being half-and-half. . . . Do you think I'd have a fifty per cent chance of success in the other sort of marriage? I'm not referring to polygamy, but if I married an Eastern man . . ."

Ming put down her cup. "Oho! This is interesting. Is he Chinese?"

"No, Javanese. But there isn't anyone particular, you understand; I was talking in theory. Hypothetically."

"In that case, I've never heard a more elaborate hypothesis.

88

Julie, I don't know. I really am ignorant about Javanese ways of life. You should ask Mr. Djung about that kind of thing. Now do tell me more about your hypothetical man, will you?"

But I had gone far enough—too far: I was appalled by my indiscretion, and soon I took my leave, with Ming standing at the door to watch me go. Her expression was a mixture of perplexity, amusement, and disquiet. I felt great warmth for her. She was really fond of me: I was really fond of her. . . . But I wanted to be home where I could be quiet, where I could go to bed early and think about Ahmet.

As I came up the path through the front lawn, Mrs. Dutoit called, "Is that Julie? Hurry up, dear, Ahmet's waiting for you."

This was unheard of. As I entered, wondering if it was some sort of joke, Mr. Dutoit took off his spectacles and lowered his newspaper, and said, "Ahmet was here a minute ago, asking for you, I believe. Now where *is* that boy?"

"Julie?" called Yvonne from the dining room. "Hurry up, Ahmet's here, waiting for you."

It was scarcely a surprise by that time; he was helping Yvonne with the much used coffee tray. She winked at me as she carried it in to her parents. Ahmet said:

"I've been waiting for you."

"Yes?"

He did sound hurried. I'd never found him in the house at this hour. Pacing around, he said, "I thought those Chinese lessons were over earlier than this; I was on the point of giving up and leaving."

"But how was I to know?" A sense of grievance made me tart. "Don't let me detain you now; I know perfectly well how important time is to you."

He was surprised; he was always surprised when other people's interests were pressed on him and interfered with his. "Yes, of course time's important, but I did wait for you; why do you resent that?" He didn't pause for an answer to the question, but abandoned it as trivial. "You said you'd like to attend one of our meetings, to hear me speak. Tonight there is a meeting, so I've waited to take you with me, but now we must hurry."

We walked. I was excited by the prospect: I felt that I was about to steal a march on Jan Vries and the others. Though evening had fallen I somehow expected that we would be joining a crowd assembled in the open air, perhaps on the great parade ground, and that there would be stirring music played by a band. The reality was of course completely different: we arrived alone at the entrance to a shuttered house in one of the quietest and dullest residential districts in town. It looked as if the inhabitants had gone to bed, if indeed they were not away. I asked nervous questions of Ahmet—hadn't there been a mistake? Or were we so late that everything was over, and everyone had gone home?

"Don't talk yet, please," said Ahmet. He scratched the door lightly and said his name; immediately the door opened and we went inside, into a brightly lit room crowded with chattering people in the stuffy warm air. I couldn't see any furniture, though I suppose there must have been some, but I noticed that the light came from hanging bulbs that were unshaded, and the walls needed painting. There were Javanese everywhere. At first I thought I was the only woman in the place, but I was mistaken; a scattering of females were present. They didn't huddle together, as Javanese women usually did in the few native gatherings I'd attended. They stood around like the men, and talked without shyness. Ahmet was seized and surrounded as soon as people saw him, and I stood alone, a foreign enclave, completely ignored.

It would be false to say that the place had a conspiratorial atmosphere. The members of the meeting were too calm and smiling to give an impression of stealth or even caution—no doubt the walls were thick, and the talkers could be sure they were unheard out of doors. But I knew we were breaking the law somehow, and I was frightened. I'd always been part of some institution. I'd never been a rebel. Even when I broke the unwritten laws of morality I had done it in the conventional way, and I was dizzy at my own daring now.

It took a moment for the inevitable afterthought to arrive, when I invoked my mother, but as soon as I did I felt strong. This was splendid, after all: at last I was catching up with her. Hadn't she been a conspirator of the very first rank? She might even have belonged to some group like this. Once I'd thought of it, the fancy gained strength. I *belonged* here, I decided. I looked around at all the oblivious strangers and told myself firmly that they were my chosen companions.

They were simply people I might have seen on any street, though perhaps they were more concentratedly middle-class than that. One might have thought them the staff of any large business house, or the graduating class of a college: spectacles predominated, and nobody was shabby. This fact put rather a damper on romantic ideas. Revolutionaries, I thought disappointedly, ought to look the part more than this. Then my eyes lit on a familiar face, and with surprise I returned the greeting of Mr. Yoshida, who owned the shop where I usually had my photographs developed. What was he doing here? He seemed to be thinking the same question about me, and I would have approached him and perhaps asked him outright, if Ahmet had not remembered my existence at that moment. He broke through the cordon around him—spectacled and toothy men, with one pretty girl in a blue *kabaja*—and brought me over and introduced us all.

"You're interested in these affairs? Good," said the pretty girl, of whom I was immediately jealous. Later I learned she was a doctor, married to Ahmet's best friend in the movement, but that evening I hated her, and criticized in spiteful silence her teeth, which in truth were not perfectly regular.

The speakers were ready to begin, and Ahmet left me to Fatma's protection, in order to join his colleagues at the top of the room. Again I was surprised. We had no formal chamber to go to, and no benches: we simply sat down where we were, cross-legged on the floor. At first this made me feel patronizing, as if I were at some party where the guests were expected to play charades or a word game. But I had learned that I was not the only newcomer there: the main purpose of this gathering was to take in a few friends of members who had been screened and were judged ready to hear more about their aspirations toward self-government. The first man to talk was decorous enough. He spoke Bahasa Indonesia and I was able to follow most of it; it sounded so mild and reasonable that I began to wonder why all the secrecy was necessary. Of course political meetings of any sort were frowned on, I reflected, but there was little harm in this.

The second man used Javanese and I wasn't able to understand what he said. He seemed angrier than the earlier talker, however, and some of the people in the audience got excited and cried out from time to time, expressing approval or egging him on. It was Ahmet who gave me the surprise of the evening. He had such power! I must have sensed it in him before that evening, but now it wasn't constrained or smoldering. He talked bitterly of the shabby treatment the Indies had been given by the Dutch, referring to historical wrongs and returning to the present, where things were worse than they had ever been, he said. He threw aside any pretense of being patient: he seemed to have forgotten, or at least rejected, the official directive that had been issued to his coworkers, to wait and bide their time until the war was over. The message was not so much in his words—I couldn't understand them all, at any rate—as in the delivery. Jan Vries was right: Ahmet had tremendous drive, and was a born orator. He carried the audience with him like an opera singer. Even I was carried. It wasn't my cause, but long before the end I, too, was quivering with indignation. Later I wondered why, but for the moment that was the effect of Ahmet's speaking— of any good public speaking. Sometimes I wonder what the excitement is made of, and where it goes when the echoes have died away. Then I remember that with some people, as with Ahmet, it never dies. They carry it with them.

When he wound up the meeting came to an end, with handshaking all round. Getting everyone out of the house was a complicated proceeding. A man who had stayed on watch at the door all evening now held it open just a crack and peered out, giving the all-clear signal from time to time, upon which one or two people slipped out into the street and padded quietly away, while the rest of us waited and gave them time to get out of sight. Our turn came near the end. Batavia streets can be very dark, as they were then. Ahmet walked briskly, in silence; I guessed he was going over his performance much as an actor or singer might do on his way home, analyzing and perfecting it against the next time. I was content to trot along quietly by his side, his admiring woman, waiting until he felt like coming back to earth, but the city's outskirts were not meant for pedestrians at night, and soon I made a misstep and nearly fell. Ahmet pulled me back from what would have been collision with a tree.

"Are you trying to get back into it?" he asked, half angrily. I didn't understand, so he told me the legend of the spirits that live in trees, like others in the clouds and animals. These are not like the waringin, which is special; they are just ordinary spirits, except that they have a taste for coming out and moving around like men and women among genuine human beings. A young man may meet some lovely girl, or what he thinks is a girl, and everything goes beautifully until they happen to pass her tree and suddenly the trunk opens, the girl steps in, and the trunk closes again.

"It's sad for the young man," I said.

"Very sad. I've been told by a ricksha-puller that he had a passenger one night who did the same thing—melted into a grove by the road, before he'd paid his fare. That's even sadder."

"A dishonest spirit, you mean?"

"Our spirits have all the human vices," said Ahmet.

At the house everything was dark except for the lamp left burning above my side door on the veranda. The door was always left unlocked when I came home late. I slipped off my shoes before going up the front steps so that I wouldn't wake anyone, but as I wasn't used to going barefoot, Ahmet outwalked me. Realizing this, he turned back and gave me a hand, and together we tiptoed along the porch to his door.

Unlike mine, as he found when he tried it, it had been locked. I whispered:

"All right, come through my room," and he nodded.

Indoors I turned on the bedside lamp and Ahmet switched off the one on the porch. The evening was over, and I thought dismally, "He's going away again." He was always going away. One had moments of liberation, even joy, but the world was a sad place after all, and in the end Ahmet always departed. . . . He stood hesitant, and I realized that I had not yet paid him any compliments on his speech at the meeting.

"Thank you for taking me, Ahmet," I said, rather formally. "You were wonderful."

To my surprise his face lit up at this simple tribute. Why, I thought, he really needs praise: he's hungry for it. He said, asking for more, "You really did think so?"

"I've never heard anyone speak so well."

Then at last he took me in his arms, at last. Was it me he held, or the reflection of himself in my eyes? It didn't matter. We were the same thing.

CHAPTER FIVE

I saw myself at that time as an audience of one, watching a private little play that stole its bit of the stage from the larger drama of war. The little interloper was our love story, mine and Ahmet's, and if you argue that no one can watch a play and act in it at the same time, I can only say that you are right, but I was late in learning it. I thought I knew about love. Hadn't Martin taught me? Hadn't I taught others? I loved Ahmet more than I'd ever cared for anyone else; still, I was Julie de Jong, who had been there before: it was only a question of degree. With self-confidence, therefore, I sat back to watch the comedy work itself out yet again. The growling, rumbling thunder and jagged lightning seemed put there merely in order to provide the actors with an effective background.

One day, simply and innocently and unconsciously, Ahmet showed me where I really stood, and my double life came to an end. I was there on the stage with him, all of me: not even the most transparent *Doppelgänger* sat on the other side of the footlights. Ahmet was talking about the future, as he always did, but this time he related it to personal matters, and this wasn't usually his way.

"Next time I go to my village I shall arrange my divorce," he said, and looked at me affectionately.

I remember I was gratified. Someone loved me enough to get a divorce for me; how pleasant! But I felt the caress only as a cat does when it rubs against its master: taking, not giving. "And then," continued Ahmet, "you will be my wife, Julie, my dear wife."

This was not so good. I made a face, repeating the word. "Divorce. It sounds formidable. Ahmet, I'd rather you didn't go through with it."

"You're always generous and strong-hearted," he said, "but I'm not going to let you go on making this sacrifice of your dignity. Besides, divorce in our country is nothing like the painful thing it is in yours. My darling brave Julie!"

Cat or no cat, he was making me feel a little ashamed, as it wasn't generosity that made me demur. I simply couldn't take the idea at all seriously, that was the trouble. Me marry a Javanese? Julie de Jong go native? It was wildly impossible. Fantastic pictures popped into my head: what would they say at the hostel, for instance? I could hear the snickers already. Imagine the Palmers on the subject, at one of their parties. And life in a kampong, carrying a jar of water on my head, sitting on the ground . . . A cold fright seized me. This, I told myself, must be how a male roué feels when he is in danger of being caught by matrimony.

"You really must not think of it, getting a divorce for me," I insisted. Perhaps the old joke would help, and I tried it: "Besides, you don't have to; you're allowed four wives as it is. Why bother?"

Ahmet took my hand. "I love your courage and I love you, but we must be serious. In the world we're going to build, all this disgusting inequality of the sexes will be wiped out, and the least we can do is start protesting now. Polygamy is a dirty, medieval thing, an insult to women."

"Oh, I don't know. It has its points. Dividing responsibility for a husband . . ." I was still desperately gay.

"Julie," he said, "think what you're saying. We're going to have sons. We'll try to bring them up properly, but what if they find it pleasant to lord it over their women? If the law permits it, there's always the temptation. And you must think of our daughters even more."

I did, for the first time. It was a shock. Children at school in my classroom were one thing: my own possible children were quite another. I'd never considered a baby resulting from love-making except in the light of a threat. This may sound monstrous, but the life I'd led was hardly conducive to any other way of thinking. Yet here was my lover, Ahmet, talking of our marriage and of our children as if these were the most natural things in the world. And—my heart leaped as I realized it—they were! At that moment all the rest of it, chitchat at the hostel and the difficulties of kampong life, slipped into the shadows forever.

"I wonder," I said.

"What do you wonder?" He tightened his grasp of my hand.

"Nothing but a silly little idea. I was wondering if my mother—our mothers—had such plans and hopes about the world we were going to grow up in."

He shook his head sadly. "Not mine. She was never taught to think in these terms at all. Her mind was wickedly wasted, and that's one of the reasons we must see that it can't happen again."

"My mother," I began, and stopped for a second. "I don't know anything about mine," I said at last. Ahmet, thinking he understood, stroked my hair.

In the history books war always comes down like the wolf on the fold, taking its civilian victims by surprise. They're living their ordinary lives when suddenly the blow falls: an armed baron rides over the horizon with his serfs; the ship is torpedoed; Indians attack, whooping, at the dark of the moon when the settlement is asleep. History books will say the same things about our war, and for the other cities of the East it will be the truth. In Hawaii and Malaya and Hongkong it started with a dropping bomb that shattered the sleep and the peace of innocent victims, but the Indies are always different. The war came to Batavia at a leisurely pace, as if the climate were slowing it down.

I was preparing for Christmas, and working hard at it since

I felt it would be my last. "When we marry I shall become a Muslim," I said to Ahmet, and though he assured me he didn't care whether I did or not, I chose to think he was pleased at heart. We made a lot of plans about the marriage. The date of course had to wait on his divorce, the ceremony of which he explained in detail. "I talk it over with the kampong chief. As soon as he's been notified and is convinced I mean it, the divorce proceeds. We don't have to go to court."

"And you're absolutely sure you'll never regret it?"

Ahmet said, "No." We had the same conversation twenty times, but I still had to hear him say it. This time he added with genial scorn, "Women!"

In the same amiably superior manner he watched the Dutoit women and me as we wrapped parcels and talked about Christmas. The week before the Japanese started everything, I was busier than ever on things that look very trivial now when I think about them. I'd bought a fountain pen for Ahmet, so he would have a Christmas present whether or not he expected it. I was knitting a bed jacket for Agatha, putting into it affection and guilt, because I'd neglected her so. I had a strange kind of date with Chick Palmer: he wrote a mysterious note asking me to meet him at the club for lunch. Marge was not mentioned in it; I assumed she'd gone home, as she had often threatened to do. Belatedly I pondered the way she had behaved in Bali, and when I saw Chick waiting for me in the bar I was amazed at how he had changed. He looked worn and thin.

Sitting at a little table with drinks, he explained it all. "I don't know what you must think of me, Julie, leaving you alone all these months without showing a sign of life. I don't believe I've seen you since Phil left. Marge, of course . . . but you know how it is in this damned place. A man gets snowed under." I assured him I hadn't brooded over his neglect, but he didn't pay attention. "Phil's a pal; I don't have to tell you he thinks the world of you. I feel I've let him down, that's it. And I think you're entitled to an explanation. It's Marge. We've been—" He broke off, swallowing, and rubbed his face with one hand as if he were cleaning it of cobwebs. "We've been having one hell of a time. The fact is, we're washed up."

I stared, not understanding, so he tried again.

"Separated. We've separated. Marge has gone away."

As I said all the things one does say, I thought, panic-stricken, of Bali. Was Chick going to ask me embarrassing questions about that? But he didn't. He went on talking in a rambling, miserable fashion, saying how much of a surprise it was going to be to the town, where he and Marge were considered one of the ideal couples. It would rock the place. It was—

"What was the trouble?" I asked, bravely.

He swallowed his drink and snapped his fingers for another. "That's just it, Julie, that's the maddening part of the whole mess. I just don't know. It came as a complete shock. Marge announced out of a clear sky that she isn't happy with me, and what's more, she said she hasn't been happy for years. Now, I ask you, could that be true? Of course not. We've had our moments, like everybody else, but you can't tell me Marge would suffer silently all this time. Not Marge. Nobody would have guessed. Did *you* ever suspect anything of the kind?" I said no. "I'd like to have a good long talk with her doctor at home," said Chick. "At her age I guess a woman might go off the rails, mentally. That's what they tell me. But she went wild with rage when I sort of suggested that might be the trouble—right up in the air."

"You could hardly expect her not to," I said. "Where *is* she?"

"Oh, she's gone; she sailed yesterday for home, via Singapore. Going to stay with some of our friends there until her boat sails. I can understand why she'd want to get the hell out of here, considering. And that's another thing; I'm reassured, sort of, because if she'd wanted to stay I'd have been sure she had somebody here she thought she'd fallen in love with. You know, under that hard-boiled shell of hers, Marge is really as romantic as a kid. You'd never guess it if you didn't know her well, like I do. She swears it isn't somebody else that's the trouble, only that she isn't happy with me. It doesn't make sense, but I can't think of any other explanation. That's why I asked you out today, Julie. One woman understands another as no man could hope to. Would you say Marge had fallen for somebody else? Did you see any signs of it? She's always thought a lot of you—she always said you had more sense than most of these female nitwits, and I think if she was going to confide in anybody it would be you. Was there some other man?"

I said that as far as I knew there was no one. . . . Well, what else could I do?

The last day of that week was marred by my first genuine quarrel with Ahmet. It was not a bit like Christmas weather of course—quite hot, even for the season and the place, and perhaps that got me down and made me short-tempered. But the main trouble was that I was more than usually worried. Ahmet had been away oftener than he was present, and still I knew nothing about what he did on his trips. When he said that evening he was going the next day, it was just too much.

"For an unknown destination, I suppose, as usual?" I said.

Unwarily he assented, and I threw Agatha's bed jacket down. Needles and all, it flopped to the floor as I jumped up and raged at him.

"This is a nice love affair, isn't it? We make plans about our marriage and the next thing I know you've disappeared on God knows what errand. I wouldn't know how to find you even if the house burned down. Why should I put up with this, can you tell me one good reason?"

"No," said Ahmet.

I should have realized it was no use. This was the sort of behavior he was used to in women; he was armored against it; it got one nowhere. But I was past thinking about tactics.

"It wouldn't be so bad if I knew what you're up to." He didn't reply to this, and I dug deeper: "What *are* you doing? Any woman but me would have asked long ago. Why are you always going away; who makes you do it? And *why don't you tell me?*"

"Julie, Julie, if you behave like this now, what . . . ? You must simply take my word for it: I can't tell you. I can't tell anyone. I'm not permitted."

"Who says so?"

He shook his head sadly. "Believe that I don't want to make myself look important when I'm not. But I can't tell you."

I burst into angry sobs. "Who cares about your dingy little secrets? It's not that, it's that you don't trust me. It's insulting. Can't you see?"

No, he couldn't, or wouldn't. He went on saying gently that he understood how women are, but this time it couldn't be helped, which made me worse, if possible. I screamed at him:

"I'm not just another one of your women, damn you!" Reaching for a handkerchief I knocked over a little china vase, and I suppose the general effect on any listening ear was the same as if I'd thrown it at Ahmet. The next thing that happened was that Yvonne came to the door, her eyes wide and worried, to ask us please not to make so much noise; Mamma was upset thinking of the neighbors. I appealed to Yvonne to come in and help me, but she only batted her eyes and disappeared. This had the good result of quieting me.

Through the whole tantrum Ahmet stood there, only his pallor and tight lips showing his anger. When it was over and I threw myself down on the bed, too tired to talk any more, he went over and picked up his bag, avoiding my tear-smudged gaze.

"Are you going *now?*" I said sharply.

"I think it would be better, don't you?"

"Yes, it would. It would be so much better that I think you ought to stay away," I said. "I can hardly keep you out of your cousin's house, but as far as I'm concerned you don't exist any more. Don't worry about me; I'll—" I checked myself: I had been on the verge of saying that I would go away, but this, manifestly, was nonsense. I couldn't go away. For better or worse, I was committed indefinitely to the Indies. Instead, I said, "I don't want to see you any more, Ahmet. Please go away."

He did, immediately, and I spent most of the night crying into the pillow.

It was nearly sunrise when I fell asleep, so that my impression that someone came into the room almost immediately after I closed my eyes was not completely wrong. Whoever it was remained standing there, and naturally I thought hopefully of Ahmet, but as I blinked and saw a woman's figure, I was perplexed. The light wasn't right: it was too early. And the person holding the tea tray was not the servant, but Yvonne, pale and strained-looking.

I sat up. "Why, thank you, Yvonne, but why are you here?" Then I remembered everything, and was frightened. Undoubtedly she had come to break the news to me that her mother had put her foot down and I must go.

"I came in to tell you something," said Yvonne. She glanced in a puzzled way at the teapot, recognized it, and set down the tray. "It's on the radio and Daddy listened in, a special early broadcast; Japan's done it, Julie. The Japs have bombed Singapore and Hongkong, and they've even blown up the American fleet somewhere—Hawaii, I think. What do you think of that?"

Singapore? That was practically next door. I said, stupidly, "How could they? We didn't hear it."

"I'm not sure we didn't. I thought I heard something, or perhaps I just imagine it now we've heard the news. Do you think we'll be mixed up in this? If Japan's at war with the Allies that means she's fighting Holland, so I guess we're in it."

We looked at each other fearfully. "I'd better get up," I said, "before they arrive."

Throughout that day, though our own troops rolled through the streets in trucks or—according to neighborhood hearsay—bustled about in the army garages and barracks and departed in droves for other parts of the island, nothing that directly mattered to us took place. We stayed in the house waiting for catastrophe that didn't come. I was terribly frightened. I wonder if anyone else in the city was as frightened as I was. Mrs. Dutoit certainly behaved as if she was terrified, crying quietly now and then and showing a tendency to keep her husband and daughter within view, but I doubt if she felt anything like my blank terror. She had somebody to think about beside herself. I too should have had, of course. I should have been worrying for Ahmet's sake, but the shaming fact is, for hours I forgot all about Ahmet. Insomuch as I had coherent thought at all it was of the orphans' home. I longed to be back there, and for the world to be ten years younger; I wanted to be dressed in the old uniform and know I was part of an institution where proper routine was followed and people behaved in a tidy way, where nothing like this could happen. Not until I recollected that something exactly like this must have in fact already happened to the home did I achieve a bit of sanity. Then at last I thought of Ahmet, and like Mrs. Dutoit I wept. Perhaps my weeping was more painful than hers because of pangs of conscience; after all, we'd parted on angry terms and it was my fault, but I didn't think too much about that. My anger had been unreal for the most part, and I had an idea that Ahmet had seen through it. What mattered was that he was not there, I didn't know where he had gone, and now *they* were coming and might well keep us apart, perhaps forever.

The intensity of all this was bound to subside. By afternoon, what with more radio news and a good deal of coming and going among our neighbors, we had figured out that all wasn't necessarily lost. *They* were still a long way off, up the coast of Malaya, fighting their way against the British and some of our troops who had been flown up. Mr. Dutoit said that they couldn't possibly win the gamble, after all. They'd been audaciously tricky, but they weren't up against the poor primitive Chinese now, and they'd very soon find out the difference. Oh no, this was merely a flash in the pan.

It was persuasive; it was comforting. All of a sudden the scene was reversed, and I saw the world as it had always been, properly balanced and myself on the right, cozy side. One was, after all, a European. When Yvonne went to take a motherly, watchful look at her shop, I too went out: I felt a sudden urge to visit the hostel and see how Agatha was. I wanted European company. Agatha was not in her room, and I found her down in the reception room with a number of the other women; everyone was apt to seek the herd at that time, just as I was doing. She greeted me with a rather watery smile, her lips trembling and her eyes puffy.

"Pieter?" I asked, as I took her hand.

"He's been called away; I suppose he's in Malaya by this time. Isn't this a *mess!* Those damned Americans, being caught like that . . ." With shaking hands she arranged a cup for my coffee. "Have you heard the way it was? They were all drunk on shore and sound asleep, and the ships were crowded together in the harbor like sardines. People like that shouldn't be trusted with a navy. It's criminal."

"Don't worry, Agatha, he'll be all right. You're lucky it isn't the Germans he's fighting. I mean—Japanese, after all!"

Everyone in the room was saying the same thing. This would be a salutary thing for the Americans, we agreed; serve them right, always staying out of world wars until they were forced to come in. Coining money from other people's troubles. Letting the Germans get away with it all these months. And now look at them! We felt much the better when we said these things so vigorously; even Agatha forgot to start and tremble. I felt so Dutch that it was only surprising, not an overpowering relief, when the old *djongos* came in to tell me quietly that a Javanese man was outside, asking for me.

There on the doorstep stood Ahmet, like a comment in a foreign language inserted in ordinary conversation. I greeted him breezily. "Hello, there. So you didn't go away after all!"

"I'd just started early this morning when the news came through." He glanced without evident pleasure at the front of the hostel and in at the door, to the hallway where the servant lingered, watching us curiously. "What are you doing now?" he asked. "Must you go back in there?"

I hesitated. I can see now that everything depended on that moment. If I'd made the other decision I'd have followed a widely different path for the rest of my life, for I was already halfway back to Europe. Given another ten minutes with Agatha in the hostel I would have stayed with her; I'd have sent for my things and taken the old place among my friends. I didn't know all that: I only felt a strong pull. But I looked at Ahmet and remembered who he was, and that was stronger.

"No, I don't have to," I said. "Let's go home."

There was no drama about it.

"You know I didn't mean anything I said last night," I blurted as we walked away.

"Oh, that . . . Julie, we must be serious now. Everything is going to be changed when the Japanese get here, and it would be better to decide in advance how we—"

I halted on the pavement, dismayed. "Ahmet! You don't really think they're going to get this far?"

He, too, was surprised. "But what else could you be thinking of? It's only the question of time. They've done a wonderful job all through; they've caught everybody off guard. It was beautiful timing! What's going to stop them now?"

"Oh, you mustn't talk that way. You mustn't give up hope so easily. Look what they're up against—all the British and the Australian troops, and our own people too; a lot of ours have gone up to help. Why, Ahmet, how could Japs possibly do any more than they've done? Besides, they're tired out from all these years fighting in China—years of attrition." After the morning I had spent, the phrases of Mr. Dutoit and his friends came naturally.

"Come on," said Ahmet. I resumed walking with him, and for a minute or two there was silence. "We'd better begin over again," he said at last, "because we're at opposite ends about this, though I suppose it's to be expected. You've been with the Europeans and they've infected you; you're looking at the Japanese as if they were enemies."

"That doesn't make sense, Ahmet. Of course they're enemies: what else could they be? They've made war on us, they've bombed our ships and landed on our territory—"

"They haven't attacked *us*," he said in gentle tones. "It's not *our* war. It's war between the Japanese and the Westerners."

"But the Indies are Dutch!"

He said nothing, but gave me a bright glance, and then I understood him and began to think it over.

"But you're involved," I said at last. "Whether you want to be or not, you're involved, just as I am."

"That remains to be seen—for both of us. So far they've been perfectly logical. They want the Europeans out of the East. Well, so do we. They've attacked the Dutch, indirectly; soon they'll carry the attack into territory where they'll be at direct war with the Dutch. They're doing, in fact, what we wanted to do but lacked the strength for. Remember who they are, Julie; they're the Japanese, who once whipped czarist Russia. Don't listen to your European friends who look down on them and laugh at them as funny little yellow men. They're the strongest people in the East."

I floundered in fresh panic. "And you're *happy* about it."

"Not exactly. No, not happy, but certainly excited. One's got to wait and see. I admit I have hopes."

"This changes everything, everything. . . . Oh, you must be wrong. I couldn't bear it if you were right. Don't you see, whatever they do about you people, it will be terrible for us—for me. I can't understand you; I never will. I—"

Ahmet sounded stern. "Julie, you must not cry like that." He was probably scandalized; in his circles it was wrong to show erratic emotion like mine. For that matter, so was it

106

wrong where I'd come from. I tried to control myself, and he went on, talking rapidly: "What is there to be afraid of? I'll take care of you. They have no quarrel with us, and you'll be with me. Can't you trust me? Don't you think I'm strong enough to look after my own woman?" I could hardly answer that in any way but "Yes," and I did so, but it must have been too faint a reply to satisfy him. "I see how it is," he said. "You can't have faith in anyone but a European."

There was so much truth in this that I was stimulated to make a more convincing show of denial, and he was appeased. And yet, all the while I assured him that I was now thoroughly contented and easy, in my mind I was looking for some way to escape. I must get out, I thought; I must get away. Surely if I looked hard enough I could find an escape route to Australia, and from Australia to America, where the Japanese would never be able to reach me. There was no war in America, there couldn't be. When I got there I'd find Phil, and he'd help me make a fresh start. It was checked only an instant by the thought of his wife Lily. Never mind Lily; I had no intention of troubling her, but Phil would have to—

"All this had better be a secret for a while," Ahmet was saying as we came in sight of the house. "The Dutoits are probably taking the European point of view."

"Yes, they are." I thought of Mr. Dutoit and his cheerful jokes about the Japs, and the general hopefulness earlier in the day, now killed stone dead by Ahmet. "Are you ever going to talk to them?" I asked submissively.

"Oh yes, in the course of time. But you'll see, Julie; they'll come round without any help from me. All the Eurasians with any sense will recognize the facts, and then they'll drop this pro-Dutch nonsense in a second. I know them, you see; I know them better than you do."

Doggedly, the Europeans picked up the threads of existence and went on pretending that life was normal. Agatha,

107

the other teachers, and the people for whom Mr. Dutoit did his job—they scamped nothing: they got up in the morning and went to work, and came home at night and went to bed. If there was not much partying any more and a fantastic amount of search for the latest news, that was only to be expected.

Fate moved closer and closer. Hongkong surrendered on Christmas Day. The Japanese bombed the heart out of British naval defenses off Malaya and moved down the peninsula. The Japanese hammered at the Philippines. The Japanese did very much as they liked, with no interference from the West, and slowly the civilians in Java lost hope, though they continued to go to market, tend their gardens, and drink coffee. There was a lot of talk about unity and brotherhood and standing together in the face of a common threat. But Ahmet had been right: I could see a change setting in with the Indos. They were beginning to wonder; to think about their own identity. As the West seemed to prove itself more and more feeble, it was natural that a Eurasian should take comfort in the thought that he was not irrevocably committed to their race. If one anchor chain snapped, why, there was still another left. The thought came in uninvited: you couldn't help yourself, any more than a chameleon can help changing from green to brown. I elaborated on this thought. I imagined that I could understand the feelings of a chameleon, but perhaps I was mistaken; possibly they feel nothing, and are unaware that they are changing color. It was that way with many other Indos. To some extent it was true even of me. One morning I counted up the days since I'd last been to a gathering of Europeans, and I was shocked that it added up to weeks, though for excuse I had the continued presence of Ahmet. Whatever his duties had been, their nature was now changed; he seemed to have plenty to do, but he stayed in Batavia.

Of course there were still the Djungs: I saw them regularly. The big house was transformed now; it swarmed with people I hadn't seen before, most of whom had hurried in from their country houses to gather around their family head, Mr. Djung. They ranged from simple peasant gardeners to urban types, and some of the women were certainly Ming's co-wives, though I never liked to ask. Mr. Djung remained his calm self, and Ming imitated him. He would tease me for being a European—I got it all ways just then —and rubbed in how badly the Western forces were doing against the Japanese:

"Tell me, Julie, where's this superiority I've heard of all my life? Where is that magnificent armed might that kept the East subjugated? I see nothing in the papers these days about it, do you?"

For some time I had to take this quietly and smile, but it went on too long, until even Ming murmured in protest, and Mr. Djung dropped the joke and got down to something nearer the bone. "They're only Japs, after all. The same Japanese who've been fighting the Chinese so many years, driving them back across country while the Western world laughed at China. Nobody remembered that they never actually *beat* the Chinese. They've been trying ever since 1932, but they never finished the job. It was a comic-opera war, wasn't it? A war between two yellow nations fighting in their funny little yellow way."

"Mr. Djung," said Ming softly.

"It's different now," said Mr. Djung. "It looks different when little yellow men chase the British out of Hongkong and turf the Americans out of Manila. Nobody's laughing any more. And yet it's just the same miserable little Japs who couldn't settle China."

Since there was nothing I could say, I remained silent. A Chinese, I thought, may have more chameleon-trouble than I ever suspected.

If I never gave the Dutch enough credit for their preparations, it was because I knew so little about them. A civilian saw a good deal of mysterious coming and going; a civilian found himself more and more circumscribed in his pleasures, what with our favorite beaches wired and put out of bounds, and the necessity of blackouts. But a civilian was told very little. It was amazing to me that we should have been able to hit back when Japanese planes did at last attack us. Already a few had flown over Batavia with impertinent assurance, eliciting a few halfhearted shots from emplacements on the ground, but when they made their first —and last—hostile attack on Tanjong Priok, dropping bombs near by, our answering fire was more effective. Much to my surprise, our AA guns actually brought down a plane.

It still didn't seem real, but when they began nibbling at our islands and found foothold on Indonesian soil, I believed at last that they were coming. There was no good in talking to Ahmet any more, so I didn't. Instead, I didn't sleep well, and when I did drop off I had nightmares. Night after night I tried to catch elusive trains that either disappeared altogether just as they seemed within reach, or pulled out of the station the moment I got to the platform. In other dreams I lost Ahmet, or rather someone who, though he didn't look in the least like Ahmet, was him in essence. Only once the stranger was not Ahmet, but Martin: I knew even before I woke from that dream that it was all a lie. At times my mother was there, either in disguise or lurking in memory that was not mine but the dream's. They were not happy nights, and afterwards it always took a long time to shake off the emotion. These waking moments in Batavia are hard to describe. You are suspended in a new element. Nowhere but in that flower-scented warmth can you feel so haunted and other-worldly; the air seems full of shapes, beings, that you see clearly only for a vanishing second between night and day.

For a while *they* took a harmless place among such phantasms, but as the nights marched on they moved out and became real. I recognized the names of the islands they occupied. Then they were actually bombing ports on our coast. Sometimes I felt that they were deliberately holding off from Batavia in order to wreck our nerves, but that was self-flattery: the truth, as Ahmet explained it, was that Batavia was comparatively unimportant to the conquest. Instead of driving straight from the capital city of Singapore to our capital city, they made sure of themselves by going for Palembang and Surabaya. A wave of military debris flowed in far ahead of them—shiploads and planeloads and trainloads of wounded and civilian refugees. I thought that anything would be preferable to this dead peace, for I could feel my mind slipping, as on the day I met Marge Palmer in a line of women who stood outside a shop to buy cakes, and greeted her without remembering anything I'd heard, without thinking that she was not supposed to be in Batavia at all. It was Marge who gave me the hint.

"As you see, I'm back. The bad penny," she said, with an embarrassed laugh.

"Oh yes." Now I remembered. "You were lucky not to be caught. Where were you when it hit—Hongkong?"

Apparently this was a stupid question. "Hongkong! Who do you think I am—Houdini? No, I was in Singapore for a nice holiday, dear, and look what happened! I don't mind telling you it was absolute hell the last few days before I bullied the Navy into letting me hitch a ride. I got to Bandung that way, and so on in a train jammed with refugees. I was never so glad to see a place in my life as I was to see good old Batavia—not that I know why. It's just the same thing here all over again."

Marge hadn't lost her customary jauntiness, but she looked awful. She had extra worries, I remembered, and wondered what had happened about that, for she was chattering of Chick and her house. "It was terribly neglected while I was away; you know what men are like alone in the house, Julie."

Of course, though, the divorce would have been shelved. Not many people would hang on to a marital quarrel in face of the coming invasion, I thought, and Chick hadn't wanted it anyway; he must be happy to have Marge back. I felt a twinge of curiosity: what had happened to the

American lover? But if Marge wanted to discuss it she would, without prompting, and she said nothing.

The next day I had my own troubles to think about, when Ahmet went off in the bad old way, without explanation or promise. "Yvonne, have you any idea what he does?" I asked despairingly. "Why can't he stay home like a sensible man at a time like this?"

She said casually, "Oh, he's all right. I expect he's gone to Sukabumi." She added hastily, "Now, don't snap at me, Julie. It's only a guess, but you could have come to the same conclusion if you'd read your papers carefully. The government's been moving some of the exiled leaders around, so they can keep more of an eye on them, I suppose:—Sutan Sjahrir and Dr. Mohammed Hatta are back in Java, over there at Sukabumi, and my guess is that Ahmet's gone to carry a message from their friends, or something like that."

I felt humbled; I looked at Yvonne with awe. "How do you happen to know about all that political stuff? I'd never have thought it of you."

"Oh, I'm a born snoop, Julie. It comes of keeping the shop. You hear anything and everything in a shop, and I love it. Stop worrying about Ahmet, because he can't possibly get into trouble on a little thing like this. I'll admit he does run crazy risks sometimes, but this is harmless. He'll come back some time soon, you'll see."

He did come back a few days later, taciturn as ever, but cheerful, and clearly delighted to be with me again. I decided not to hint at Sukabumi. If that was the way Ahmet wanted things, I could behave accordingly. But I could not quite leave the subject alone. That night before going to sleep I said:

"I was beginning to wonder which of you would get here first—you or the Japs."

"Oh, I knew I would be back," he said.

We were lying on a mat on my floor, as we did whenever he spent the night with me. It was late and everything was still. The Dutoits, like the neighbors, were asleep. In the quiet room it seemed fantastic to be talking of the Japanese so surely on the way; it was like a conversation in one of my dreams. I said:

"You haven't admitted once that you're at all afraid. Are you really as confident as you sound, that it's going to be all right?"

"You should believe me by this time. I am really looking forward with hope."

"A man looks at things one way, and a woman another. No matter how you sort it out in politics, Ahmet, it's going to be dreadful in the first days. I can't forget that. They'll come rushing in, and they'll kill people, and loot and burn and rape. That's how it was in China and that's how it's going to be here. Sometimes I wish I could fight, and die before the end."

"They won't necessarily be like that here. That was China, and they were making war on the Chinese *people*. Here, what they're after is the foreigners, not us. I've said it hundreds of times, Julie. I wish you'd have faith."

"I wonder how you're going to feel if they rape me and Yvonne, and you have to watch. What will you think of the brotherhood of man then, I wonder? Or if they hit Mr. Dutoit, or Mrs. —"

He put his hand firmly over my mouth and kept it there until I stopped sputtering. "You take the newspapers too seriously," he said. "You shouldn't believe the capitalist press."

To be truthful, I was not as distressed as it sounds, but it was one way to make him say over and over the things I was anxious to hear. "Why should these soldiers behave like angels just because they're Asiatic?"

Patiently he said, "I don't expect them to be angels. I only expect them to distinguish between friends and enemies. And now, darling, let's get some sleep while we can."

"But my friends are Dutch."

"Not all of them," said Ahmet.

I was confused and torn. When I saw Mrs. Vanderlip next

day and she was full of fight and confident, I didn't think, as I would have done earlier, that she was a silly old woman with a malicious tongue who ought to be taught a lesson. Instead, she upset me by saying:

"What nonsense these people are saying about our servants turning on us! It all depends on how one's treated them. I do believe my *djongos* is utterly devoted; he'd die for me." I wanted to cry. It was unbelievable that my eyes should be wet for Mrs. Vanderlip. But at least I'd found a way to make everything bearable; I had only to remind myself that this was the kind of atmosphere my mother would recognize. She'd have risen above it. She wouldn't have been afraid.

The end was pure anticlimax. We went to bed keyed up to face the worst: we woke in the morning to find that the Dutch had surrendered before the battle ever got as far as us. Batavia had been declared an open city. The only thing we were expected to do now was watch while the men who had been left to defend us were marched off to prison camp.

No doubt it was a great relief, but I was unreasonable. I felt aggrieved; I'd been made a fool of. "Now what?" I demanded sharply of the family: to hear me you would have thought they were in some way responsible for the surrender. No one took the question seriously: no one replied; each spoke his own thoughts.

"There now," said Mrs. Dutoit. "And after all our worrying, too. I wonder if they'll open the shops today?"

"I'm going straight down and make sure mine's locked up," said Yvonne. Mr. Dutoit muttered that one hardly knew what to think with all this chopping and changing. Ahmet said something about getting in touch with certain people immediately, and I of course immediately raised objections:

"You've no idea what might be going on in the city this morning; you'd much better wait and find out."

"It won't wait, Julie; we'll have all sorts of things to do.

. . . Can't you see what's happened? The Dutch have surrendered. We're on our own, after hundreds of years. *The Dutch have surrendered!*"

And then, of course, I did see. I sat there staring at the facts, and so did the Dutoits, and so did Ahmet. Of us all, only he looked quite sure and happy.

CHAPTER SIX

The woman who stopped short at sight of me in the passage
was Mina. I had only time to halt in my turn and say, "Why,
hello, Mina, how—" before she reared back like a scared
colt, pulling aside her skirt, and nearly spat at me, her
eyes blazing. Silently I walked on. I should have known
better than to have slackened pace or given any sign of recognition, but the meeting took me by surprise, since Mina's
habits in the old days had never brought her to the hostel.
Things were different now: I cautioned myself to keep it in
mind. The Europeans were moving around town like water
in a draining bathtub, circling and rushing here and there, trying to cover lots of space, however pointlessly, before the Japanese scooped them up and carted them away to concentration camp. There was time for these futile adventurings. The
only good thing you could say about the internment was that
it was going slowly, and that there were no more nasty sur-
prises every day—or so we thought—since the worst had happened. At the beginning when the Japanese came in everything had been in a hysterical rush, especially the beatings and
lootings and beheadings, impulsive sins taking place in the
open for everyone to see even when he didn't himself suffer.
There is no use talking about it now. In any case the Dutoit
house and family got off easy because our street wasn't grand
enough to attract looters at the beginning, and later the Japanese imposed more discipline on everybody. Local toughs
were treated severely, and so were even their own troops,

if the rules were broken and if somebody with authority happened to be on the spot. There was a crazy kind of intermittent justice about it, that grew less intermittent every day. Sometimes Ahmet managed to help out too, when we had to argue a point with a Javanese working for the Japanese. He was known, and his word carried a bit of weight. It was good for him when he could do something constructive like that, because for a long time he seemed dazed with shock at the way our liberators were behaving.

In short, though they were still harsh and cruel, our world was no longer in chaos. We civilians, too, had a pattern imposed on us at the beginning, by the Dutch authorities in their farewell message. They told us to behave well and treat the Japanese with courtesy—as if there was any chance we would not, terrified as we were—and to observe new rules of conduct, which included bowing low every time we passed a Japanese sentry or met a Japanese officer in the highway. Some people thought of this behavior as tactful co-operation, others condemned it as collaboration, but for most of us it was simply necessity.

I think that most Dutch officials, even after the handing-over ceremony, expected that they wouldn't have to change their way of life to any painful degree. They assumed that they'd be permitted to go on living in their own houses, though of course, they thought, the Residency would be taken over for the Governor General's opposite number: after all, this was a reasonable act of war. Moving as they liked about town, they talked to each other of ways and means, cutting down expenses, paying their servants with IOU's that could be redeemed after peace was declared. I heard of this from Mr. Dutoit and Ahmet; Ahmet for a while was apprehensive that things would indeed work out just that way. The Dutch reasoned that as this kind of arrangement held good in the European cities now occupied by the Germans, it would naturally follow in Indonesia, since the Japanese and the Germans were working together. It wasn't to be like that, though. Ahmet told us why, when the internments began. Indonesia wasn't thought of by the Japanese as a nation in France's class. The Dutch themselves had kept her a colony.

"It's their own fault. They held us down, in the position of a piece of property, a piece of booty. They held us by force, and now somebody else has taken us away by force, which leaves the Dutch here with no claims as honorable prisoners of war. They are simply the former owners, who are now in the way. Of course this isn't *our* opinion; it's the attitude the Japanese are taking, but we agree with the Japanese in one thing, that the Dutch have no right to be here at all."

I remember that Mr. Dutoit listened in fascination and fright to these remarkable sentiments. He nodded as if he nearly understood, but would prefer not to. He cleared his throat and asked:

"But what's going to happen to them, and to us?"

Ahmet hesitated, I suspected because he didn't know as much as he was pretending to.

"It's not for us to say," he admitted. "The Japanese are in charge. But they won't be unreasonable; there's no plan to kill off the Europeans. No doubt they'll do what they did up north, put them into safe camps, out of the way, leaving us to get on with our business. As for you, Uncle, you shouldn't talk nonsense and act as if you classed yourself with the whites. You are a Javanese civilian. You have a new future, with our nation."

Mr. Dutoit looked more scared than ever, as well he might after a lifetime of modeling himself on the Dutch, but he only cleared his throat again.

"They have been as stupid as ever," Ahmet continued severely. "Only a Dutchman would be arrogant enough to think he could keep his privileges now. It's our country, not theirs. They will have to grasp that fact."

No one would know, hearing him now (I thought fondly), that up until the evening before he had shared the Dutch belief that they were going to get away with it. He'd told me so. He'd been mystified by the sight of Dutch people still going to the club for swimming and tennis, sauntering like lords in the streets, or driving in their good cars. He had begun to wonder whether the new conquerors weren't going to be merely so many more lords, in league with the Dutch, ready to share in the spoils and keep the Javanese where they were. There was nothing yet in Japanese behavior to reassure any Indonesian on these points, though they talked in print a good deal about liberation. But now relief had arrived. The blow fell and the air was filled with European lamentation as the whites were carried off. Ahmet sighed and relaxed. As for me, I lamented, but my reaction was forgiven me. It was only natural, the Dutoits told each other. They, too, were appalled, though for caution's sake they didn't show their feelings.

After meeting Mina in the hostel I told myself not to lose my temper. Mina was to be pitied, not resented, I said over and over, like an incantation; nevertheless I was very angry. Why should she feel herself entitled to put on the airs of a bereaved patriot? She still had Jan Vries. At least she knew he was near by, though to be sure he'd been locked up with the other Volunteers. She knew he was safe: he had been seen and accounted for, whereas Agatha had no idea what had happened to Pieter. He'd been missing since shortly after his regiment was sent to Malaya and engaged in action with the enemy, as the report had it. Yet Agatha behaved normally, refused to entertain any idea of disaster, and treated me as she always did, even if from her point of view I had ratted on my community. It might have been galling for her if she'd permitted herself to think that way, to see me walking around freely. She knew that *my* lover was well; worse, that he was contented with the Japanese occupation. She must have felt poignantly humiliated, as the other Europeans did, about the situation generally . . . and though Mina would not have believed it, so did I.

I couldn't help knowing that the Dutch had surrendered far too easily. Stories kept trickling in. Where the girls at the hostel got them I don't know—for *my* gossip I depended on Yvonne, and she never let me down: every day brought a fresh crop. It wasn't a pleasant story. It looked as if we'd been deserted by a lot of cowards: all the European troops—British, American, Dutch, Australian, anyone with a white skin—had rushed wildly to the south coast and made his escape in some crowded vessel, sailing off to Australia. To be sure, our shame was mitigated by stories from people who met and talked with some of the troops as they left. The men *had* gone unwillingly, these accounts said: they had resented their marching orders and complained that they'd never had the chance of even one fight in defense of the country. But the question remained: what about the higher-ups who had sent them away? I couldn't get any satisfactory reply to that, and the chorus of scorn was soon taken up and swelled by the Japanese information service, which—with radio broadcasts, newspapers, and placards—joyfully rubbed it all in.

So I seethed at Mina, who had dared to look at me as if *I* were responsible for this humiliation. With a last curse at her I paused at Agatha's door.

It was open. I heard sounds of movement in the room, yet for a minute I hesitated, working up courage to say that I was there. Agatha might have gone over to the other side since I'd last seen her; she might now be thinking of me as a traitor because I wasn't packing up, like the rest of them, to go into internment. It would not have been surprising if she had. Still, I couldn't stand forever in the passage, quaking, so I drew breath and called her by name. "It's Julie," I added. Abnormally sensitive, I detected the tiny pause that followed before Agatha said, "Come in." I resented it, and reflected that it was perhaps just as well if we parted now, before we came to open quarreling.

Agatha, tousle-haired, stood over an open suitcase, peering into it with an odd expression of perplexity. She had stuck a pencil over her ear and evidently forgotten it was there. Clothes and books and bits of furniture lay around, out of place; on the unmade bed and the side table and the chairs.

The potted plants had been allowed to die of thirst, and everywhere was dust. She only glanced at me before turning again to her packing, but she said amiably:

"Clear yourself a space and sit down. I'll just carry on with this if you don't mind. Sorry it's all so dirty, but it hardly seems worth while now bothering to tidy it up."

"Why do you have to? Where's the *djongos?*" I moved a small carving, an empty ink bottle and two brassières from one of the chairs to the bed, and sat down.

"The *djongos* has gone, back to his village," said Agatha, angrily jabbing a rolled-up petticoat into a corner of the case. Her anger was not directed at me exclusively: its address was universal. I knew the feeling. "One couldn't expect anything else," she went on. "At least he was decently civil up to the end; in fact I think he was sorry. But the cook has been incredible, talking aloud to himself about how the Dutch can't fight, and it took only a handful of Japs to beat the whole lot of us and so on. Of all the infuriating people, these Javanese . . ."

"Answer back," I suggested, speaking from much recent experience. "Ask him what he's got to say about a handful nowadays. The Japs keep pouring in as if they were coming out of an anthill."

Agatha shrugged. "Who cares? As soon as I blow off steam I forget about it; at any rate he's gone, too, by this time. And I can hardly lecture the whole nation now, when I'm being pushed into prison any minute." She rubbed her forehead. "Strange how my mind works. I'm obsessed with silly little things. I keep thinking, Poor old *djongos*: I wish I'd given him his tip before he went. Julie, if you ever happen to run into him—"

"I'll take care of it, Agatha."

"Thanks. And now this packing worries me so, you can't imagine . . ." She put a piece of clothing into the case, paused as if thinking it over, and pulled it out again to cast it aside on the bed. "No," she said as if to herself. "Definitely not a cocktail dress . . . Julie, help me." She spoke like a child. "There's something the matter with my brain; I can't make decisions. I haven't the slightest idea what I'll need in concentration camp."

I stood up, saying, "I'll try, but I haven't any idea myself."

"No," Agatha said dryly, and gave me the same swift glance I'd got before. She added, "The necessity doesn't arise in your case."

Agatha was not Mina, and I had no inhibitions. I blazed out: "Look, if you really do think of me as a criminal, Agatha, say so here and now so I can go away nicely."

She looked taken aback. "Don't be silly; who's talking about criminals?"

"Then how about treating me like a human being?"

"Oh dear." Agatha dropped what she was holding and threw her arms around me. "Julie, I'm sorry, I'm so sorry. I didn't really mean a thing."

"Well, you acted—"

"I know I did. Priggish and nasty. I take it all back and apologize. I really do think you're behaving just the way you ought to in the circumstances. Really I do, and I wish you all sorts of luck."

I was still stiff. "Then why did you—"

"Because I'm jealous," said Agatha. "Can't you see how it must be, watching somebody who's lucky enough not to be in this horrible fix with us all? Sheer jealousy. You shouldn't pay me any attention."

She shook me a little, fondly, and I smiled and dropped back to the chair, and said, "All right, but if you only knew! It isn't as easy as it sounds, I can tell you. We nearly got caught in the net, the Dutoits and me. They missed being interned by the skin of their teeth."

"I did wonder," said Agatha slowly. "I've heard about lots of Indos who *are* being put in. Especially people like your Dutoits, Westernized and Christian and all. Who got them out of it—your boy friend?"

"Oh, Ahmet hasn't any pull," I said. The note of contempt

in my voice startled me, though it could also be described as fond. I paused for a second to listen to it, and continued more carefully: "I think myself it was the flag that did it. We—we hung out a Nationalist flag Ahmet gave us." Agatha's mild, speculative gaze was embarrassing and made me stammer. "We got credit for that," I went on doggedly, "and I suppose they overlooked the things they don't like about people like us. As for me, I seem to be lumped in with the Dutoits as a member of the family, which suits me."

"Yes, it's a lucky thing," said Agatha. "I won't have to worry about you, now you're fixed up with Yvonne and her people."

Warmth crept into my heart where I hadn't felt it for a long time. "I don't know how it's going to work out, but Agatha, if I can possibly do anything to help you while you're inside, I will, I swear it."

"Bless you, Julie, I'm sure you will."

"And it can't possibly go on for too long," I continued. "I suppose you've all heard the Djojobojo prophecy here in the hostel?"

Folding and refolding a dress, Agatha shook her head. "No, we haven't. It sounds like some *dukun's* story; don't tell me you've taken to visiting a *dukun* now? That would be going almost *too* native." She was using the vernacular word for witch.

"It's nothing to do with a *dukun*. I take it half seriously, I don't know why—because it's so comforting, probably. Djojobojo was a king in Java I don't know how many centuries ago, and he made this prophecy that Java would be conquered and held enslaved for two hundred years by a race of white men. Then the white men would be driven out by yellow men from the north. Then—"

"You're making it up."

"No I'm not, that's the strangest part of it. It's a genuine tradition, Ahmet says, and I've found for myself that nine out of ten Javanese are talking about it and believing it. It goes on that the yellow men will stay in power over Java for enough time to grow one crop of rice, after which they'll be driven out in turn."

"And who does the driving out?"

"The Javanese themselves."

"Oh, pooh." Agatha went on packing. "I'll believe that when I see it. What nonsense!"

"Presumably we all live happy ever after," I said. "We were talking about it at home last night, and according to the way we figured, it takes three months to grow a crop of rice. So that means you'll have only a little more than two months to spend in camp, Agatha."

"How nice . . . Do you mean to tell me that Javanese want to believe that story? I thought they loved the Japs. I thought the Japs were their liberators. Is the gilt off the gingerbread already?"

I hesitated. "It's not all that cut and dried. It never was, really. They don't like anybody much, I suppose. Not the Dutch and not the Japanese either. They want to be on their own . . ."

"But they've been *liberated*. Is there no gratitude left in this country?"

In spite of her exaggerated sarcasm, Agatha watched me sharply. Poor girl, I thought—I'm her only contact with what she considers the knowledgeable world, God help her. I had nothing like the amount of inside information she believed I had, but I did my best.

"It's this way, Agatha. The people I know, mainly Ahmet of course, are Nationalists. They'll take any help they can get if they think it takes them further along the way to independence for the Indies, and you can't blame them for grabbing at what the Japs promised—freedom from the Europeans. So—"

"I *can* blame them. I do blame them. They're incredibly stupid if they think they'd have been an independent nation all these years if it hadn't been for us. Why, you've only to look at the record before the Dutch came—nobody had any conception of a united Indonesia; it was a lot of little warring states, being overwhelmed by any sea power that came along. *We* united Indonesia. *We* taught them all they know about survival, about medicine and modern culture and decent roads and—"

"We didn't teach them more than we had to for our own sakes."

Agatha began to reply hotly, thought better of it, and breathed deeply before speaking. "Naturally, you've been hearing a different point of view lately," she said in mild tones.

"It isn't as new to me as all that. Remember, we used to argue about schools for native children? But it's a waste of time talking about such things now. The main fact at present is that I don't think Ahmet's as happy as he expected he'd be."

"*No?* Why not?" Heavy sarcasm again.

"Oh . . . Part of it's fine, of course; I mean, he thinks it's fine. All the exiled leaders are out again and they've had great reunions. But—you won't tell him I said what I'm going to say; promise you won't?" Agatha reminded me that there was little likelihood of her holding long cozy chats with Ahmet or any other Javanese for some time to come. I went on, "Of course; sorry. It's just that last night I was talking to him about what we always talk about, self-government, and when I asked how long he thought it might be before the Indies got it, he said we mustn't expect it in a hurry because of the war. We have to wait until Western imperialism is defeated, and have faith. . . . Agatha, does that remind you of anything?"

"Poor Ahmet." For a minute neither of us spoke. Then she clapped her hands together smartly. "Well, this is all very fascinating but it's not getting my packing done. Come on, woman. Help!"

When the case was finished and strapped up, I said good-bye. Deliberately, we were unemotional about that: I said, "By the way, you know Marge Palmer slightly, don't you? Well, if you meet her give her my love. And, of course, if they put you into a camp with any of my kids . . ." At the thought of the children I did lose control, just a little: my voice shook. Going into camp didn't seem so bad for the grownups, especially with Ahmet telling me every day that it was for their own protection, and that the captivity wouldn't go on forever in any case. But most children would be bewildered and probably frightened, missing their routine and their familiar toys and lessons. Agatha spoke in a bright, firm voice that put me back in balance:

"Oh, I'll start up classes in camp: we'll all be back at work within a week. All but you. Now run along; you don't want to be here when they come, do you?"

"Heaven forbid. All right, Agatha—good luck, and I'll see you soon."

I kept a sharp lookout for Mina as I left, but she kept out of the way.

The sun glared as it always did when there was no rain, but as I walked home it seemed to me that a pall hung over the city. There was litter in the streets, and the little gardens were neglected and decaying. Soon, no doubt, the houses left empty by large-scale internment would be taken over by Japanese, but for the moment the only buildings kept in order were the big government houses and the Hotel des Indes, already full of high-ranking officers and heavily guarded by sentries. My prejudiced eye found nothing that seemed cheerful, though I passed little groups of Javanese laughing together, and here and there I saw small children at play. The world reflected only the colors I chose to see: I couldn't believe anyone was really lighthearted. There was no novelty left in the banners slung across the roads on fluttering ribbons, bearing slogans about the Co-Prosperity Sphere, and exhortations to work hard for the new era. Printed jeers against the Dutch imperialists were an old story too. Words, words, words—and all the time, I reflected, the machinery was running down: the Japanese were poised on our island like birds in transit. They used what they needed and took what they wanted, and when the time came, they would go on.

I was sorry for Agatha and for Ahmet, too, and I was miserably lonely.

Passing a Japanese sentry, I bowed as we had learned we must: the gesture had been a bitter duty for a week or so, but now it was automatic. The man himself was a typical specimen, and appeared to me shockingly ugly with his unshaved face and teeth botchily filled with gold, his baggy olive-drab uniform and strange rubber boots in which the big toe was separate from the others. He was so insultingly *small!* How could, how dared these little short-legged gnomes set themselves up as conquerors over our tall, strong Dutchmen? Still—there it was; those were the facts: they had conquered. They ruled us. It was an aspect of my shame I couldn't admit to Ahmet, but my eyes were wet, and it seemed to me that even my indomitable mother would have understood that.

Soon afterwards I was spending a long day at home, with no work to do and no prospect of my job's ever starting again. Ahmet had gone to a meeting, with Hatta's coterie, as I understood it, and I envied him his dedication. You can nourish yourself on a cause, I reflected, even more than on love. When Ahmet came back I would be all right, but in the meantime there was the long, empty afternoon. Ahmet never had empty afternoons. If I went on like this I knew I would begin thinking again about Agatha and the other Europeans, trying to get themselves adjusted to concentration camp, though I was determined not to look back in this sterile fashion. At any rate Yvonne would soon be home, and that would help.

Yvonne was late. Mrs. Dutoit and I tried to keep ourselves occupied with talk and coffee, but she was really frightened by the time her daughter walked in, just after sunset. Mrs. Dutoit flew out at the object of her loving worry and scolded her with all the anger relief can inspire.

"These nights of all times to be careless! Do you want me to have one of my migraines? Are you trying to kill me? As if we didn't have enough to put up with! If you had heard

some of the stories the neighbors were telling this afternoon—"

"I could match any of them," Yvonne said pertly. She was
getting thinner and she looked tired out, but nothing
quenched her spirits. She winked at me. "Honestly, Mamma!
I'm a big girl now, and what do you suppose my assistants
chatter about all day if it isn't rape?"

"That will do, Yvonne. You know perfectly well that sort
of language is forbidden. I never wish to hear that word in
my house again, do you understand?" Mrs. Dutoit was recovering. Her protests were automatic, and when Yvonne
muttered: "You'll be lucky if you don't have to, one of these
days," it went unrebuked, especially after Yvonne went over
and hugged her mother's stout waist.

"I'm really sorry, Mamma, but it couldn't be helped tonight, and I made a lot of money. Two officers bought a lot
of my things—old stock I haven't been able to move for years.
Then, just when I was putting up the shutters, another cus-
tomer came in, a Jap woman. They're bringing some of their
women in now. Comfort girls."

Mrs. Dutoit promptly moaned again that she didn't know
what the world was coming to when a decent, respectable girl
like Yvonne had to be polite to that sort of woman, but again
there was a tinny sound to the protest, and Yvonne didn't
attempt to argue. The unexpected fact was that the shop was
doing well and Yvonne was enjoying what she described as
a genuine boom. The Japanese went in for buying sprees, she
said, as if they hadn't seen fully stocked shops for ten years.
All the retail dealers were making money. The conquerors
must have been starved for the simplest things, cotton goods,
watches, shoes, and above all, foreign-style women's clothes.

"I don't know what they do with half the stuff, and I don't
ask," said Yvonne. "Just so long as they keep buying I'm
happy. Already I'm running around every morning trying to
scrape up more things to sell in the afternoon."

"But they do pay?" asked her mother. "That's what I don't
understand; why they bother to pay when they could take

what they wanted without giving anything in return, the way they did at first."

Her words evoked unpleasant thoughts of those days, and we were quiet for a minute.

"It's different now," said Yvonne. "They had their fun, but now they've been told to settle down and make friends, I suppose, and why shouldn't they hand out money for the stuff? It's not money to them—not real money. The only thing that counts with a Japanese is yen."

Just then Mr. Dutoit came in, making a dramatic entrance for once. His shirt was torn and dirty, so that his wife screamed in proper wifely horror. Mr. Dutoit sank into a chair; we hovered over him, pelting him with so many questions that for some time he couldn't get a word in. At last he could be heard saying, "Terrible, terrible," and we subsided and let him have the floor.

"It was terrible," he said. "I'd been to my office—there's nothing to do there, but I feel I should keep an eye on things as long as they let me; when the war's over they'll have to pay my back salary, at least I'll put in a claim. We're all going to do that. Only today I was talking it over with—"

"Never mind that; what happened to your shirt?" asked Mrs. Dutoit.

"Oh, it was terrible. Just as I started home a gang of Japanese came into the building with tools and weapons—spanners and guns and a pickax; I can tell you, I thought my end had come. But they paid no attention to any of us; what they were after was the company strong room on our ground floor, which somebody must have told them about. I can't imagine who would do a thing like that. Mr. Heensma himself locked it up just before he went out and got himself rounded up with the Volunteers. It might have been that office boy; I never did trust him; remember I said so at the time we took him on?"

Yvonne's sigh had no effect. For a man usually taciturn, Mr. Dutoit was thoroughly enjoying his chance in the spotlight. He would not be hurried, and it was at his own rate of speed that he told how the Japanese tried and tried to open the strong-room door, but met with no success until they lost their tempers and shot the lock out. The noise they made, he said, was terrible, terrible; the door gave way at last, and in went the looters.

"A minute afterwards, money filled the air. I mean that just the way it sounds. Money filled the air, flying out of the door and hitting the floor, packets of notes and showers of silver."

"But why should they throw it around like that?" asked Mrs. Dutoit. "You mean they didn't want it?"

"That's the most terrible thing of all; they didn't. All they wanted was gold. There *was* gold in the safe, you see; some coins and even a few bars, I believe, and they grabbed that and threw out the rest. They're crazy. It was like some terrible dream, but I wasn't alone in the dream, I wasn't the only one watching. You know that crowd of coolies you always see hanging around and following looters like jackals? There was a crowd there on the spot, their tongues hanging out at sight of all that money, but they didn't dare move so much as a finger without permission. They got it all of a sudden; the Japs yelled at them to come along and take what they wanted, and then stood there laughing like lunatics, and applauding, and cheering the coolies on when they fought. It was like—no, it wasn't. It wasn't like anything I've ever seen before in my life. The coolies wrestled and grabbed and hit each other and rolled in the dirt and cursed. . . . Terrible." Mr. Dutoit shook his head and wiped sweat from his face. Yvonne was leaning forward, hands gripped together and eyes glittering. With passionate yearning she said:

"Oh, why wasn't I there? Oh, Daddy, why didn't you wade in and grab some of it for yourself?"

"But I did," said Mr. Dutoit in his mild little voice. "That's how I tore my shirt. I got a bad bump on the head too, but . . ." Diffident as ever, he dug into his pocket and brought out a wad of notes which he handed to his wife. "Count it, my dear," he said. "I didn't have time."

Yvonne's boom and Mr. Dutoit's windfall helped us for a long time, and hadn't come to an end before I was aware that the family was fretting again. The fear of coming to the end of their resources always haunted the Dutoits. If I hadn't understood them I'd have thought they were being unreasonable, since they weren't destitute, but they had been brought up like any family at home, with a philosophy of thrift that I recognized. Thousands of people in Europe were going through the same thing. The tidy system of pay checks and savings in the bank had been blown to pieces. Nest eggs were unavailable because the banks had been closed by Japanese decree. Yvonne's income seemed good, but its very goodness made it suspect; at any rate it might disappear overnight. The whole affair taxed the Dutoit nervous system almost unbearably, and mine as well, for wasn't I responsible for a considerable portion of their daily expenses? I sometimes felt crushed by helpless guilt, and at those times everything a Dutoit said sounded like a direct accusation.

"We've managed so far," said Mrs. Dutoit one day, to nobody in particular, "but *nothing's coming in.*" To her this was so dreadful a state of affairs that she simply had to speak about it, but I interpreted it as a personal reproach. I was not paying my way, I said in harried tones to Ahmet when we were alone. He was mystified by my lack of logic.

"Neither is anyone else in the country," he retorted. "How could you expect to be able to pay your way, as you put it? We aren't starving. Just accept things and wait; it's the only thing to do."

"But there must be some way I could help the Dutoits. Yvonne brings home money. Why can't I think of something?"

"You are so Western, so much in a hurry." Ahmet spoke absently. He had developed a habit of not listening to my complaints. His mind was on national affairs, and individual troubles never interested him much, even when they were mine.

Ahmet was growing even less happy about the Japanese

control; he was trying hard to get used to a new conception of the Co-Prosperity Sphere. The first Japanese he actually met were a shock. He'd hoped to find the Japanese superior beings with something more than the practical ability, courage and strength they'd shown when they overthrew the Europeans—men of understanding and generosity and idealism. After all, somebody in Japan had formulated those excellent slogans; somebody had a policy. It's natural, I suppose, until one learns better, to expect individuals of another nationality to live up to every quality the nation's got a name for: a shock of disappointment is inevitable, but it was too bad Ahmet's first face-to-face encounter with Japanese should have been on such an entirely different plane than he'd expected. He went to keep an appointment with one of the officers, to talk about the future of the party and methods of co-operation: after being kept waiting two hours, he found his man drinking and unable to make sense at all. Poor Ahmet when he got home wouldn't tell me in detail what happened, but I heard enough to guess.

"Such bad manners!" he said, over and over. "He was uncouth. I would never speak to a servant as he spoke to me, and he seemed to have no idea of who I was, who had sent me, or what was needed." After smoldering for a bit in silence he added passionately, "Not even the Dutch have ever treated me like that."

For a few days he was deeply depressed, and spent long hours in private conversation at the house with his colleagues. Fortunately the next meeting with a Japanese went a good deal better. This Lieutenant Kiyama was sober and well-educated. A part of his duty was to deal on a friendly basis with the Nationalists, and Ahmet found him easy to get on with, but even Kiyama wasn't exactly encouraging.

"They are still putting everything off," Ahmet said.

Watching all this coming and going made me envious, and more restless than ever. I thought I might work for Ahmet's people in some capacity or other, but he wouldn't agree.

"Just now everything is at a halt. Now is not the time for

volunteers. We are waiting, and none of us is really busy. You must wait, too."

Sometimes I was ashamed to find myself harking back with regret to those days when I'd made the decision to be a Javanese rather than a European. This was such a disloyal thought that I hastened to put it away. Nevertheless I went on wondering how the Europeans were getting along. All of us knew where the internment camps were. Little by little, by dint of comparing and pooling bits of knowledge, those of us among the non-prisoners who were interested had found out where our friends were, and were sometimes permitted to send in supplies of food and clothing. I did what I could for Agatha. Direct messages were not allowed, but in the ancient way of prisoners the internees set up underground communications—through local people working for the Japanese, and tarts who slept with the soldier guards, and carefully hidden signals of various sorts.

Of my old world there remained outside only the Djungs, but at first I followed Ahmet's advice and stayed away from them. "It's for their sake as well as yours," he said when I protested. "If a Chinese gets a name for being hand in glove with Indos, he's that much more suspect, and the Chinese position is tricky enough as it is, without your bringing in complications."

It sounded thoughtful, even sweet, but—Ahmet had never shown much fondness for the Djung name. He didn't know them, and I had the feeling he didn't want to. He was prejudiced in general against rich Chinese, I reflected, and decided to forget his warnings, and went to their house. No lightning flashed and no thunderbolt fell as I pushed open the gate and entered the big, ugly garden. I had been half afraid of finding a Japanese sentry at the entrance, and the house itself occupied by some Japanese official of high degree, but everything was quiet and I didn't see uniforms anywhere. There was a long wait after I pulled the bell, then the door opened a crack, and a cautious eye peered out before I was admitted. The smiling man who welcomed me was a servant I recognized. The entrance hall stood bare and empty, until he called out over his shoulder and told my name. A moment later, with a swoop and a chorus of cries, the children ran down the stairs and surrounded me. On their heels came Ming and Mr. Djung, smiling and gracious as ever.

Back in our old places, sipping tea, I was able to sum them up, to put my finger on what had puzzled me at first about their appearance. They were muted. Ming wore plain blue linen and no jewels, and Mr. Djung, for the first time since I'd met him, was dressed in a long white Chinese gown. Any Japanese who happened to see them in the road would have dismissed them at a glance, as one more worthy but not interesting couple.

"Well!" said Ming. "How is it going?"

"Oh, not too badly. Here I am, as you see," I said. "And what about the Djung family?"

"The same." Ming dimpled. "But my husband finds it delicate work sometimes."

We both turned our eyes on Mr. Djung, who nodded slowly. "We are being careful," he said.

I didn't probe. I was sure Mr. Djung was feeling his way, stepping on eggshells, and collaborating as hard as he could, and I didn't see why he should not. It was unutterably pleasant to be with them again, in a friendly, familiar house. We talked about mutual acquaintances, most of whom were European: the Djungs knew more about them than I did, and gave me a wealth of news. The Palmers were all right, Mr. Djung said. Hennie Scheffer had been ill but he believed she was better now. Neither Djung knew Agatha, and had never heard of Agatha's young man. But as I was about to take my leave, Ming dropped a bombshell into the conversation.

"You won't care about it now," she said casually, "but I have a bit of news for you. I would have let you know earlier, but I remembered a conversation we had once—have you forgotten?—about Javanese marriage laws and so on. I knew then that anyone else didn't matter to you. You're a sly girl, not mentioning your Ahmet."

Mr. Djung said something in Cantonese, rather sharply, but Ming only laughed and shook her head at him, and replied in English, "Julie and I understand each other. It's all right." She turned back to me. "Did you know," she said, more seriously, "that your friend Mr. Brewer is here? Because he is. He's in the military camp out at the airport."

CHAPTER SEVEN

It makes me marvel, looking back, when I realize how well most of us, under the pressure we sustained, managed to remain more or less normal. The main part of the time we behaved remarkably like ourselves, but I admit that at this particular moment I was knocked off balance by Mr. Djung's bit of news, and was staggered far beyond what was warranted by the facts. No doubt part of the effect was due to the idleness I'd lived in so long: no doubt, famished by days of inaction, my brain fell on that crumb of gossip and made of it a feast. Before the Japanese came I wouldn't have reacted violently to Phil Brewer's—or any other man's—name, yet now I trembled with excitement to think that Phil was in Java, only a few miles away at that moment. The situation seemed to mean far more than Phil himself. In hasty imagination I was out of the whole dilemma, as if by virtue of his presence everything that had happened following the attack on Pearl Harbor had been wiped off the slate.

Fortunately, however, I didn't leap up with an exultant cry or otherwise betray this temporary aberration. I continued to sit there, only in spirit running after my racing thoughts, which was a good thing, since the Djungs, unlike me, didn't easily lose their grip on reality. I admonished myself to be as careful as they were, for after all, everything was just as it had been five minutes earlier, and danger was still with us. The Japanese *had* attacked us and conquered the Dutch: they *were* in power, and Phil was no magic talisman to bring back the old comfortable life, but a prisoner confined to a military camp. I couldn't reach him; as far as practical help was concerned, he might as well have been where I'd been picturing him all this time—in the States. Swallowing my joy, I managed to be calm as I asked Mr. Djung:

"How could that have happened? Where did *he* drop from?"

Mr. Djung shrugged. "We can only guess, but there are plenty of ways he might have come back. Perhaps his government sent him on a flying trip to Malaya—a mission— and he was still there when the Allies made that last rally. He would then, perhaps, have volunteered for active service, and it was his bad luck that he entered at just the wrong moment . . . Something like that, don't you think? What sort of a man is Mr. Brewer—would he do that? I never knew him very well."

I nodded. Yes, it was what Phil would have done; he'd have been eager to get into things.

"Then there you are," said Mr. Djung, with a little gesture of finality. "Poor Mr. Brewer. What bad luck!"

Ming had been watching me covertly. She said, "I don't suppose there's any chance of somebody being mistaken about seeing him? Poor Julie's quite upset, I think. You're pale, Julie."

"Not at all," I said. "What's Phil Brewer to me?"

Mr. Djung was saying testily, "No mistake, no mistake possible." He was proud of his private intelligence service, but a moment later he remembered to have kind thoughts, too. "Remind me, Ming, to do something for Mr. Brewer out there as soon as it's feasible, and let us hope he doesn't get too hungry in the meantime." He added to me, "You see, I've been making a list of my friends on the other side of the wire. Later I'll try to send in food, but I don't want to call attention to myself in that way just yet. The Japanese don't like Chinese to show too much sympathy to the Europeans, but after they've handed over to the local people, feeling won't be so bitter."

"If they ever do hand over," said Ming skeptically. Her husband quickly corrected her:

"The time will come, Ming, have no doubt about that. The Japanese have been keeping many of their promises." Ming sniffed, but he went on, "You don't see them holding government posts any more; that was just an early precaution. They're putting in Indonesians as fast as they can find trained people."

Ming was unrepentant. "It doesn't mean a thing. As long as they're here you'll have some Japanese official standing behind every Indonesian, pulling him around and directing him like a *wayang* puppet."

"No, that's not true. Sukarno, for instance—he's no *wayang* character. He's head of the Central Advisory Board of Putera now. He doesn't take orders from anybody." Mr. Djung spoke to me rather than to his wife, fixing his eyes on my face earnestly. He wanted me to make note of what he was saying, and I knew him well enough to understand why. Though Julie de Jong was of little importance at the moment, she could bear witness as well as the next person, when or if the time came when such evidence might be needed, that Mr. Djung's behavior and sentiments had been impeccable. It didn't matter so much to him who won the war as that he should be prepared with his defense at the day of judgment. Preoccupied though I was, I listened with mingled amusement and admiration. Mr. Djung never changed, I reflected, but I was impatient to get back to the main topic. I did it as tactfully as I could.

"Nobody wants you to take risks," I assured him. "Whatever you do, don't stir up trouble and suspicion. A man in your position *can't* help European prisoners; it wouldn't look right." Mr. Djung murmured in a gratified manner, and I continued, "But nobody could possibly object to an inconspicuous person like me carrying presents to the camps. For instance I've already been sending stuff in to Agatha."

"Her friend, the teacher," Ming explained in an undertone to Mr. Djung.

"And I can do the same for Phil Brewer. Nobody would object to that, I should think."

Ming said in teasing tones, "I can think of one objector—your other friend, Ahmet."

"I'll have to talk it over with the Dutoits," I said, thinking aloud. "We pool everything nowadays; I couldn't take any of our food without their consent, but I think it'll be all right. He'll be wanting butter and meat and eggs . . . Oh well, I'll manage somehow."

This broad hint was immediately followed up, as I hoped it would be: I knew the Djungs had laid in a good stock of foodstuffs. "We can do something about that," Mr. Djung assured me. "If you don't mind taking it, we can help make up the material comforts, ha ha."

I took my leave soon afterwards, and on the way home swung back into pure excitement. To think I had a friend again in this city! That Phil Brewer wasn't lost forever! Perhaps, then, the world itself was not lost, and I was no mere waif among strangers, but Julia de Jong, the same Julia who had lived and breathed before the catastrophe. I'd only been dreaming lately, after all; I'd been wandering blindly in utterly new surroundings, but it would not last forever. There was hope . . .

Again, I had to rein myself in and stop thinking along such treacherous lines. I was appalled by my own thoughts: what possessed me? Why was I telling myself lies? All this was rank ingratitude, if not treason. Why, I was a happy girl. I was a Javanese, living in my own country. I loved and was loved, and had recently been liberated to boot. A heroic existence lay open to me, since, side by side with my husband, I would share his vision and watch the break of a glorious day. My mother would have been proud of me. Only the most stupid sort of reactionary would waste time regretting the bad old days when there had been no Ahmet, no liberation, and no hope, when we'd been in servitude to the imperialists.

I excused myself by reflecting that I hadn't been regretting; I'd been remembering. "There is a difference," I argued with my conscience. "It can't be wrong merely to slip into reminiscence, and I did once think of myself differently. Facts are facts. I was Julia de Jong of Holland then, and Phil Brewer was my good friend."

A good friend, I repeated stoutly. I recalled, so sharply that I almost smelled it on the spot, the scent of his pipe smoke. Whatever would he think if he could see me now? Certainly I was changed. I wore Javanese dress, a blue *kabaja* and sarong of cheap print, for like the Djungs we of the Dutoit house had taken refuge in drab clothes. But my hair was still drawn back from a center parting as it had always been, to a low heavy chignon in back. Phil had often teased me for clinging to such an unmodish style when all the other European girls wore short, waved bobs. He would ruffle my hair, and I'd scold him and smooth the dark wings with both hands. It was almost a ritual.

But in other ways I'd changed. I looked much more careworn, and my stride was different. I now walked with a purposeful step because I had to go such long distances on foot. We hadn't money for rickshas, and the trams were impossible. Incidentally, I reminded myself, I would have to get up very early next morning to walk to the airport camp.

It's hard to explain why I was determined to make that trip. I couldn't hope to attain any contact with Phil. Besides, I knew—we kept track of such matters, we who had friends locked up—that it wasn't one of the days set apart by the military authorities for handing in parcels of food out there. Still, I had to go: the necessity filled me and left no room for any other thought. I looked on it as a reconnaissance journey, I suppose, but whatever the reason I was obsessed. However, I kept my own counsel at home, and this, too, was strange, considering our little community's custom of bringing whatever we heard or learned during the day to the evening table and offering it to the others, along with our food. Each evening we got Mr. Dutoit's account of the events, trivial or important, of his day. Yvonne retailed her girls' chatter, Mrs. Dutoit told the rumors she had collected while shopping, and if we were lucky Ahmet might give us some hint of his adventures, when he wasn't feeling cautious or—as Yvonne once bad-temperedly called him—self-important. I was the one who usually had nothing to contribute, since I hadn't made a place for myself in the modern world. I'd always felt a little niggling shame for this deficiency, though I knew the whole thing was rather childish, and it was strange that now, when I had an item of genuine interest, I should have kept it to myself, but I did. I merely remarked that I'd called on the Djungs and pretended not to see Ahmet's glance of surprise that I should have done this against his advice. The family asked questions. Yvonne wanted to know how Ming was looking—glamorous as ever?— and all of them listened politely, but without interest, as I told them Mr. Djung's ideas of what was to come. Mrs. Dutoit preferred her favorite fortuneteller's prophecies to any other, and I suspected that Yvonne had the same bias, even though she scoffed at her mother's superstition. Nevertheless I talked at length of Mr. Djung and said nothing of Phil Brewer, insincerely telling myself that his name would mean little to the Dutoits or Ahmet. Also, I said nothing of my plans for the next day.

I admit that I didn't feel quite right about this omission. Guilt went with me, and on the way I wondered why I had kept silent. The attitude was bound to give offense to the household, ultimately, and I wouldn't be able to explain it to them, since I didn't understand it myself. The little worry had plenty of chance to expand to a big one as I plodded on: I hadn't bargained for the time it would take to cover all the distance. Soon a blister formed on one heel, and after two hours I was hungry, but I felt I was making good progress, for I was at last outwalking the residential suburbs. More and more frequently I passed scattered shops in otherwise empty fields, until there came a stretch of flat ground with no buildings at all, and I had the eerie feeling that I wasn't making any more headway. I was alone in the road for a little while, a sensation that after so many days among crowds rather frightened me. Still, it couldn't possibly be much further, I thought. At last there were signs of life— a figure on a bicycle, carrying a tray on his head, who approached and passed me, a Japanese army vehicle going far too fast, and a slow-moving oxcart.

Shadows on the horizon that did not move proved to be sheds of some sort. In due course I recognized them, with sinking heart, as two large sentry boxes, one on each side of the road. Undoubtedly the inhabitants of these were guardians of the approach to the camp, and it was a hundred to one they wouldn't let me go by. Too late I recalled the rules; except on parcel days, civilians without special permits were forbidden to walk anywhere near the barbed-wire fences of prison camps. Japanese guards, high up in the observation posts that had been built at intervals around camp perimeters, could not see everything at once. The cruder attempts made by prisoners and their friends outside to communicate had long been discouraged by the sentries' shooting when they saw suspicious behavior, such as outright signaling or throwing objects over the fence, but these precautions were evidently not enough, and pedestrians were forbidden the vicinity except once a week. Even on that day it would be a courageous if not stupid person who turned his head to look openly at the prisoners as he came by. To stoop and pick up something from the ground would have been suicide. All this I knew perfectly well, but I kept going. In a few minutes, almost certainly I would be turned back. Still, I didn't give up hope.

And then, just before I entered what I estimated would be the danger zone, I had an inspiration, born of the sight of wheeled traffic. Any sentry who happened to be looking my way would have seen a stupid countrywoman stopping short, as if suddenly realizing she was near forbidden grounds. I turned in my tracks and hurried off the way I had come. Around me an occasional vehicle stirred up dust—armored cars overtook and left me behind, a limousine carrying an officer and a heavily made-up lady met and passed me on their way to the camp—and then, surprisingly soon, I saw what I wanted—a horse and cart. It might mean that my luck was in, for I'd been prepared to wait hours if necessary for such a thing. All Japanese sentries of whom I'd had experience concentrated their suspicions on people who went on foot, and as a matter of fact this was logical, since no one in a car could get close to the fences. The camps were placed as far as their situation allowed from the vehicular road, at least two hundred and fifty yards, sometimes further away than that, but walkers could swerve in nearer, as if accidentally, and a walking spy might be able to pass a verbal message. The sentries, therefore, practically ignored drivers and passengers in cars.

The cart drew nearer. I saw a typical Javanese farmer holding the reins, wearing a dusty jacket and turban. He was carrying in the cart a load of green untrimmed timber, with a woman and a number of children perched on top. When I hailed him, he pulled up readily and listened to the request I had prepared in Bahasa. I expected an argument with perhaps a refusal at the end of it, but he didn't object at all; he wasn't surprised either. I suppose it wasn't the first time somebody had asked him to do such a thing, if he made the trip regularly. His wife wasn't any more startled than he was. She leaned forward at one stage to ask courteously:

"Does the lady know it's not an open day at the camp?"

I replied, "Yes, I do know, but it doesn't matter. This time, you see, I only want to locate a friend—"

"Step up, miss," said the farmer, and gathered his reins. The wife held out a helping hand, and I jumped and sank down gratefully next to her on the fresh boughs, squeezed between her and a small girl. We jounced on, very slowly, and finally came to a halt between the sentry boxes. I might have been nervous, but my attention was fixed beyond, where the camp stood. Behind the fence a group of men lounged idly, staring out at nothing, like other prisoners I had seen. A stocky little soldier commanded us to climb down for a routine search, and I recalled my gaze, staring modestly and safely at my feet as we waited. The guard walked all the way round the cart, jabbed its load two or three times with his bayonet, peered underneath as if some secret might be hanging to the axle, and indicated with a jerk of the head that we could proceed. It wasn't really a tense period—we all went through such moments every day, if we went out at all—but I never got used to it; there was always the same speeding up of the heartbeat, the dry mouth, the premonition that this time at last the beast would slip its leash. But no. We were up again and the horse was trotting slowly down the road past the camp.

It was no different from the others. There across the yard were the same dwelling places, in this case converted warehouses fitted out with army cots, some of which were standing out in the sun, probably for airing. I saw makeshift clotheslines strung from window to window, even from bed to bed, with garments dangling on them. For some reason this had a powerfully touching effect and brought tears stinging to my eyes. Heaven knows why, but I hated to think of all those young men doing their own laundry.

But I looked my fill. It was the first good view I'd had of such an institution, having always rushed past Agatha's camp with eyes fixed severely on something straight ahead. So I stared in the natural direction, through the fence, and the guards did not think of objecting. For one thing I could hardly have looked elsewhere without twisting my neck like an owl, and for another I was only a farm girl, traveling with my family and a load from one rural spot to another. The Japanese soldier who grinned and winked at me as our cart rumbled past him on the road probably thought it a good thing for peasant morale that I should see white men cooped up like fowls. Shyly I smiled back at him, wondering as I did it why I'd come at all, and what I hoped to accomplish. I'd known all along that there wouldn't be any chance of looking for Phil outright, but I was bitterly discouraged at sight of the men crowded behind the fence. They looked bewilderingly alike, and none bore any resemblance to Phil. Shirtless, wearing khaki trousers or shorts, most of them sporting beards, they were utter strangers. I must have known some of them, I reflected, but it had been a long time since I'd seen fair heads and pink faces. And if Phil was one of those who had grown a beard—

Yet when I did spot him there was no doubt in my mind. There he was, taller and heavier-built than many of the striplings around him, though I could see that he had lost considerable weight. He wasn't lounging at the fence with the others, staring out at the cart: he was taking exercise by walking up and down. He would pace toward the fence, check himself as smartly as a British guardsman, swing around, and set off on the return journey. He had made one complete tour and was coming back when the cart caught his attention and he paused. I held my breath. Yes, he had seen me, for he lowered his chin in a particular way that I recognized, and peered more intently.

This was it—but I wasn't prepared: I didn't know what to do next. I must signal somehow, without inviting a shot from the Japanese. Suddenly, just in time, I remembered that old joke we'd had about my hair. Now as he gazed, I took the chance and turned my head, looking for the Japanese who had just winked at me. I found him—he'd been marching as fast as our slow horse walked—and as I returned his friendly look I raised my hand self-consciously and smoothed my hair, as if worried that it had been jolted out of order. We had progressed to the very edge of the boundry by this time, but Phil understood: I could tell that from what I saw from the corner of my eye. He was talking hard to the man next to him, and managed to give a little nod in my direction.

Out of sight of the camp I thanked the farmer and his family, and paid the sum I'd promised, and set forth on a long, roundabout way home. It was no chore now: I even forgot the blister.

People who've never lived in occupied country would no

doubt be mystified by this whole performance and conclude that the only explanation was that I was madly in love with Phil Brewer. Of course that was not it at all. As I've said, Phil represented to me the West; he came as a message, reminding me that even though I'd had no news, not even a bombing raid from Allied planes, the place was still there. The vacuum of my existence had begun to terrify me. Even though Western civilization was an illusion, as Ahmet often told me and I tried hard to believe, I'd invested more than a score of years in it. I needed reassurance. I did truly sympathize with Ahmet; I loved him; I agreed with him that imperialism had been wrong for Indonesia, but—it was my whole life he so lightly proposed to jettison, and that is not as easy as it sounds, to throw everything away and start over again. Even in peacetime it would not have been easy, and the war had made it harder, snatching away my past before I'd quite renounced it. And now, just when I had despairingly accepted that every future day would be like the one I was living through, a dull marking of time, came a welcome shock, like a lightning flicker up the sky from some source beyond the horizon. My heart leaped with it. There might be an end to this eternity after all, and I might still have the power to choose. That was the important thing—the power to choose. The glimpse of Phil reminded me that it still existed. And I was confident that his glimpse of me meant even more to him. His prison was far smaller than mine.

"Where have you been?" cried Mrs. Dutoit as I appeared at the door. It was very late, and no doubt I was an alarming sight, sweaty as I was and streaked with dust. I'd expected the family to be in the dining room at the table, and had thought I might perhaps have a chance to hurry to my room and take a bath before appearing. Instead, they'd waited and worried for me. I could tell from the way Ahmet started up that he was really concerned, but he said nothing, leaving Mrs. Dutoit to ask the questions. I told her where I'd been, quite simply; I felt no more need for caution or secrecy.

Ahmet was impassive, but the elder Dutoits shook their heads over my recklessness.

"A girl going all that way alone!" said Mr. Dutoit in shocked tones.

I saw Yvonne's eyes, widened in surprise, turn slyly toward the silent Ahmet, then as he gave no sign of reaction she winked at me. I washed, and joined them at supper. Mrs. Dutoit kept saying reproachfully:

"You should have told me you were going to be away all day, Julie," until Yvonne defended me.

"Oh, Mamma, these days how can anyone tell in advance when she'll be able to get home? Of course Julie counted on getting a lift, and then she couldn't."

"That was it," I said, grateful to Yvonne. I was eating greedily, as if I hadn't a care in the world, but really I was ashamed of having been so thoughtless. I added, "You must promise not to get worried again, Mrs. Dutoit. I'm not worth it, and anyway I know how to take care of myself."

"Still, a girl alone, and these lawless days," muttered Mr. Dutoit. His wife said:

"I'm surprised you allowed it, Ahmet."

Ahmet said in tight tones, "Julie doesn't consult me about her actions."

"You're in for it, Julie," said Yvonne, and though she spoke lightly, I knew it was the truth.

I brazened it out as long as I could. I asked outright if we could afford to send any food to Mr. Brewer and said that the Djungs had promised to help. The Dutoits and I talked about this, and of ways and means to get me there on my next visit with less fatigue, and then I said good night. Ahmet and I had been careful to observe certain amenities of behavior, not so much to deceive the Dutoits—we couldn't have done that anyway—as to avoid embarrassing them. For example, we never retired together, but had founded a little tradition. I would say good night to the family and go to my room, and when everyone else had gone to bed Ahmet would quietly follow. It is a fair sign of how preoccupied

I must have been that I should have expected that night to be left undisturbed by him. I was still wrapped in a private excitement, and paid no attention to other people's feelings, even my lover's. But Ahmet, naturally, had a private excitement of his own, and he must have been almost unbearably exasperated to find me, when he came in, already asleep. Without preliminaries he spoke loud enough to wake me.

"Julie, tell me the meaning of this."

I shot up to a sitting position. "Oh, you scared me. What is it? What's the matter?"

"That is what I want to find out," he said. "What does all this mean? Tell me, what are you trying to do to me?" He stood very straight, breathing hard, his eyes narrow. "What is this American to you? Why haven't you ever told me how you feel about him?"

At last I came to my senses, and saw with clarity what my behavior looked like. As fast as the words would come I said, "Ahmet darling, it isn't like that at all. It was only that I was so glad when I found a friend I thought I'd lost. I—"

"A friend." He gave a snort of angry laughter. "Truly we have different words for the same thing." I grew angry in my turn, not because I thought Ahmet was unjust but because attack automatically calls forth defense. I said loudly:

"Phil is a friend, an old friend, and I've never denied it. I can't imagine that he has anything to do with you in any case."

"Now this is outrageous. This is too much." Ahmet spoke to the empty room around us as if calling the spirits to witness. It was his habit when he had something exciting to say to pace the floor, and now he began to do it, striding up and down. The action brought to my mind Phil's restless captured-tiger walk behind his prison fence, and to my surprise I began to cry. But tears did not move Ahmet, who gave no sign of noticing them. He talked furiously, using words I hardly understood, for he stumbled over them in his rage and

148

his accent grew more marked. He spoke of hypocrisy, infidelity, lackeyishness, revisionism, feminine irrationality, European irrationality, ingratitude, and hypocrisy again—at which I cut in on the flow.

"I am *not* a hypocrite, and I certainly haven't been unfaithful either."

"No, because it wasn't in your power, because there was a fence between you and your lover, that *American*." He spat out the word like a curse. In my tense state this suddenly struck me as unbearably funny: I giggled.

"Ahmet, my darling Ahmet, aren't you being an awful fool? If you'd only give me a chance to explain! Come on, sit down and listen."

He remained standing, but he listened. Drawing a deep breath, I told him as well as I could what had happened, and why I had reacted as I had. I said a lot about what life had been like for me lately. I had not said these things before, but now it came pouring out, and if I didn't tell the whole truth, concealing the fact that Phil and I had once been lovers, I saw nothing wrong in that. My relations with Phil hadn't had anything to do with the day's adventures, I reasoned. It would have been the same with any former acquaintance who turned up so surprisingly. What I had to explain to Ahmet was the whole unsatisfactory situation I found myself in—adrift in a country not my own, in love with a man of another nation whose very tongue was not mine, bereft of my work. I didn't know if I was making any impression at all. He remained motionless for the several minutes I talked, and though I used eloquence I began to think I was failing, when I stumbled on one argument that went deep, saying:

"It's not your fault that the world takes it as a matter of course when women throw off everything they've learned and everything they have, to marry. We've got to give up our childhood and girlhood to become wives; we're supposed to assume our husbands' lives and interests like new coats, new skins. That's the way of it and I don't complain, but I do think you might try to understand how it isn't always easy. It's painful and difficult at times, Ahmet, and I suppose that's why I behaved badly today. I made a grab for—well, for a bit of the past that I knew."

Ahmet gave me a startled look, his face softened, and he sank down to his customary sitting position on the floor to think it over. For a while we were both quiet. I realized that I was about to be forgiven. What I must do, I told myself, was to be suitably grateful. I must not quarrel any more; I must keep my temper on a tight rein.

"I'm sorry, Julie," said Ahmet at last. It made me happy that he was no longer angry. I did love him, I didn't want to quarrel any more, but I had learned today that there were reserves in my heart. The task ahead of me was to keep them separate from daily life. "There are still many bad old habits I'll have to break," Ahmet was saying. He went on to apologize for having behaved like a reactionary husband, for having forgotten that a woman is a person like any other person, with her dignity to maintain. "I've treated you as if you were a slave," he said humbly.

"But you haven't. I don't want you to talk like that about yourself," I protested. "You've always been more than fair to me. I was just trying to show you why—" I broke off and held out my arms, but he ignored the invitation.

"No, I haven't done what was right about you. Look at how I've neglected your request for the past weeks when you begged me to find you some share in our work. Selfishly I've been putting you off, over and over. I see now that I was exploiting you, taking advantage of you, keeping you at home because that is where I wanted you to be."

"You couldn't help it."

"I could have tried. I didn't. What happened today has been a lesson I hope I'll never forget." He stood up. "I promise you faithfully that it's going to be different," he said impressively. "I'll make it up to you. Tomorrow I'm going to take you to see Lieutenant Kiyama."

"Why? I don't want to see any Japanese, Ahmet."

Ahmet said, "You will when you understand what it's about. Kiyama has asked me to find people who can help with the reconstruction of the country."

"But how can I do that?" I asked timidly.

"You can be very useful."

"I don't see how."

"Lieutenant Kiyama will explain," said Ahmet. For the first time that evening he smiled. His voice was kind and loving. "Poor Julie, you won't have to wander around Batavia any more, trying to fill the empty days. You'll have better things to do than dig up worn-out friendships from the bad old times."

He bent down to embrace me. It sounded very nice, but I was wary. If Ahmet expected that a job with his Japanese friends was going to prevent my taking food parcels out to the airport camp, he was mistaken.

"Dear Ahmet," I whispered, returning his embrace. I loved him very much.

CHAPTER EIGHT

———

"Where is this Lieutenant What's-his-name's office?" I hoped my voice did not sound quavery. At any rate Ahmet gave no sign of noticing as he said:

"It's Lieutenant Kiyama. You must learn to remember it. The office is in his house, because of the nature of his work; it's better right there, under his eye."

I was about to ask for specific information on the lieutenant's work, but a new thought put it out of my head. We were entering a long street of solid white houses that I knew well from former days. They were not the most imposing dwellings in town, but they were prosperous-looking. From those houses or others very like them had come many of my pupils, and as we made our way past one porch after another I was possessed by that sense of unreal recognition called, I believe, *déjà vu*. First, second, third, fourth—I counted them off, meekly padding after Ahmet. As we approached the sixth one I knew without being told that we were aiming for it. There was a guard at the door, but his presence could not mislead me. This was the house where Mrs. Dekker had lived, poor Mrs. Dekker who drank too much and had kept her child away from my class. This was the house to which I had gone, centuries ago, to expostulate with her about the error of her ways. In that drawing room I had drunk coffee and eaten cookies. In which camp was Mrs. Dekker now? How long had it taken for her to stop suffering for her daily allowance of drink? But by this time she must have recovered from the pangs of deprivation; for her, at least, imprisonment must have been a good thing.

Yes, Ahmet had turned in at the Dekker entrance. "You'll find a knocker like a dolphin on the door," I told him. He looked at me in surprise and asked how on earth I knew, but I only smiled mysteriously.

The flower beds had not been altered, and there was the dolphin knocker, but indoors I would not have known where I was. Much alteration had gone on, after a pattern often adopted by Japanese residents in European houses. A false floor had been built over the drawing room's to accommodate the *tatami*, or soft matting, of a Japanese house. At the door where the new platform came to an end, two or three pairs of shoes lay scattered about. The servant who had opened the door to us indicated the platform edge and paused. We had learned the way to behave; we took off our sandals before we stepped up on the matting barefoot and followed him into the room. People have often told me that the Japanese have an exquisite sense of beauty and simplicity, exemplified by their houses' lack of clutter. That day, however, as I looked around remembering Mrs. Dekker's household and the cool shady room this had been, I thought the lieutenant's arrangement glaringly ugly. The chrome table and metal filing cases had certainly not improved it—but then, it was an office nowadays, I reminded myself.

We were alone. The lieutenant was out, the servant had said, and according to Ahmet's experience he might well leave us to wait there for a long time. There were no chairs, of course, but I could have squatted on one of the rather dusty cushions scattered about the floor: however, Ahmet wouldn't permit this. Apparently we were expected to be respectfully uncomfortable until the great man arrived, waiting upright on our feet, so I resigned myself. Looking around, I took in more details and recognized a few relics of the Dekkers that I had missed before. Surely I had seen the windmill picture that hung between the side windows. And the little ship from Amboina, made all of cloves, still sailed bravely in its glass case as it had done on my last visit, though now it sat on a green metal cabinet and the glass was badly smudged. I became sadly pensive over the Dekker child, wondering who if anyone was giving her lessons now. Suddenly the guard at the door barked like a dog, I heard a stamping of booted feet, and then there was a pause during which I imagined the lieutenant pulling off the boots. But he did not enter. He called out something that sounded amiable as he passed the door, a greeting aimed at Ahmet, and we heard him going upstairs.

"He's gone to change his clothes," said Ahmet, low-voiced. "They usually do that when they come home unless somebody superior is expected. They're not really used to trousers at all, most of them."

The lieutenant pattered down the stairs and we stood to attention, side by side, as he entered the room. Solemn moment though it was, I nearly burst out laughing, for somewhere—probably in Mrs. Dekker's bedroom wardrobe—he had found garments of a nature new to him, and had put them on; a woman's suit of lounging pajamas, made of rose-colored silk and trimmed with ribbon. Kiyama was a tough little man and that morning he was wearing a three-days' beard. With his shaven head he looked such a virile type above the neck that the contrast was unbelievable. Not to mention the effect of short bent legs under the soft pink trousers, and the leathery neck in a girlish, low-cut collar. . . . I bowed low as Ahmet presented me.

The interview followed unexpected lines. Kiyama spoke Dutch and could have addressed me directly. Instead he posed all to the questions to Ahmet, who had to relay them while the lieutenant watched me sharply. Most of the answers Ahmet felt qualified to give without first referring to me. Naturally I resented this procedure somewhat, but I understood why he did it: this was the manner in which Japanese treated women. Thus, even when I heard him make little mistakes in the facts, for example adding a year to my true age, I bit back protests and did not contradict, because I knew I must not offend the lieutenant or give him cause to think I was badly brought up. Patiently and silently I stood by while Ahmet told Kiyama of my training and experience in teaching, as well as the bare facts of my birth in Holland. He told of my conversion to nationalistic sentiments in Java, at which the lieutenant made an approving noise. He ended with a little speech drawn completely from his own brain, about my enthusiasm for the Japanese liberation of the islands. Through all of this, Kiyama's keen little eyes did not change expression. Now and then I met their gaze, then lowered mine again. I had come to the conclusion that all Japanese facial types could be classed roughly as two, the broad Mongolian with snub nose and the narrow, dark aquiline. Kiyama was aquiline.

"So!" he said, as if he were shooting me with the word, and he then addressed me directly. Apparently I had graduated into the rank of human beings. "You want to help us?"

I didn't particularly. Still, too much was at stake for me to indulge in the truth, so I assented.

"In what way had you thought you could help us?"

I looked to Ahmet for assistance, and he said, "She could teach, sir. We're going to open the schools soon." But the lieutenant shook his head.

"She's a Dutch-speaking teacher, and Dutch is no longer to be allowed." There was a pause. I was feeling relieved, when he put up his hand commandingly. "Wait," he said, though no one had moved. "I know: she must learn our language."

I protested. "How could I learn it well enough? It would take years. I couldn't teach in a new tongue."

Kiyama smiled mechanically, in Japanese fashion. "We need not put you to work in a school. There are other ways in which friends can assist each other."

Ahmet was impassive, but I must have looked puzzled. However, the lieutenant seemed to think something had been settled, and after he had given Ahmet a few directions, he dismissed us.

"What *am* I going to do?" I demanded as soon as we were in the street. "I'm awfully disappointed. I thought I could start earning right away, and now I've got to go to some tiresome training school instead."

"Oh, they'll probably pay you a little salary to tide you over—partly in rice, partly in money; that's what they do." He did not seem disturbed, but he wore an expression I had learned to recognize and dislike—his secret look, I called it. "You should be feeling a little happier," he continued. "That bourgeois conscience of yours—is it more comfortable?"

"Much more, thank you." I smiled to prove it. "But I'd still like to know what's going to be expected if—or when—I ever finish this funny course in Japanese. How long will it take?"

"If you're an apt pupil it shouldn't be more than eight weeks."

He took me to a government building where a female clerk made us wait a while and then handed me an arm band rather like the one Ahmet had been wearing since the beginning of the occupation, made of coarse white muslin with Japanese characters brushed on in India ink. I understood that these gave my name and number and indicated that I had a job with one of the departments. My feelings about wearing the band were mixed. It would be good to have the prestige it gave when I dealt with soldiers and guards and small officials generally, but wearing it was like branding myself as a collaborator.

"Nonsense," said Ahmet when I worried aloud. "Who would blame you for that?"

"Practically everybody."

"If you're referring to Europeans, they're all in camp and won't see it."

"They'll see it all right, on parcel days. I can imagine how they're going to talk. . . . But never mind. I know it's better to have one than not."

Ahmet sulked, as he always did when I talked about the

European prisoners. But we both forgot the little quarrel when I discovered that he had procured a bicycle for me, the greatest luxury one could have in Batavia. He led me to the machine shop where he'd found it, and I was absolutely delighted.

"You had to have one," he said, trying to look as if buying bicycles were the most ordinary thing in the world. But I knew it wasn't; I wondered how he'd managed to acquire it. Any bicycle was priceless, even an old battered one, and this vehicle produced by the Chinese dealer was practically new. No money passed: the Chinese just said, "Good," and grinned at us as we wheeled the thing away.

"How did you do it?" I demanded, out of earshot.

"Never mind how I did it. Wong won't suffer, you can be sure."

"But you can't possibly pay what it's worth. How did you manage?"

"Perhaps I know the right people."

I blurted out a question I had long withheld. "Ahmet, is Lieutenant Kiyama one of the *kempeitai?*" This was a Japanese word for their secret police, who held much the same position as the German S.S., and were equally feared and hated.

"What if he is?" said Ahmet.

I didn't quite know how to reply. Kiyama hadn't really seemed so frightful. And it was wonderful to have a cycle, especially because I had grown up in Holland where everyone practically lived on wheels. "Oh well," I said at last, "if one's going to collaborate, I suppose it's best to go straight to the center."

The Dutoits were excited by my new possession, too. "Bring it into the house whenever you aren't riding it," Mr. Dutoit advised. "Otherwise somebody's going to steal it the minute you take your eye off it."

"I'll take it to bed with me," I assured him. Yvonne said:

"You're going to let me ride it to work, aren't you?"

Ahmet broke in severely on the chaffing: "Julie's to use it herself, to go to class with."

But my first errand was to ride over to the camp at the airport. If Ahmet felt chagrined he gave no sign: my ingratitude was punished in less personal manner—this second call on the camp was a flat failure. To be sure, I did discover that one could look through the fence as easily and safely from a bicycle as from a cart, but for some reason only a few of the men were outside the huts that afternoon; I didn't see Phil. The only satisfaction I got was the knowledge that I would now be able to reach the place in reasonable time.

I was afraid to walk into the classroom. The omnipresent guard at the schoolhouse door gave a sort of salute to my arm band, slapping the stock of his rifle smartly as I passed, but I was still afraid. This was my first overt act of collaboration, I said to myself, and I wondered what the other students would be like. As soon as I was among them, however, I was reassured. They too looked worried and hangdog; there was no insolent self-confidence among them. Indeed, some of the faces were vaguely familiar, and I realized after a while that I'd met the men at the secret meeting Ahmet had taken me to, so long before. Others—a few—were Chinese, but most were Indonesian, and a large proportion of those bore the indescribable atmosphere of the mission school—this, no doubt, because we were drawn from the literate class. Several of us were women and one other of these was Eurasian.

There was never another class that lacked what's called school spirit as thoroughly as ours, until later. During the first days we treated each other with deep, poorly concealed suspicion. Each one arrived alone, opened his notebooks, studied with fierce concentration, and when the hours were over went away with no farewell sign except a furtive glance at the others that said clearly:

"When all this is past history, don't you tell on me or I'll tell on you."

Without doubt these sentiments would not have changed

throughout the course if we hadn't been bound together, in spite of everything, by a common resentment of the teacher. He was a remarkable specimen of Japanese, small but with the arrogance of a giant. I sometimes wondered if he was not a maniac, for he screamed at slow or faltering recitations, and some of us declared that he foamed at the mouth. Merely shrieking and bouncing up and down on his feet did not satisfy him on the day an unhappy youth made a mistake over an affix. The teacher's shouted abuse did not help; he stayed stuck at the affix until the teacher stalked across the room like a turkey cock and slapped the boy across the face.

This was really beyond the limit. Everyone was so still you couldn't even hear them breathing, while the unlucky boy—he was an Indonesian, a bank clerk—turned as red as Chinese sealing wax. I fully expected him to run amok. Instead he drew a deep breath, fought hard for self-control, and found it by simply standing straighter. The teacher seemed unaffected by what had happened and merely ordered him to sit down before turning attention to another student.

As soon as lessons were over we collected outside in the street to discuss the matter, in low, shocked tones. The slapped youth became a hero; we took him to a coffeehouse to treat him and talk it all over again. Japanese stock had never before been so low; when we went back to our respective lodgings we carried the word. Though I made a sensation with the Dutoits when I told the story, Ahmet was singularly lacking in the indignation I'd expected him to show, saying only:

"Of course, what else did you think might happen? I thought everybody knew that Japanese do slap people. They're always slapping; it's their way. They even slap each other, and nobody thinks anything of it. It's a regular routine, a part of scolding."

"But don't *you* think it's outrageous?" demanded Yvonne. Ahmet sighed.

"Oh, if you like I'll call it outrageous. But slapping . . .

They can do a lot worse to a man. They can and they do."

I said, "Ahmet, have they ever slapped *you?*"

Ahmet did not reply.

One day, pedaling fast, I halted with a skid at the door of Yvonne's shop. I had hurried all the way from camp to bring my news. Carrying the bicycle bodily indoors through the hanging beads, I called Yvonne out from the rear regions. "Why, hallo there. Aren't you sweaty! What's the matter?" she said.

"Nothing that need worry us, but I've just been to camp—you know, handing in stuff for Agatha."

"Didn't they let you give it, or something? Come on, tell me."

"As soon as I can catch my breath," I said. I picked up one of her fans and began wafting it before my wet face. "Yes, I handed it in without any trouble, and besides, I saw Agatha." The note of pride in my voice was peculiar to camp visitors when they had succeeded in catching a glimpse of a friend—a good deal of life was made up of such tiny triumphs over the Japanese system. "I saw her perfectly plainly, and I'm sure she saw me," I went on, "but of course she couldn't make any sign. But that's not the point. I also saw Marge Palmer. Oh, for heaven's sake, Yvonne, stop shaking your head: you remember Mrs. Palmer. You always say you don't, but you do. Why, she's the one who sent me to you in the first place."

Yvonne's face cleared. She said, "Oh yes, the American. All right, but what's so special about that? She's in camp—well, of course she's in camp. She had to be somewhere, didn't she?"

"Wait a minute. Marge Palmer is pregnant! What do you think of that?"

Yvonne shrugged. "I'm sorry for her; what did you expect me to say? I'd hate to be pregnant in camp. Still, they've got doctors and—"

"You don't understand: the Palmers weren't able to have

kids. Marge used to talk about it a lot, how she wanted a child and what a tragedy it was, and how it was probably her husband's fault for being sterile, and—"

"And she found out she was wrong, didn't she?" She chuckled. "It took a war to prove it. She's probably happy anyway, but we'll have to make a special parcel for her once in a while; she shouldn't have to live on the diet they're getting in there. . . . What's the matter with *you*, Julie? It isn't the first time you've seen a pregnant woman."

"She's months along," I said." I said. "I mean, she must have been that way when they went in, by quite a time, judging from the size of her now. She'd left Chick, you see; she was in Singapore until just before it surrendered, and then she came on here until *we* surrendered, and so, when could she have . . . ? There was a man she met, that time we went together to Bali. . . ."

"Oh," said Yvonne. "Yes. I see what you mean." She whistled. "What a mess!"

I walked around the little shop, absently fiddling with things. "It isn't any of my business, but one can't help thinking. I don't see any other way it could have happened, and I don't expect Chick does either. He's there in camp with her. After they'd made it all up, too, and were getting along so well. It must be hell for her."

"And for him."

"Yes, of course, for him too—hell for both of them."

For a while neither of us spoke, gripped as we were in pity that, as it happened, was not justified; but we couldn't have known that human nature inside prison camp is not at all the same as it is outside, that Chick had quickly forgiven his wife, and that as a matter of fact they'd never been on better terms than at that moment. Yvonne fetched a deep sigh.

"It's a tragedy all right, but Julie, you've got bigger things to agonize over. There's nothing you can do for them except send stuff in. Let's promise each other not to forget food parcels, at least."

"All right," I said gloomily. With love, I gathered up my bicycle and carried it out to the street.

With the grubby bit of folded paper in my hand I felt as if I held a load of TNT. I stared down at it, too shaky to try opening it. I was terrified of the whole thing—the note, the man who had brought it, the whole implication of this adventure. Though like everyone else in town I knew that prisoners did manage now and then to smuggle out word to friends, I'd never expected it to happen to me. I didn't bother to speculate on which prisoner could have sent it.

Instead, I asked myself if the messenger was trustworthy, since if he wasn't I would certainly suffer. I'd never seen him before. There he stood smiling foolishly, a very young man in ill-fitting Japanese uniform. But he too seemed to feel nervous, for he glanced around as if the veranda was uncomfortably public, as in truth it was—the servant had given me no hint of the nature of my caller, but merely left him there and gone to fetch me.

"Come in," I said, and we went into my room.

I thanked heaven Mrs. Dutoit wasn't at home: She would have felt that her lodger was recklessly imperiling the household. Then I remembered my arm band and calmed down. It was protecting me in a manner never envisaged by the authorities who had granted it to me: this visitor might quite well have been coming to see me on official business. "Sit down," I said.

He did, uneasily, like many Japanese who weren't used to chairs. He accepted a cigarette, flashing gold teeth at me, waved toward the note, and said, "Read."

I recognized Phil's writing: "Darling, darling Julie: What a wonderful surprise to have glimpses of you. I can't tell you what it was like that first time when you rode by on the cart with your new boy friend." The idiot! I laughed and stopped trembling as I read on. "The food you send is wonderful, too. You can trust this man. Don't try to write. Tell him how you are, how things are going. I'll try to persuade him to call on you again. It gives me a lump in the throat to see you on your bike every week. I love you so much, darling. P.S. Do you think you might possibly manage more butter next time? Can't imagine what you are using for money. You are really marvelous."

"Well," I said brightly to the man in uniform, "that's very nice. Thank you so much."

He bowed from the waist, saying, "You want me to tell Brewer anything?"

Softly the servant padded in with cups of tea. I waited until he had gone. "Yes, please—tell him I won't forget about the butter, and that I'm very happy to have his letter, and I'm safe and well. You understand?"

"Yes, I understand." He drank the tea noisily, sucking it through his teeth. I was about to make some polite remark about the weather when he stood up to go, saying, "All right; I try to come again." He smiled like a kind old uncle, though he must have been a lot younger than I was. I asked him about himself and was relieved to hear he was a Formosan and not a Japanese at all—Formosans, I knew were not necessarily fond of their masters. Something handsome in the way of a tip would have been the thing to give him, and I didn't have enough money to do that, but I remembered in time that I owned a ring I'd bought once in the goldsmiths' district, and I gave him that before he went away.

Once he was around the corner and out of sight, relief made me so weak I had to sit down. But it was good to think I'd had a letter from that mysterious country inside. Once more I read Phil's letter, and replied in my thoughts.

"You've changed about me, Phil. It makes a difference, being hungry and dependent, doesn't it? I know all about that. But it's too late for you and me. It's too late."

Romantic nonsense! Laughing at myself, I burned the paper carefully in an ash tray, and threw away the fragments out of doors. Ahmet would soon be home.

Above all things the Japanese, according to frequent announcements and declarations, wanted to make their language and culture popular. Japan the Savior, Japan the Leader, Japan the Light of Asia, had to sell herself, but her ambassadors went at it maladroitly, as if the idea could simply be handed to the Indonesians and they would gobble it up. In fact they did not gobble. They were dismayed to hear that school lessons formerly taught in Dutch were now to be in Japanese rather than Bahasa. They wondered indignantly why their children must now learn Japanese history in the time formerly given to Dutch history, and what the aim could be of teaching them Japanese customs.

"We have perfectly good customs of our own," one of Ahmet's friends explained to me in a hurt manner. "This is not independence as I see it. We've only exchanged tyrants." He expatiated on the subject for a long time—in Dutch, of course—and I could see that Ahmet was with him, sharing his resentment but not his surprise.

"You're perfectly right, but I wouldn't worry too much if I were you," I said. I'd been thinking it over. "They don't seem thoroughly consistent about all these plans. For instance, take the latest statement—that we're all going to change over to the Japanese language inside a year."

"It's not exactly a statement, just a rumor," Ahmet broke in. I shrugged.

"Statement or rumor, it comes to very little anyway, because the fact is they don't really *want* us to talk their precious language. You've only to see the suspicious way the guard reacts when I speak to him in Japanese; if it weren't for this arm band I'd probably get into trouble."

Ahmet's friend said, "Surely you're only imagining that. Why, the latest out of their headquarters is that they're going to publish the daily paper in Japanese characters before long, and if they take to broadcasting in Japanese, most of us won't have any notion whatever of what's going on."

"All that's official. It doesn't work out in practice," I said.

"You'll see for yourself; they really hate any of us talking the language. They feel it's too good for us."

"Are you really getting on so well that you can talk?" asked the young man, in admiration, and Ahmet was proud as he said:

"Julie's remarkable at languages; she's picked it up very quickly."

I blushed and changed the subject.

One day the teacher selected me to take a message to Lieutenant Kiyama. I found him sitting at his desk in the Dekker drawing room with a stack of flimsy papers before him. Since our first interview I'd seen him only at a distance, once or twice at the school building and several times in his car, driving past me on the road. A quick glance around the room showed me that nobody had given it a good cleaning since I'd last been there. The lieutenant had not, evidently, followed the example of many other officers, who had found themselves housekeepers among the local girls. I wondered why, and decided that his special position as a leader of the *kempai* service probably made him suspicious of women. But he was quite polite to me.

"Ahhh yes, Miss Julie." He took the note and read it while I stood waiting, then he put it down and said, "So. I will not reply immediately, and you may wait. Sit." He gestured at one of the cushions and I obediently sank down on it. The lieutenant shuffled through his papers, hissed absently between his teeth, and scribbled a note or two. Then he slapped the desk and stood up smiling. It was a real smile.

"So, now we have lunch," he said. I stammered some sort of excuse, but he overruled me by ignoring it and gave orders to the servant.

I was confused and surprised when he poured out a glass of sherry. I'd expected that he would want me to do that, and all the other little services of a host, but he understood foreign ways, at least to a certain degree. The servant brought in a little short-legged table and set it up between me and Kiyama, who sat on a cushion of his own, his legs crossed in the easy way we foreigners found impossible to imitate. As soon as the food was brought, ready served in little plates on two trays, the lieutenant began talking to me in Japanese. So that was the idea! Clearly this was an unexpected kind of viva-voce examination, and I braced myself to do as well as possible.

The food looked dainty, but I'd never seen anything just like it. My portion of rice, for example, sat in a dark red lacquer bowl and was not only stone cold—a fact the lieutenant seemed to accept as natural—but had been modeled into a peak and was colored green with a sprinkling on the top of grated coconut.

"Do you admire it?" asked Kiyama, noticing my distrustful inspection of the edifice. "I have my own cook who knows Japanese ways, and he makes little pictures of the food. That, for example, is Mount Fuji—the famous Mount Fuji, very beautiful. Eat more, Miss Julie; you haven't a very good appetite."

Now and then, talking, I hesitated for a word or an idiom, and he prompted me in a kind, patient manner. In the same way he corrected my mistakes, so that by the time the meal was finished I had gained confidence and talked with more fluency.

"Enough," he said abruptly, changing back to Dutch. "You have done very well, Miss Julie. The teacher does not exaggerate in his reports. You lead the class." Modestly I looked down, murmuring something or other about being glad, and he went on, "We must consider how best to put these talents to use, but enough of work for the day."

Sipping tea, he made conversation. I was agreeably surprised to find him a well-informed man, who had evidently spent quite a lot of time on the Continent. He knew Holland, that was evident, and it was just as clear that he knew Germany even better. But as we talked, I felt less and less easy about the situation. My thoughts drifted back to those officers who had taken mistresses in the town. By this time we civilians of course had a good picture of their customs in this respect, and I knew one of the girls who had been chosen to keep house for a naval captain—she was a Eurasian named Maida, who until recently lived quite near the Dutoits. Mrs. Dutoit and other women always shook their heads and clicked their tongues over Maida, but Yvonne and I defended her. Teasing Yvonne's mother, we would accuse her of envious feelings for Maida.

"Not that it isn't natural," Yvonne said, a wicked eye in Mrs. Dutoit's direction. "Did you see that girl when she came home yesterday to bring things to her mother? All dressed up, and much fatter than she used to be."

"She looked happy, too," I chimed in. "She probably loves her friend very much."

Mrs. Dutoit bridled and called us evil-mouthed girls.

The Japanese were indeed domestic types in their way, who missed their wives and homes, and seldom lost time reproducing similar milieus as closely as possible.

"More power to them," Yvonne and I always said stoutly, when our elders talked about how disgraceful it was. But now I had second thoughts. Lieutenant Kiyama was being so very kind, so complimentary, his glances were so particularly admiring that I couldn't ignore the implication. When he began asking careless questions about Ahmet, I really was flustered. Fortunately his telephone rang at that moment, and I was able to thank him and take my leave before he had finished his conversation with it.

"Well! That's a new problem," I said to myself as I pedaled away from the Dekkers' house.

I had covered about half the distance home when I heard a noise unusual in that tightly disciplined town—loud, excited talking in the Indonesian language, mixed with Dutch, that most natives used. It came from a crowd of people standing near the corner where I had to ride across the street. As I got off my bicycle and pushed it with me toward the crowd, other people, too, hurried to join in, so that it swelled rapidly. By the time I got there the nucleus was almost hidden, but I could see that it was composed of students in uniform, listening to one of their number furiously haranguing about something. I asked the nearest boy what it was.

"Those Japanese," he said. "It's too much! Now they've told us we must shave our heads like the students in Japan. We won't. We'll die first."

I wanted to laugh. It seemed a trivial grievance for so much passion, but it was obvious that the crowd did not agree with me. Everyone was on the students' side, and cheered the speaker as he went on.

"Have we become outright slaves to these people? Where is our spirit? Where is our independence? They promised to make us free, and now look!" His hearers shouted in angry support. "They are denying our nationality!" he asserted, and there were more yells. "They have beaten us!" he said. "They have humiliated us in front of our brothers! And now they want us to become altogether Japanese, with naked heads to show humility."

So much enthusiatic rage sounded in the answering roar that I decided to be prudent and leave the party. I wondered as I rode away why no police had yet intervened to break it up, such gatherings being as expressly forbidden under the new regime as they had been under the old. But even after I had traveled past several streets I saw no policeman or Japanese soldier anywhere. It was as if they were deliberately hiding, and I was puzzled.

The news had gone ahead of me; I found Yvonne already at home when I got there, talking about the same thing. "They're having riots all over town," she told her parents, "And I thought I'd better get back. Anything might happen—the students are awfully angry. It's something about having to shave their heads."

I waited in confidence that Mrs. Dutoit would laugh as I had wanted to do. To my mild surprise she didn't even smile, but shook her head gravely as if her sympathies were with the rioters. When the family group was complete and the subject came up again, I asked:

"Please, what is so terrible about having to shave your head if you're a boy? Somebody explain, will you?" The four of them looked at me blankly as I went on, "Don't the Japanese themselves do it because it's so much cleaner—a matter of hygiene? It sounds reasonable enough, doesn't it?"

Ahmet said, "No, Julie, it's a personal thing. It's the very last right a foreign army should try to take away. The style a man uses for his hair is his own affair, and any order telling him what to do about it encroaches on his liberty."

"But all Japanese orders do that already. Isn't the occupation itself one big encroachment?"

There was another perplexed pause, broken by Yvonne. "I think it's something to do with religion too," she said. "When you strike at a Muslim's custom of keeping his head covered, you're asking for trouble. It's hard to explain, Julie, but I know just what's involved. I *feel* it."

"That's it," said Ahmet. I nodded and they were all relieved. This was an aspect even I was capable of grasping. "You'll see," Ahmet added. "The Japanese are going to regret this. It's their biggest mistake so far."

When we had gone to bed I said, "Ahmet, suppose a Japanese—an important Japanese—happened to like me and asked me to sleep with him. How could I get out of doing it?"

"That sounds like a sort of game," said Ahmet, amused. "I'd say that it's a woman's question, though—the kind one woman asks another, so why bring it to me?"

"Because it isn't a game, exactly. Somebody might be going to bring it up." I hesitated. I didn't mean to be coy about it; I was really afraid of Ahmet in one of his jealous rages. Still, I had to know, so I said, "I might be mistaken, but I think Kiyama's got his eye on me." I waited for the fireworks.

They seemed slow in coming. For a second or two I wondered if Ahmet had not fallen asleep, but then he said, "Kiyama, eh?" in an odd, reflective voice.

"Yes, the lieutenant. Your boss."

"My boss for the time being only." Ahmet's voice had sharpened. He sat up and folded his arms, staring straight ahead, and the expression on his face was not at all what I'd expected. He looked as he did when he was planning the next move for his Nationalist comrades: it was his secret look. He repeated in a slow, reflective way, "Lieutenant Kiyama."

"Yes. That's him. What am I going to do?" I would rather see him angry, I told myself, than the way he was. I didn't understand it. He turned and looked at me and the faraway look went out of his eyes.

"Well, Julie, I still think it's a woman's question," he said. "Women know how to use some sort of magic, don't they?—to handle men in these matters. Besides, it may never happen. You may be mistaken. We won't worry until the time comes, will we?"

His arms were around me, comforting me, coaxing me to forget the problem altogether, and I tried willingly. Half an hour later, however, with Ahmet sleeping peacefully by my side, I was still awake, still worrying. It was not only the lieutenant who bothered me now, but—of all things—the thought of the hostel *djongos*, who had come to the house a few days before and begged me to find work for him. "Please give me a job, *njonja*," he'd pleaded. "I'm sorry I ran away, but I was frightened."

"But why have you come back from your village? You'd be far better off in the country—there's nobody here now to hire foreign-style servants."

"No, no, we're not better in the country, *njonja*. We're hungry." He'd put his hand to his stomach. "There isn't enough food any more; the Japanese are there as soon as our crops ripen, taking everything away. Find work for me, *njonja*. I'll do any kind; I don't have to be a *djongos*; I'll take my pay in food. Find me work, *njonja*."

I'd had to send him away. I couldn't hire him; we had other people with stronger claims on our loyalty, and when I explained that, he was reasonable about it and went off without further complaint. He had good manners, the old *djongos*. But now the thought of him haunted me, and when I fell asleep I dreamed something new about my mother. She was there in some sort of disguise—that is, though she was some-one else, I knew it was she as I always did. She was saying:

"Remember one thing, Julie. In war, nobody is right."

What did it mean? Before I could argue with her, or ask her why she had played such an active part in her war if war was always wrong, I woke up. Of course I woke up; one always does before things are settled in dreams. Awake, I tried to comfort myself, thinking:

"That wasn't really my mother speaking. Anything I dream comes out of my own head. *She* would never have said that."

But I still didn't like it, and least of all did I like the idea that I made up my own dreams. If I had to believe that I would be lonely and bereft of all comfort. I put the thought away.

CHAPTER NINE

If I hurried, I would be able to reach Yvonne's before the girls' lunch hour was over, and she would be alone. It was not acutely necessary to see her, but I had something on my mind, so it was with exasperation that I found Ito standing around in the shop as he so often did, joking with Yvonne in his atrocious Bahasa. He was supposed to be a sergeant, but we had long since discovered that rank did not mean the same in the secret police as in the Army. We called him Ito because that was the way his long, unpronounceable name started out; besides, he was the sort of man who seems to demand a nickname: he was plump, with gold teeth, his face shone with good humor. According to Yvonne, a greater rascal never lived. His chief job had something to do with controlling supplies of cloth, and that is how she got to know him, since her work often took her to the central office where licenses to buy were dispensed to retail merchants. Petty officials like Ito were venal, and kept their eyes conveniently shut to black-marketing when they found it profitable; little bribes were the order of the day, and Yvonne played the game alertly. Ito had become, literally, a household name with the Dutoits. A regular Ito saga was in the making, but Yvonne was careful to stay on his right side, and so for her sake was I, even today when I didn't want him there.

"Is Lieutenant Kiyama well this morning?" he asked me, with the reserve he always showed in my presence. Kiyama was far more important than people of Ito's rank. I said:

"I suppose so, but I haven't been to work today; I was given the time off."

"You are lucky. I wish I could be a secretary, don't you, Yvonne?" said Ito. But in spite of his jaunty air, he was uneasy in my presence. No doubt he feared I might make trouble for him with his superiors by carrying tales. It wasn't long before he left.

"I'm sorry to scare away the boy friend," I said sardonically. "I know how fond you are of him."

Yvonne chuckled and waved her sewing hand with the needle in it. "Think nothing of it; he'll be back tomorrow. What's new?"

"Well, something queer is happening," I said. With Yvonne I always blurted out anything that was on my mind: she was the only person in town that I trusted absolutely. I'd come to the conclusion months ago. Yes, months. Incredibly, the Japanese had been in Batavia for a year and a half.

Yvonne glanced at me shrewdly over her spectacles and turned her attention again to the silk dress she was finishing off by hand for the wife of some Japanese colonel. She asked, with bent head, "What's queer? I thought you were going to see Agatha this morning." It was the way we had fallen into referring to our camp visits. Within limits it was accurate enough.

"I did, and something funny is going on up there. I don't understand it." The stool I sat on afforded a view through the bead curtains to the street outside where my bicycle was propped. Though it was still my most precious possession, I no longer found it necessary to carry it indoors wherever I went: most people would have been afraid to rob me now. "It's the way the women acted," I went on. "I mean the ones I know especially, of course—I saw Agatha and Marge and some of the other teachers. Yvonne, I could be wrong, I thought they all snubbed me."

This sent Yvonne into a fit of laughter. Unsmiling, I waited. She said, "Oh, Julie, you're an absurd girl. How can anybody snub you through a fence, and at that distance, too? I wish you'd tell me."

"It can be done," I said stubbornly, "and it was done today. I'm serious, Yvonne. When you've walked past the fence as often as I have, you can tell if the people inside are glad to see you or not. You can tell a lot of things. Remember that time I was sure something wrong was going on, and we found out later that there was dysentery in camp."

"That was different. You must have known because they looked ill."

"No, I could tell, that's all. I can guess the moods. When I go to see Phil it's the same, I know when he's discouraged and when he isn't. Anyway, this morning what went on didn't call for second sight, I can tell you. They actually turned away their heads, trying not to look at me . . . I felt as if I'd been tried and condemned for some crime. I can't explain exactly, but I'm worried. I know something's the matter and it's something about me. What can I do?" I stood up and paced across the room and back again, coming to a halt before Yvonne. I said in lower tones, "Yvonne, do you think they could have heard—anything special?"

A look of pain and apprehension came into Yvonne's eyes, but she spoke brusquely. "Stop talking such nonsense, my dear; how could they have heard anything about you? They couldn't possibly. Julie, you must try to stop this worrying. Promise me you'll try. Now you just go home and take a shower and rest. It's more tiring than one realizes, going to camp. And just remember that nobody is talking. There's no nasty gossip about you in camp—or anywhere else, either."

It had been a relief to put it into words, but as I finished the trip home I reflected that Yvonne didn't know much about prisoners and couldn't be depended on to judge. She didn't have my experience; her trips to camp were very few, and lately she hadn't been at all, whereas I visited both Phil's and Agatha's week after week, carrying parcels. I knew, as she didn't, that the setup was not as rigid as it had been in the beginning. You felt nearer to the inmates nowadays, because the guards didn't make such a point of guarding. Though they would still have objected violently to outright signaling or calling back and forth, in a dozen little ways a thaw was evident. This no doubt was because the guards were used to the visitors, and we in turn had lost much of our first fear of them. Even though the men among them whom we got to know were sometimes removed and new people put in their place, the situation remained relaxed. I don't know exactly why. It wasn't because things were better generally. On the contrary, there was a constant deterioration in conditions. Nevertheless the attitude was more friendly on both sides; familiarity had eroded much roughness. I thought of the war as an independent organism with human characteristics of its own. It was getting on in years; like all aging creatures it was losing some of its ferocity. I smiled at this, pleased with the conceit, but then worry crept into my mind once more. Whatever Yvonne might say, those women at the camp had behaved in a very odd manner, and I couldn't doubt they were angry with me. Of course Mina had hated me long before the internment, but Agatha hadn't, nor had Marge. I wondered what the reason for their anger could be. Then I told myself that I could guess at it, and a cold hand grasped my heart.

However, this was mere speculation. I must drop it. I made a firm resolution to do just that. The puzzle could wait, along with many other unsolved riddles, until the end of the war, though time was slipping by and the day of the end seemed to jog ahead forever and ever, a mirage I was tired of watching. On the heels of my resolve came another sneaking fear: had Phil, too, turned against me? My next trip to his camp would show.

However, once I was at home a cool shower cheered and calmed me, as Yvonne had said it would. I ate a little and went to bed and rested. Later I actually enjoyed putting on a new dress, even though it was in honor of an appointment I didn't look forward to. Mrs. Dutoit invited me into the family sitting room for coffee and I found her alone. It was clear from her high spirits that she'd been pursuing her particular hobby, visiting a fortuneteller who was all the rage these days among people who shared her tastes. Her mother's penchant for the occult irritated Yvonne, but I couldn't see why Mrs. Dutoit shouldn't be allowed to play with prophecy and astrology if it comforted her, as it obviously did: I wouldn't have got anything out of it and neither would Yvonne, but if Mrs. Dutoit had faith, why spoil it for her?

"Let me tell you my news," she said enthusiastically. "I've just been for a session with Hamid, and he was perfectly wonderful, Julie. He was inspired. I have exciting news. He says if we can only hold out just a little longer, about a hundred days, our troubles will be over because we're going to be rescued. Just think of it; why, that's hardly any time at all. Hamid says the signs are *definite* and *positive*. There now!" She sat back in her chair, beaming as if she'd just bestowed on me the world's largest diamond. I was glad Yvonne wasn't there, for she would certainly have reminded her mother of other times when she'd brought home similar prophecies, none of which had ever come true, with an equally fervent faith. I thanked Mrs. Dutoit and made excuses, returning to my bedroom to finish dressing. Everybody must have his pacifier, I reflected as I brushed my hair, and everybody managed to find one sooner or later. Mr. Dutoit drew comfort from cronies, with whom he had taken to sitting all through the evening in a friendly wayside café where the proprietor was satisfied if he bought one cup of coffee. The older generation had found a sort of content in spite of all the trials of the occupation; routine, sleep, hope—they needed these to keep their minds off such realities as scanty diet and complete isolation. It wasn't only their generation; we young people too had taken refuge in preoccupations. Yvonne enjoyed her battle with the world for a living, and in her quiet way she was winning, too—even amassing wealth. Ahmet had his political vision and the intrigues through which he was confident of attaining its promises . . . with himself in a high place among the powerful, I added in my mind spitefully. I had lately been harboring many malicious thoughts like this about Ahmet, though I was always sorry afterwards, and felt guilty. I couldn't seem to resist them. They came into my head all the time except when he was with me to exorcise the devil. I shrugged off this one.

What pacifier had I? In the mirror the brush paused in the air while I thought. But why was I hesitating? It was Ahmet, of course; I had Ahmet. I had him to love and tend and fight for. The brush returned to its work, but my eyes no longer sought themselves in the reflection; Ahmet himself came in and interrupted my thoughts.

He greeted me cheerfully, smiling as he rarely did nowadays, until his eyes fell on the new plum-colored jacket I was wearing. His step faltered for a very short space, but then he came on and sank into a low chair, saying in casual tones:

"Nice dress; the color suits you. You're going out?"

"Yes," I said, not adding that I had had these plans since the day before. I drew the outline of my lips carefully with a stick bought from the special canteen used by Japanese officers. Not until my mouth was properly painted did I go on. "There's a lot of correspondence to catch up with at the office, so Kiyama's sending the car."

"Good," said Ahmet genially. "It happens that I, too, have an appointment."

Neither of us mentioned the discrepancy in my story, though it was clear that secretaries did not put on new clothes to spend an evening taking dictation and filing letters. Our times together were full of unsaid things like these, details that we shrank from bringing into the open. No doubt such unuttered facts were responsible for the poison in my thoughts, but it couldn't be helped. Ahmet went into the bathroom and undressed for a shower, tossing out his garments one by one through the door as he pulled them off. Like a good housewife I picked them up from the floor, folded them neatly, and put them on a chair ready for the wash. During

177

the lean, anxious days I'd learned to treat clothing with exaggerated care, and now, though the hard times were over and the bedroom chest contained new clothes, I couldn't break such habits. When everything was tidy I went to join the Dutoits again. I clung to them when Ahmet was in the house. I felt safe with them, and felt sure that if Ahmet were ever to turn on me—though it was impossible to suppose he would—they would defend me. Yvonne was home now, and we sat comfortably together, chatting of trivialities, until Lieutenant Kiyama's car arrived. No Dutoit commented on the car, or Kiyama, or anything personal at all when I took my leave. It was for their benefit that I called toward our room, "I'm going now; goodbye, Ahmet," and his answering cry, impeccably friendly, followed me out.

In those unpleasant moments alone, at the times I was hating Ahmet, I told myself that if I lived a hundred years I would never forgive him for having let me in for the position I occupied now. Why hadn't he put his foot down, or at least dissuaded me from taking the step? Why had he not intervened like a strong man and taken me away? He hadn't even contradicted me when I spoke of the advantages we would all enjoy if I went ahead. But of course all this was unreasonable. Instead of railing at Ahmet I should have aimed my curses at the situation that trapped us both. In fact Ahmet was simply unable to do anything. None of us could help ourselves, least of all him. If anyone could be blamed it was me; it must have been my mother's legacy that made me react as I did to Lieutenant Kiyama when he first showed that he was attracted. At that time I could have discouraged him without—perhaps—causing awkwardness for anyone involved. Kiyama was no rapist. In his country, as he told me more than once, people adopted a more comfortable attitude than we did toward girls who sold their favors for the good of the clan. It was considered a noble thing to do, and no doubt Kiyama thought I would be delighted at the suggestion that I go to bed with him and thus join the heroines of the East. And it is only fair to say that I was *not* entirely distressed. Oh, there were good reasons for what I did, plenty of them. If I'd turned Kiyama down he would probably not have been very angry, but there wouldn't have been a job, I'd have had no special standing any more, and Ahmet might have come under the cloud with me. That at least is what I argued in my mind, but I knew, the whole time, that all these reasons were, none of them, the basic one. I wanted to be Kiyama's mistress because he was powerful. That was my nature: that is the way I was, and I suspected my mother had been the same. It explained what otherwise might have mystified me: why she changed sides so often in her war. She, too, was attracted by success.

When the time came to tell Ahmet I was going to take a job with Kiyama, I had done it in a way that saved him face. I'd said only that the lieutenant wanted me to be his private secretary. If Ahmet wanted to read more into the announcement, that was up to him, but he did not have to feel himself forced to interfere. And he had not interfered; he didn't even try. After all, what could he have done—rushed into Kiyama's house and made a scene? Of course not. Any action against Kiyama might have been disastrous, whereas as things were, life was going well for all of us. It was good most of all for Ahmet, because he made me work for him, in the most delicate, imperceptible way imaginable. Once in a while I was able to get him some bit of information he needed, as when he asked, "Has Kiyama said anything in your hearing about Hatta?" Hatta, one of the Nationalist leaders, was in a dangerous position because he worked for an undercover anti-Japanese organization. If Kiyama were to suspect this and mention it in a dispatch, Ahmet wanted to know immediately. But the only time the lieutenant had occasion to use Hatta's name the mention was harmless, and that is what I told Ahmet. Ahmet also coached me sometimes in suggesting ideas to Kiyama, but it was such ticklish work that I was afraid to do it very often. In crazy fashion, sometimes the game was played the other way round, and Kiyama began probing me for information as to Indonesians. It took considerable agility to turn aside these questions, and I learned to think quickly. I must never help Kiyama; I held on to that principle, if only that. Ahmet was my love. I was on his side. That at the same time I could be so resentful and bitter against him was a mystery I have never solved.

There were other advantages than espionage in my connection with Lieutenant Kiyama. I brought home reasonable sums of money, more than I would have earned in some other work, and that was good for the Dutoits. Also, when I went out with Kiyama I often met other women who belonged to officers, geishas and comfort girls and even lawful wives, who were now being allowed to come over and join their husbands. I told these females about Yvonne's shop, and a lot of them ultimately became customers of hers. She was rapidly becoming a power in the mercantile world of occupied Batavia; not that she wouldn't have made her way in any case, but my efforts helped a little. And for myself there were various good things; security, and pretty clothes, and the knowledge that I was important. It was a satisfaction to have power: I admit it.

I didn't dislike Kiyama. I admit that, too. I might even go further and say there were certain things I liked very much in him. There was his way with a woman, offhand but fervent at times, that struck a chord in me; it made up for his short-legged body and comically broken Dutch, though a woman doesn't like it when her lover is funny. Kiyama, in bed and out, was master of the situation. I liked his strength. But it wasn't always pleasant to be his mistress. He had no head for alcohol: two of the tiny cups used by Japanese for *sake*, their hot rice wine, sent him into tears, and he would behave like a baby, sentimentally begging for comfort and reassurance as if I had been his mother. I found this disgusting. I didn't want to be Kiyama's mother, but the helpless captive of his conquest. The only man who had a right to my protective love was Ahmet.

All in all, however, Kiyama wasn't bad. I had no serious reason to complain.

A car was still a rather unusual sight, and children stopped playing and stared as Kiyama's swept past. Our adult neighbors, too, watched my departure in such state, but there were no incidents like those at the beginning, when some of the more indignant among them shouted epithets at me. It was just past the evening prayer hour, when prewar Batavia had been almost quiet and certainly peaceful, but that was all changed now: the air was full of reverberations from a magnified, eloquent voice that was broadcast from a nearby radio tower. Once again, for the third time that day, Sukarno was orating to the people, by special order of the government. I did not have to listen: I knew what he was saying, because it was always the same. Help the war effort. Demolish imperialism and the exploitation of the underdog. Co-operate with the liberators. Bend every effort to win the war. We must use our muscles and purify our spirit and sacrifice ourselves, if necessary, to do this. Help the Japanese! I could never be quite immune to the singing magic of Sukarno's voice; I doubt if anyone could, but he was talking utter nonsense nevertheless. The word "co-operation" was particularly ironic, for the Indonesians were never given the option. They were forced to co-operate, all of them, though the most extreme cases were those wretched men who were rounded up by the thousand and sent away from home to work out their lives at hard labor—men who had done nothing wrong, whose bad luck it was to become mere statistics.

I didn't hold any resentment against Sukarno, though. Like that of the rest of us, his co-operation was extorted, not given freely. In Ahmet's opinion these political exhortations pleased the Japanese without hurting the cause, and one branch of the "Center of People's Power," the great amorphous organization Sukarno nominally headed, was actually working out well for the Nationalists: this was the Volunteer Army. Until now, Indonesians hadn't been taught how to fight, this being the last technique in the world that the Dutch wanted them to acquire. The Japanese, however, got to work on military teaching as soon as they could, organizing and training the youths themselves with the intention of using them in the war against the Allies. It suited the Volunteers to pretend that the Japanese cause was theirs, but among the men was a secret understanding that they would put their new skill to a very different use as soon as the time was ripe. In many ways our conquerors were surprisingly naïve.

"I'm glad you came early," the lieutenant greeted me. "I have heard within the last hour that I must entertain a brother officer who has been here from Hongkong on a tour of inspection. He arrived only a few days ago—a man named Captain Yoshio. Order a room for us at the Pearl."

"Yes, Lieutenant; for how many?"

He paused and thought. "He has no friend here," he said, meaning that the captain had no woman, "but that needn't matter. It's too late for invitations to other officers, so you'd better come along to fill the room."

I thanked him, though it was a matter of indifference to me whether or not I had dinner with them. Geisha evenings were boring to a non-Japanese who hadn't been brought up to feel their attraction, and were especially boring for women in any case. I knew, because Kiyama had told me, that in Japan well-brought-up females didn't attend geisha dinners, not because they are considered vulgar, because they aren't, but because geishas are trained to cater only to men. The whole idea of a party was to amuse men, make them feel important, and even a Japanese man doesn't feel as important when his wife is there as he does with other women. But in wartime things were different. Besides, I wasn't the lieutenant's wife. Judging from what he told me about her, we couldn't have been less alike.

At the beginning the evening promised to be much like many others I'd spent with Kiyama at that geisha house. The manageress met us at the door with two pretty waitresses, all three on their knees while they cooed greetings and compliments to the lieutenant, as if he'd been a god instead of a small man with short legs. We took off our shoes and pattered softly along, led by the women to the room we'd reserved, screened off from the rest of the place and furnished—or, rather, unfurnished—in the best Japanese style. A table with dwarf legs occupied the long middle, with tasseled cushions marking where we were to sit, little cups and chopsticks waiting on the table above each cushion. The captain had not yet arrived.

"He's made an appointment with someone," Kiyama said, after talking rapidly with the manageress in their own language.

"For dinner here?" I asked. It seemed rather cool of a stranger to do that, but he said:

"No, no, not dinner. This woman says the other man is coming in at nine o'clock. It is all right—some business he hasn't had time to finish, I suppose. He is going back in the morning."

The waitresses fluttered around, kneeling abruptly whenever we happened to look at them or they had to walk in front of us where we sat on our cushions. They brought in a record-player. They stared at me and whispered, giggling. Giggles are not rude in Japanese, but polite. In any case I didn't mind; I knew they still weren't used to the idea of women eating right at the table with men, as if they were human beings too, though the waitresses must have learned by this time that it was customary procedure among Europeans. Kiyama chatted with them and told them what he wanted in the way of entertainment; music, and dancing, and a girl good at conversation to keep his guest happy. This meant a girl good at riddles and jokes and repartee generally. Japanese are lucky, I reflected wryly, because they were trained to laugh all the time even when they weren't amused. A Japanese could get through a boring evening without pain, but my poor mouth got awfully tired of smiling. I reminded myself that there were hopeful aspects about this party nevertheless. Usually when we had a late evening such as this promised to be—"late" in Batavia meaning anything after ten o'clock—

Kiyama didn't choose to make love, but took me straight home from the restaurant. Probably the wine he drank at dinner would have died out before we left, so I didn't have to contemplate tears and all that. Instead, I'd get home like a good girl, and could go softly to bed, past Ahmet asleep on his mat, with no blot on my conscience and no defensive spite in my soul.

When Captain Yoshio arrived I was ready to greet him with warm gratitude, but I restrained myself, for that wasn't the way people behaved at Japanese restaurants. For quite a while, during which the lieutenant and the captain said polite things to each other and bowed and bowed, it was as if I wasn't there at all. Finally the lieutenant presented me, we sat down at the table on our cushions, and the waitresses poured the first cups of wine. We had music too—a geisha played on a lute, and another girl sang. After a while the food was brought in, and I felt relieved. The wine was hot, as it should be with Japanese food—I don't know why, but that's the custom—and it worked fast on both men, who were getting noisy. It's only fair to say that no one in the place thought any the less of them for that. Japanese when they drink really set out to get drunk; that's the object. They haven't got the European idea that alcohol is something to struggle against, something you dare to do its worst. A Dutchman swallows his liquor with defiance, as if he were undergoing a test to see which is the stronger, but a Japanese doesn't think strength has any part in the affair. He lets his wine take him where it likes. So I had no reason to feel embarrassed by the men when they sang and shouted and laughed like hyenas, but I was bored until the food they took made another change and quieted them down.

Now and then, of course, they talked of their work. Their speech was too fluent and fast for me to follow, and I soon stopped trying, but I gathered that the appointment the captain had made was indeed, as Kiyama had assumed, with a man working in his department.

"I want to get a picture of how the new organization is

going along," I heard him say, or thought I heard. Then they were off again, speculating on the sentiments of the people in this district and that. When they talked of sentiments they were referring to the attitude of the public toward themselves, the Japanese, since in their estimation nothing else about the Indonesian had any importance. Accustomed to this point of view, I felt no surprise, only more and more fatigue as the evening dragged on. We had finished our dinner: nothing remained on the table now but a teapot, and at this stage of the proceedings any ordinary party would have come to an end, but, as I knew, we had to wait for the captain's man. The manageress brought glasses and poured brandy for the gentlemen.

They drank, and a waitress filled the glasses again. Some of the geishas had come in to help make the time pass, and after another glass our two little gods became amorous. Geishas always protest that they are not prostitutes, and I am willing to believe anything they feel so strongly about, but many of them don't object to a bit of dalliance, or if they object they are so well-trained they don't show their feelings. The men dallied. Finally Yoshio slid down on the floor because he found it easier to lie flat than to sit up, and put his head on the lap of one of the girls, while Kiyama, roaring at some joke he himself had just made, pulled me over to him. I was compliant, of course: I never struggled against this sort of thing. Public orgies aren't what I really care for, but I never argued with Kiyama. Resignedly I lay back against his arm, marking time until I could get away, and then came the interruption I'd been hoping for—the manageress, announcing with superb aplomb, as a woman who had seen everything before and could not be less interested, that Captain Yoshio's friend had arrived. She moved back, giving way to the friend walking in, and I had a shock. He was an Indonesian I knew. With him was Ahmet.

For a second Ahmet didn't see me, or, rather, he didn't take in the fact that it was me sprawling there at his feet with Lieutenant Kiyama's arm around me. Then as I shoved myself free and sat up, he really looked. A terrifying flame leaped into his eyes. Fascinated, I stared at the veins that stood out on his forehead. I was so frightened that I stopped breathing and waited for something—a crashing blow, an earthquake, I didn't know what—that would bring life to an end. Then the other Indonesian, very quickly, said something into Ahmet's ear and my lover recollected where he was, and with what other people beside me. His eyelids dropped over his eyes and his face turned stony. He did not move. It all happened in less time than it takes to say. I was trembling, but it was over, and the world still revolved.

Now that duty called them, the two Japanese collected themselves with commendable speed. Kiyama sat up straight, and Yoshio, as his girl had scuttled out of the room like a sand crab, did the same. Kiyama actually recognized Ahmet and greeted him genially, and asked both Indonesians to sit down and have a drink. They politely refused the drink. Conversation followed along the lines the captain had indicated, a discussion of the People's Loyalty Organization. It had only lately been created, and I was aware that Kiyama had great expectations of it. The plan was to sweep away all the earlier organizations that had been founded with the same ends in view and replace them with this. Under Japanese direction, Indonesians already trained in their kind of political work, eager young men like Ahmet, were going to set up centers in every community in the land, cities and kampongs and all. The scheme had a wide scope, but was no better than all the earlier ones because of its shaky foundation. It was no use preaching to committed Nationalists that their Japanese masters were better and kinder than the European tyrants they had supplanted. That the Japanese people came from the East instead of the West could not change the fundamental objection: the Indonesians wanted no master at all. At least one Indonesian at that moment was ready to blow up the entire Japanese nation. From the temporary haven of Kiyama's shadow, I watched Ahmet with slowly ebbing apprehension. Every minute gained, I felt, was something to be thankful for. Anger, like drunkenness, doesn't stay at its high point.

The talk went on and on. Yoshio was covering up for his loss of dignity at the beginning by taking a strong line and scolding the Indonesians, for faulty organizing and general slackness. It meant very little and his hearers knew it; this sort of pep talk was commonplace. Still, they had to wait submissively for the peroration. At last it came:

"I am not at all satisfied with what I have seen," declared the captain. "Things are being badly neglected in this area, and I intend to say as much in my preliminary report. That is all, gentlemen. You may go."

Not long afterwards our party too left the restaurant. Wrapped as I was in my own troubles, I hadn't noticed that the captain's criticism had been a slap in the face for my employer as well as the Indonesians, but Kiyama didn't leave me in ignorance very long. As soon as he had seen his guest into the government car and bowed it away, he began railing. All the way back he kept it up:

"What does he expect of us here, considering the stingy attitude they hold towards us in Tokyo? We're the poor relations of the whole department. It's all very well for Yoshio to talk, with his fine soft job in Hongkong. When a man like that wants something he's only got to ask. It's different in this damned backwater."

"I'm sure you do your work better than anyone else in Japan," I said soothingly.

He paid no attention to what I said, nor indeed to anything that had to do with me. Brooding over his wrongs had driven out every vestige of amorous appetite, and I realized from the direction the car pointed that he was going to leave me at the Dutoits' house. At this I nearly lost my nerve; I nearly begged him, for the first time since our relations had begun, to take me home with him, but I didn't dare. Instead, I might creep into Yvonne's room, I realized, and take shelter with her, but somehow I couldn't bring myself to do that. Pride held me back. I couldn't call on an outsider for help in such an affair; the thought of it was repulsive. Behave like those frowzy hags in Holland at the water front, shrieking for help from the neighbors on Saturday night when their husbands beat them up? I'd die first . . . And the thought crossed my mind as I walked softly up the path to the house that I *might* very well die, at any minute. It did not take much exaggeration to believe it; I wondered if it might be by strangulation or the knife. Somewhere in my jumbled notions was a shameful sort of anticipation of violence. I make no excuse for it. I can't. No doubt it owed itself to that same part of my character that made me admire Kiyama for being one of the conquerors of Asia.

Indoors as well as out in the garden everything was still. The last echo of the lieutenant's engine died away. On the veranda I listened with painful intentness for some sign of life, but there was none. I couldn't even hear Mr. Dutoit snoring. The light over my door was still burning, and after a short hesitation I approached until I could see that there was no other lamp still turned on inside, not even the little one by my bed that the servant usually left lit. Only the tiny red glow of the mosquito coil glared like a small animal from the floor; otherwise the room was a cube filled with pure black emptiness. Where then was Ahmet?

He had left me alone before, after other quarrels. He must have stayed away, I thought, rather than risk murdering me, or perhaps it was even simpler; it might be that I'd become loathsome and he had gone away for good. He might have left the city altogether. I could understand that, but my heart sagged in my breast. It was no use standing at the door thinking up worse and worse happenings, and I stirred at last, and crept like a whipped dog to the bed. In the dark I put off my clothes and lay down, miserable and wide awake.

It was now so silent that I could hear what I had missed before, the sound of a second living thing breathing. I sat up and snapped on the light, and there was Ahmet lying on his floor mat, as he lay every night. It was Ahmet after all, and Ahmet sleeping. How could he sleep tonight? I turned off the lamp and settled back, trying to understand. I thought I could see what had happened: however violent he had been when he got home, in the waiting bedroom he had time to think. Laboriously, doggedly, he had built himself a tower to hide in. Brick by brick he put it up, reminding himself of how and why it came about, that sight of me in Kiyama's arms. He had been aware of it all the time—another brick—but had ignored the knowledge—one more brick. He had even found the situation useful. He was more to blame than I. He must put away his personal grief because that was a violation of justice. Finally, when the tower was finished, the tired Ahmet had fallen asleep.

Without a doubt something very like that had gone on in our room. The struggle was over, and I knew we would never speak of it now. I was safe, or at least as safe as I had been that morning, but the realization brought no comfort, and for a long time I cried quietly, until I too fell asleep.

CHAPTER TEN

―――――

"Is it bad?" I asked in properly muted tones.

Kiyama said, "Of course it's bad, you fool. I've been ordered to return to Tokyo, can't you understand?" He struck the telegram in his hand sharply and talked in loud, staccato tones as he walked up and down. "To make a full report of my activities here since I arrived. It's evident they suspect me of serious misdemeanors, and I know what's at the bottom of it—that fox Yoshio: it is his work. Remember how he sniffed around? He's had it in for me ever since. He was determined to ruin me."

The bedroom was furnished according to Kiyama's ideas of European *décor*, all chromium plating and colors that clashed. I had grown used to its ugliness, and didn't see it now. I sat up in bed, arms around bare knees, waiting dutifully for my host to tell me it was time to go home. The dutiful act wasn't difficult to sustain now, for it looked as if I need not play it much longer, but I was a bit nervous for other reasons. If Kiyama was in trouble with his superiors, might I too be embroiled? Little weights I'd had on my conscience—unimportant betrayals of office affairs to Ahmet, occasional suppressions in reports—suddenly became heavy.

"That upstart!" Kiyama kicked a small table out of the way. "I should have got in ahead of him with talebearing."

I said, "Are you sure it's Yoshio? His visit was a long time ago. Mightn't it be some other thing we haven't had complaints on, that's happened since then?"

"I tell you, I know it was Yoshio who's done this to me. He doesn't like me. He never did. These things always take a long time." The words gave me a frightening insight of all the cold plotting, tangled intrigues, struggles for bits of power that made up life in the secret police. "Besides, remember that I know what goes on at that head office," he added, shaking his finger at me. "I know who are my friends and who my enemies."

So it really was Kiyama, not me. I sat back, relaxed, while he continued to pace and mutter. Finally, in private gratitude, I made another attempt to soothe him: "This isn't necessarily the end of everything; all they said in the telegram is that you're to go home and make a report. If you really haven't committed any crimes—which we both know you haven't—it might all pass off without a lot of trouble. Otherwise they'd have arrested you, not sent for you."

This had the desired effect: he admitted there was something in what I said. Nevertheless, he said, it was disturbing that he had been recalled. At best he would be transferred to another post, and he'd been contented in Batavia. I listened to all this and made the appropriate noises. I owed it to Kiyama to be sympathetic, but my silent thoughts were busy with my own possible future. What was going to happen to me? It now seemed that I'd made a grave mistake when I joined him as a mistress as well as a secretary. I thought with fleeting wistfulness of the rest of my class at the Japanese school, now safely embarked, probably, on jobs that had appeared at that time to be less rewarding. Oh well, it was good while it lasted, and I hadn't really had much choice. No doubt Yvonne would be glad of an extra helper in her expanding business, though it would be a comedown: I'd enjoyed my special position in the family. It was nice to think, however, that my relations with Ahmet were bound to improve with Kiyama out of the way. . . . Speculations darted through my head like scared fish, but I sat quietly and kept my eyes on Kiyama.

"But you *will* be all right?" I asked during a pause. "You're really not in danger?"

He had talked himself into better humor. "No, it's not so bad. I'll be reprimanded for some error I haven't been guilty of. They won't be able to find any cheating in my record, and that's bound to count. But it will take a long time to work back to a post as good as this. That cursed Yoshio—if I ever get a chance at him!" He broke off to think broodingly of revenge.

"What sort of position do you think they'll give you now?"

"Why ask such foolish questions? If I knew exactly what's going on in their heads, I wouldn't be upset. But Yoshio's not the only one who can play at games, especially if I'm there on the spot. . . . You're worrying about yourself, I suppose?" he said, his voice changing sharply. Kiyama was never a fool.

"Of course I'm worried. But I know better than to bother you with my affairs, especially now when you're powerless to do anything for—"

I had used the right line, because he grabbed it. "Powerless? Who said so? No, no, I still have plenty of influence in certain quarters, as Yoshio will find out. You needn't worry, little girl. The navy people here will do whatever I tell them, and we'll get you a good place there to tide you over. It won't be a bad thing for them. I can honestly say you're a good worker—a good girl."

This was welcome news, but because I felt I owed it to the lieutenant to show grief, I wiped my eyes. Gratified, he said:

"I believe you're really sorry to see me go. Fond of me, are you?" Yes, I said, I was fond of him. He went on, "But what are we to do? Yet—it's beautiful, in times like this, that you can feel kindly toward a former enemy. It's noble . . . Julie, would you like to come to Japan? I could arrange it."

I didn't want to go to Japan. Though I no longer kept it as a living hope, I was convinced in an impersonal way that the lieutenant's island would some day get a trouncing.

"Many, many thanks, but I couldn't. Think of your wife's reaction. I couldn't do that to her."

"My wife? But—Well, I see how it is. A foreign-born woman has a different philosophy; one knows about that. Never mind. For a European it *would* be awkward at this moment." And so it ended, with both of us promising to meet again some day when the vision of Pan-Asia became fact and the world was at peace.

I worked for several weeks with the Navy, but I didn't like it. Every day I sank deeper in a mass of unfiled papers. Many of them were written in Japanese, and defied every attempt to classify them according to my Western system. I should never have been given the job, I thought despairingly. I wasn't sure if I was permitted to resign, but I intended soon to try, and was feeling very sorry for myself when a summons arrived and gave me fresh hope. I was ordered to present myself at Kiyama's house—the Dekker house—for an interview with Kiyama's successor, another lieutenant, named Shiga.

He was a man I don't remember particularly, for he had no noteworthy features. I waited, standing, while he read some flimsy paper and then read it again, softly whistling the latest geisha tune. Then he said, looking up:

"There you are. I see by this report that you have done a little confidential work for our department, not long ago. I understand you are not really needed over at the naval offices and I should like you to do a bit more along the same lines. The duty will take you to Hongkong: here are your orders."

"That was the way he put it," I told Ahmet that night. Even more than Kiyama's departure, the emergency had served to put us on good terms again. It was no time for grudges, and we lay together and whispered like the lovers we were. "He said 'orders,' and I didn't like the sound of it. Kiyama had his faults, but he would have given me a chance to turn down an assignment I didn't want."

"You don't like it, then," said Ahmet, brushing aside the mention of Kiyama.

"No, of course I don't. For one thing, it will take me away from you, and also it's so nasty, watching and prying into the affairs of somebody I'll be working for. I'll be a common spy." The words reminded me of something important, but there was no time to investigate the thought.

"When does he want you to go?" Ahmet's voice trembled slightly.

"Within a week—whenever they've got a place in some plane going to Hongkong. I probably won't know until the last few hours. You know how they do these things." We lay silent, staring up into the dark. "He said this Saito, the man I'll be working for, is suspected of handing over secrets to local characters—Chinese. Then, presumably, the Chinese slip word to the Allies in Chungking. I'm to get evidence."

"No!" said Ahmet suddenly. "You can't do that. We'll fix something up. You could run away. Yes, that's the way we can do it; you could go and hide out in my village."

"It wouldn't work, and you know it. Just think a minute. I've been over all that myself—they'd be at this house within an hour, questioning everybody. They'd beat up the servant and probably the Dutoits as well, and certainly they'd get at you. It's no good."

Ahmet went on arguing, but he knew I was right. We couldn't take that risk with the Dutoits' safety, let alone with that of his friends, and at last he admitted it. I said:

"It won't be forever. Shiga said it isn't a permanent transfer; as soon as I get enough on this naval officer in Hongkong, the *kempeitai* there will take over, and then, you see, I'll be shipped back."

"And they'll simply give you another assignment just as bad," said Ahmet angrily. "I see there's nothing to be done, but . . . All this is happening to you and I can't do anything to stop it. I'm a prisoner, that's the worst of all. If I could stir up a rebellion, if it would save you—but I can't, and it wouldn't. I'm no good to you. I meant to take such care of you, and now look. It gets worse and worse."

I thought I had never been so happy. A little frozen lump in my breast was melting away after many months of burdening me. I took Ahmet's head in my arms; I rocked him like a baby, and talked of the future when everything would be all right.

"It can't be helped. My poor little boy, it can't be helped. Just wait," I said, again and again.

"If you told the truth, you'd admit that you're excited by the change," said Yvonne. She sat on her heels on my bed while I packed a bag. I said absently:

"Does it show so much?" and held a dress up against myself, looking in the mirror. "No, I won't take this one; it's shabby."

"Does it show? You're walking around with visible wings on your feet, and if Ahmet hadn't been there this morning I would have told you not to rise into the air until you're on the plane."

"Well, I can't help it, can I? I shouldn't feel any pleasure, I suppose, but I've always yearned to see Hongkong. And we've had such a dull time lately."

Yvonne laughed. "Don't mind me. I don't blame you, I'm only so envious I could scratch your eyes out. Think of me when you're having a wonderful time up there, drinking champagne and dancing all night. Spare a thought for poor, faithful Yvonne, going through her dreary routine day after day—"

"—arm in arm with Ito," I finished. Yvonne made a face.

"One of these days I'll have to kick Ito out. He gets on my nerves. Let's see if I've got things straight." She studied the list I had written for her, of my prison-camp commitments: she had promised to take care of them while I was away. "I notice you send more sweet things to Phil than Agatha; is that all right?"

"I hope so. I go by rumor mostly, and the notes Phil's

managed to slip out. The shortages aren't all the same in the different camps: he wants sugar and sugar and sugar, but for Agatha I haven't anything to go on except that I know they always need meat, butter, or oil, things like that. And Marge has got that baby now. I don't know . . . It's decent of you to bother, because I know what a hard job it is, even with the bicycle. Look, I'm putting this note on the table. It's for Phil, if the guard ever comes again—I never know from one time to another if I'll see him again. There's nothing special in it, you can read it if you want; I just tell him I'm going away for a while, to keep him from worrying when I don't turn up. I can't communicate with Agatha at all. Let her worry—but I don't think she will. Half the time she doesn't turn out to look at us when we go past on parcel day."

"Why bother to send her stuff, then?"

"Oh, I couldn't cut off her parcels. They need that food. Whatever's the trouble, we can straighten it out some day."

"Some day, some day," said Yvonne impatiently, and an unfamiliar look of defeat shadowed her jolly face for a moment. "We might be better off if we stopped hoping for that," she said.

In the middle of all the turmoil, months after I'd got out of the habit of thinking about my mother, the idea of her inevitably came back. I was a long time picking up the strings: it wasn't until I went to bed one night, almost sure I would be called for the plane the next day, that I remembered her. But of course, I said to myself: this is nothing new. My mother had gone through the whole business, no doubt, many times. She too must have felt misgivings, even revulsion, when she was given a mission of the sort I now held. The reflection held a little comfort.

Bowling along Queen's Road in a ricksha, huddled in a coat I had just bought at great cost, I shivered. If this was Hongkong's famous balmy weather—and it seemed to be: nobody else looked cold—I thought it much overrated. We were having one of the fogs they were so complacent about, and there seemed no getting away from it indoors either. The Li family, in whose house I had lodgings, kept little lamps burning in all their closets so that fungus wouldn't form on their shoes and leather cases, but even so I regretted having had to leave my room with its heater, where I could at least draw curtains against the wet, gray out-of-doors. As the ricksha coolie ran, I passed through layer after layer of cold mist that seemed banded in density. My complaints, however, drew no sympathy from Mr. Yamashita, the little man in civilian clothes who had taken care of me at the airport and since.

"Hongkong is never cold. I don't believe you can be a Hollander or you wouldn't say that," he said. He had once lived abroad, he told me, in Europe and America as well; he loved to talk reminiscently about those days. "In the Netherlands you really get winter weather," he said approvingly, "not like this little chill in the subtropics. Ice on the canals as far as a man can see. You've been spoiled, Miss de Jong. How long did you say you've been living in Java? Your blood's gone thin, that's the trouble; it always happens to you people. My place in Hokkaido would be too much for you. You'll see, when you've settled in, that we have a wonderful city here for climate. The forces send their wounded convalescents here as a reward. Why, it's paradise."

What Yamashita didn't realize, and what I certainly didn't mean to tell him, was that his precious people had spoiled paradise from the minute they moved in on it. I was bitterly disappointed in the island. Of course I'd been foolish to expect it to live up to the glowing stories one heard before the war. Hongkong was bound to show the inevitable scars of liberation, and one occupied city was sure to be much like another. I'd fallen into the trap of wartime isolation, believing that my little community was uniquely plagued, and that everywhere else was as it had always been. I'd expected the restaurants and shops and flower stalls of Hongkong to be there still, as they were before, when the British reigned. I hadn't been the only fool, though: Yvonne was the same. I told myself that even if I found it possible to write to her, I mustn't say anything about my disillusionment. I must not describe the spirit that hung over Hongkong just as it did Batavia, of makeshift and sullen caution. I wouldn't tell her that the glowering sentries of Batavia had brothers here; that many Hongkong shops, too, were boarded up, presumably forever, as they'd been the same since the occupation started, and that this city too had a miserable stink of shortages. The only safe description I could give was to say that the streets, unlike those of our own, went up and down instead of being level, and that Chinese didn't resemble Indonesians very much—but then Yvonne already knew that. To speak admiringly of Hongkong's mountains would be to ask for trouble. The authorities had removed all scenic picture postcards from the market.

Huddled in my mood as well as in the new coat, I felt no urge to look at the people in the streets, though there were many of these: evidently the population of Hongkong felt compelled to spend much of their day shuffling along out-of-doors. I was still sulking when a miracle took place and the sun came out. For a long time it had been boring and burning its way through the fog blanket: now, like a sudden spear thrust, it came through the mist, the gray curtains rolled back, and the world opened. The change was startling, as all that was drab turned to gold. For the first time bushes and trees became brightly green. Even the stonework walls glowed, and people who had looked like tied-up bundles became beautiful. Below us, at the end of the steep street, the harbor water that shifted and rippled was no longer of a sullen gun-metal color, but became green-blue, with crisp white crests on the waves. I sat up straight, drawing a deep breath, and as the chill tints receded I felt warmth spreading through my body. So this was Hongkong! I must have smiled, for two or three people, looking in my direction as we passed, beamed at me.

Stopping and starting with the other traffic, my coolie padded on. To our right, the mountainside now sloped upward more gently. Even so, the footpaths leading up had still to be graduated with flights of stone steps. We were past the ravine above which a funicular tram ground its way to the Peak: looking back, I followed its flight with my eyes until it topped a curve that hid the rest of the course. I'd made the journey myself the preceding day with Yamashita, though the weather hadn't been propitious and the expedition seemed pointless once we'd arrived. Fog shrouded the famous view, and we saw nobody but a lot of guards, nearly all of whom demanded a look at our passes.

"It used to be a very special district, the residence of the British aristocracy. There are beautiful houses," said Yamashita as if in apology for having brought me.

"Let's walk around a little and look at some of them, then," I said, but he'd explained that this was impossible in wartime: for tactical reasons, only a few officials lived on the Peak, and the public wasn't encouraged to come. Wind swirled around our lookout point, the guards kept staring, and I was glad to take the next car down. Certainly it was better here, I reflected, on the lower levels. The coolie was bringing me nearer and nearer to the sea: now he drew up and halted at the curb, near a heavily guarded open gate— the entrance to the dockyard where I was to work. With a tingle of excitement I dismounted and walked in, flourishing the pass Yamashita had given me.

It wasn't a bit like my introduction to a job in Batavia when I had an interview with Kiyama. Here everything was bigger, less personal. A Japanese office manager glanced at my credentials, and if he was curious as to why I should have been sent all the way from Java he didn't show his feelings. He only looked me up on a list, grunted, and led me to a semidetached alcove off the main room where at least a dozen other people sat at desks: I was to be alone here, he said, with a little privacy. For a while I sat there looking out at the big room, feeling self-conscious but summing up the surroundings nevertheless. My coworkers were a mixture; men and women, Chinese or Japanese. The Japanese girls wore Western dress, and looked, as Japanese women always did in my hostile opinion, thick-waisted and stubby in it with their short bowlegs. In a little time, however, I got used to their appearance and even admitted to myself that they could be charming. I was beginning to yawn when the manager brought me a stack of letters written in Dutch, and directed me to summarize them in English. I was disappointed; it seemed an anticlimax, since my true object was Captain Saito and he was nowhere to be seen. I could hardly ask the manager where he was without betraying too much interest. Later I found out from the other girls that the captain was in Canton and would be away for several days.

Obviously it was going to be just as difficult as I'd prophesied to Yamashita. I intended to repeat my complaints that evening when he came by for a report, in the house where he'd arranged for me to live. It was a luxurious house, since my host Mr. Li was a rich man who owned one of Hongkong's biggest department stores. Before the war he and his rather haughty wife wouldn't have dreamed of taking in a lodger, but he found it wise to come to terms with the new masters of the colony and willingly did anything Yamashita suggested. As he would have said, Why not? Like Mr. Djung, Mr. Li was philosophical on these matters, ready to accept facts without worrying about principle. It was only natural, however, that Mrs. Li should have been standoffish with me. She had every reason for resentment, especially as she had leaped to the conclusion that I was Yamashita's ladylove. The past few days, fortunately, had disabused her of this notion—my mentor and I were obviously not on loverly terms—and the air cleared remarkably. Like her husband she could understand a woman's collaboration out of prudence, as long as her heart wasn't in it. That evening when Yamashita called, Mrs. Li actually smiled at me before she left us alone.

"How did it go?" Yamashita asked, his clever little face eager with craft and pleasure. He loved his job. I said:

"It didn't go at all, and I can't see any future in it. That great barn of an office—how can I sniff around it? In Batavia everything was cozier."

"Jakarta, you mean," he said. It was a mechanical correction that all the Japanese made when necessary, ever since the Dutch name of Batavia had been replaced, as a courtesy to Indonesian Nationalists, by the ancient name of a fishing village that once stood on the same site by the sea. I found it hard to remember the change, especially as other places were always undergoing the same transformation.

"Jakarta then," I said impatiently. "Mr. Yamashita, I don't believe I'll even be introduced to this man Saito, let alone get to know what he's up to. Just what is he suspected of? It might help if I knew."

Yamashita said severely, "You are not here to ask questions, but to carry out orders. You want to know too much."

"Rubbish. This isn't a guessing game," I retorted. I wasn't afraid of the little man, and he realized that this time, at least, I was within my rights.

"Oh well," he said. "I suppose it would save time. . . . This officer's sympathies are suspect. The impression he makes on our people is of being far too fond of the Chinese. We want to know how far this fondness takes him."

"It's a strange situation."

"Not so strange as you think. There is something about these Chinese: they get under your skin. You have to keep an eye on yourself, I can tell you, if you stay too long in China. That's why the authorities recommend replacements so often among officials posted to these cities. With Saito it's not so easy as all that: he's got a mixed background. He was born in Manchuria, I believe; at least he spent his childhood there. He speaks Mandarin fluently and has a lot of Chinese friends. In peacetime we didn't mind. Even during the war, at the beginning of the Incident, Saito was considered valuable for the cause because of his language facility and his understanding of the natives, but now times have changed and we think his pro-Chinese sentiments are taking him too far. In at least one case where he had to adjudicate between Japanese and Chinese civilians, he awarded judgment to the Chinese!" He paused, to give me a chance to express scorn and horror. I compromised with a solemn shake of the head. "One thing leads to another," Yamashita continued. "We have caught wind of leakages of information, and these might well prove traceable to Saito's department. In fact, we *must* trace them there, and that's why we need you."

"But how can I possibly—"

"That is your problem, but I don't think it's as hopeless as you believe. One can't expect results after one short day on the spot," said Yamashita.

So I marked time and did my summaries as patiently as I could, and a few days later was rewarded with my first look at Captain Saito when he came into the office and paused on the way to his private room to chat with the manager. Without my knowledge I couldn't have guessed that this man could possibly be disloyal to his country. He was a perfect example of a naval officer, Japanese style—not as rigid as the military but equally correct in demeanor. He was slight and soft-spoken, and seemed unassuming. The heavy black eyebrows might have given his face an alarming appearance, but didn't. He looked scholarly and serene.

"Why, he's nice," I thought in surprise.

I put him out of mind in order to concentrate on a feminine problem: clothes. I'd speedily found that my Javanese outfit was not suitable for Hongkong. The clinging sarong was an annoyance when I climbed up and down the city stairways: I understood now why Japanese women hurried to change into Western clothes once they'd tried to manage with kimonos. But for myself it was different. A return to European dress would make me uncomfortably conspicuous. At home, I asked Mrs. Li for advice, and she said promptly:

"Chinese dress, of course. Mr. Li's clerk can bring out some cloth tonight and our tailor will make it up for you. You'll look nice, I promise."

So it was done, and there I was in a second change of style. Mrs. Li had been right about it. Going to work every morning in my straight blue linen gown, I sank out of sight in an ocean of office girls. It was a pity Ming couldn't see me, I thought; she would have been so amused.

Translating, I often had to call for help from my Japanese colleagues; soon we were all on friendly terms. I ate my lunch with the other girls and listened to their chatter, hoping to hear something helpful about Saito, but all I learned was that they liked him. I had given up hope of ever getting further when one day he came out of his office and asked the manager, in audible tones, why that Indonesian woman had never turned up.

"I need help with this," he said, indicating a paper. "It's all in Dutch, and I've waited and waited for that woman. What's happened to her, anyway?"

In the general buzz of mirth, I hurried over to be presented. He took it cheerfully, demanding why I was in disguise. "A man can't be expected to understand these mysteries," he said. "Well, come in, Miss de Jong, and solve these problems."

It turned out that the captain had a large file of correspondence dealing with Indonesian affairs, and I had the run of it. Much of the material was confidential, but it didn't occur to Saito that I shouldn't see it—in any case that is what I was there for, to make it comprehensible to him. I found my studies fascinating for a private reason: one letter after another indirectly proved that certain rumors current in the Lis' circles were founded on fact: the Japanese Navy had indeed suffered heavy losses in the Pacific, pounded by American forces. As the story unfolded I found it hard to hide my joy, but I did. Even when I was at home with the Lis I was careful. Mr. Li tried to pump me, but I was careful.

"What's the truth about the Coral Sea story?" he demanded. I counterdemanded:

"What's the Coral Sea?"

"Come now, Miss de Jong, you know as well as I do. There was a big battle there last week, and a large part of the Navy was sunk. You're bound to have heard about it, working at the dockyard."

"I wouldn't be working there very long if I talked," I said, and Mrs. Li unexpectedly came to my rescue at this point:

"Julie's quite right. You're not to worry her."

But Mr. Li and I exchanged glances, and he smiled in a satisfied manner.

It was through the Lis that I encountered Captain Saito socially. They took me with them to dine with their friends at a restaurant. It was a grand party in honor of Japanese with whom the rich Chinese were careful to be friendly: among these was Captain Saito, escorting a good-looking Chinese girl named Yi. He recognized me of course, and bowed and talked a little, but soon we separated to take our places at different tables. My neighbor was a Chinese, a friend of the Lis whom I knew, and I asked him who the girl Yi was. He shrugged.

"Before the war no one had ever seen her," he said, "but she seems pleasant enough. Some of the types these people take up with aren't really presentable, but this girl is well-spoken. She comes from the north—Tientsin. Of course Saito knows that part of the country well."

During the tea-drinking that always ends a Chinese party, I worked my way over to the group surrounding Saito. He was chattering away in Mandarin, and he must have been amusing, for the hearers laughed repeatedly. After a particularly merry burst I asked the woman next to me what he was saying.

"Oh, he's very funny," she said, beaming. "So naughty! He's making jokes about the war, about Japanese propaganda. Not many Japanese would make fun of that. He's such a nice man!"

I should have reported this incident to Yamashita, but I didn't.

Later, I discovered more about Saito from another Chinese, Moy. He gave me the answer to a question that had long been puzzling me; why the *kempeitai*, with all their other duties, should be so down on this one particular man who did not seem especially important. Mr. Moy, a member of Li's group, was a great gossip; one of those people who always know everybody in town.

"Saito?" he repeated after I'd asked. "He's got a dangerous enemy, that's the trouble. Everybody who was here at the beginning of the occupation knows the scandal, but you're a stranger and of course you wouldn't have heard. In those days a lot of the Japanese behaved in a very highhanded way. One of the worst was a military officer named Nuri. If you haven't met Nuri you are lucky. As soon as he got here he started grabbing everything in sight—best house, biggest businesses, girls, everything. At the time, Saito was in charge of civilian affairs, and he blocked some of Nuri's turnovers, and they had a big fight about it. You know the Army and the Navy don't get along together at the best of times, and this was quite a struggle. Saito won his point, but Nuri was determined to get even, and they say he's still working at it. The chief of the *kempeitai* is a good friend of his, so things don't look too healthy for Saito."

"What a lot you know, Mr. Moy!" I exclaimed. It was not out of premeditated flattery: I was really impressed. Moy flushed and laughed.

"Not at all, my dear young lady. Naturally we unfortunate residents keep our eyes open, especially in times like these. We're ground between the millstones and so we learn to watch the great folk. Don't we?" He grinned at me.

The more I found out about Saito, the more futile my presence in Hongkong appeared. If he was innocent of treason, as he seemed to be, it was sheer waste of time for me to go through the motions, day after day, of working at his office. All this elaborate planning to catch out a man whose only crimes were honesty and indiscretion . . . I wanted to return to Java, where I belonged. I wanted to tell Ahmet what I'd found out about the war. I argued with Yamashita:

"Saito isn't betraying secrets, I'd stake my life on it. Surely you can see that it isn't necessarily due to treason when military secrets leak out. You can't expect to keep a place like this isolated—Hongkong's really just part of the mainland, with people slipping in and out every night. Everybody guesses things, everybody chatters. These Chinese are born spies: why blame poor Saito? Besides, he's a *nice* man."

Yamashita was irritated, and said so. "You women can never keep your eye on the important point. Remember, your sentiments haven't anything to do with the case. Your mission is to find out the truth."

"But I've done that: I've found out the truth. Saito isn't a traitor. He simply gets on well with the Chinese."

"Such as Yi? Or didn't you know he had a Chinese girl friend?" The little man's sly smile irritated me. I replied crossly:

"Of course I know about Yi. I've met her. Are you trying to say there's something sinister in Saito's having a Chinese housekeeper? Why, you've got one yourself."

He glared. "You keep your eyes on your own affairs, young lady, and forget about mine. I warn you, I don't like your attitude."

I might have been more worried by Yamashita if I hadn't known what I did about what was happening at the front, and hadn't been reassured as to its truth by my employer. It was all strange, but one of the strangest things about my stay in Hongkong was that I felt free to discuss such matters with Saito. If I'd been questioned by my employers I'd have sworn in all sincerity that Saito was thoroughly patriotic. To tell the truth, he was no paragon of wisdom. For one thing, I thought him astonishingly naïve about Japan's ambitions. He really did believe the propaganda his government put out concerning Japan's high endeavors to bring freedom and happiness to all Asia. Whenever he talked in this vein I found it prudent to remain silent, but sometimes I tried in a gingerly way to question some of the details in the grand scheme. It was hard for me, a resident of one of the liberated Asian countries, to swallow the whole story: I felt compelled to show him a bit of the other side of the picture. Once I said:

"Yes, but you know, I saw the way your people behaved when they first moved into Java, and it wasn't a sight calculated to prove that the Japanese meant well. Do you yourself think that's a good way to liberate oppressed colonials?"

He brushed it aside. "I make no excuse for the fact that soldiers behave like soldiers. These are comparatively small affairs when you compare them to the grand design, and I am sure the Chinese here, for example, do appreciate the good we have accomplished. Remember, the West was exploiting them cruelly. Western nations tore the land apart and turned a great nation into colonies for themselves. It was our duty as brother Asiatics to liberate them. It has been a dream of my own ever since I was a child in Manchukuo; even then I longed to do my part to abolish these great injustices. Your lovely country of Java was another victim. Can't you see the beauty of the plan?"

He would never admit that Japan's domination was simply more of the same. We were living in an interregnum, he argued. It would all turn out for the best; I would see. . . . Sometimes we had these talks at his house, with Yi hovering over us, pouring tea. She used to listen to him with wide eyes and an absolutely expressionless face. I wondered once or twice what she really thought of it, but then I concluded that she wasn't thinking at all. She was probably musing on the current price of black-market rice.

Yamashita had gone into the sulks. I saw little of him and didn't miss his company. My uneasiness grew, however, as I thought of what might happen in the near future. Surely the war was drawing to a close, and I couldn't imagine what might happen in occupied territories such as this one when the end finally came. I had a vague picture in my mind of vast, marching lines, Allied soldiers sweeping in triumph through the streets much as the Japanese had marched in their "victory parade" through Batavia. But what was to happen before that?

I got a sort of answer soon after I asked myself the question. One morning I was at the dockyard, sitting at my own desk, when I heard the sound of planes. There was nothing novel in the sound itself, since Japanese aircraft were always buzzing about over the bay, but that morning there seemed more noise than usual, and then all of a sudden there was none at all. It was as if they had all flown straight up and away, out of earshot. At the same time, our office manager showed signs of agitation. He ran from window to window, scanning the sky, until he was interrupted by a telephone call. As he hung up the receiver he barked out commands to us all: we were to take shelter, he said, in the lower regions of the building. Following a routine we had often practiced, we picked up the more important papers we happened to possess and marched in orderly file to the basement. We were all there but Captain Saito: Saito was not in the office that day.

This was my first air raid, and I would probably have panicked if it hadn't been for the calm behavior of my companions. They'd had much more experience of war than I, and showed little agitation. In fact nothing much happened, at least in our district. We heard, without seeing, the swooping arrival of the Americans: we heard but didn't see the smoke of a few "crumps," and then a signal was given from the hooters and we went upstairs again. No harm had been done to us, but our superior officers were in a grim mood, and there was much hurried consultation in the higher echelons. Later we got reports of damage on installations, and some deaths. It all made me more thoughtful than ever.

"Captain Saito," I said the next day, "if the war should happen to swing against your nation for a bit, what would happen to the timetable? That is, wouldn't things be prolonged beyond the date the government figured on?"

His bright eyes regarded me for a moment of silence before he said without expression, "They'd be bound to be prolonged, I should think. But nobody is surprised by setbacks. They occur."

I tried again a week later, when we'd had another air raid that was more disastrous than the first. The news was worse, and the captain looked drawn and tired. I actually felt apologetic, but my future was at stake: I couldn't afford the softer sentiments.

"Another silly question," I said apologetically. "I was talking to Mr. Yamashita—I don't believe you know him—and he said that the Japanese could carry on for another ten years if necessary. If this is true—"

"That's nonsense," said Captain Saito, as if the words were jerked out of him. "We couldn't possibly last ten years, or even five." It was the speech of a man irritated beyond endurance by stupidity and falsehood, but he added in calmer tones, "You understand, Miss de Jong, that there's no necessity to quote me to your friend Mr. Yamashita."

I assured him that I wouldn't, and I meant it. "But Captain, if the worst were to happen," I went on, "and you didn't succeed this time, how much longer do you think it's going on? You see—we have so much at stake, we natives."

We looked at each other while I waited. God knows why he answered frankly, but he did. "If the worst happened—though it's impossible to think it might, you understand—even then the end wouldn't come for another two years. I hope that reassures you. But it's idle talk, since it is not going to turn out like that. We are succeeding. We are driving on to victory," he said.

That afternoon, in the hour of daylight that was left after the day's work, I went for a walk along the mountain's lower slopes. I had a good deal to think about. I'd begun to wonder if they had not forgotten me altogether in the Batavia secret police department. It would not be surprising if they had. After all, I was only an unimportant person with a rather obscure job to do, and I wasn't doing it properly, at that. I could hardly wonder that there was never a reply to the messages I kept sending. Perhaps Yamashita wasn't even bothering about sending them, it now occurred to me—he was quite capable of acting as he thought best in a matter of the sort, and he made no secret of his disapproval of me. Yet even if I'd been able to find something derogatory about Saito, something they could use, wouldn't they have forgotten about me? The war was not going well for them: Saito couldn't be the only one with the brains to see that there was another outcome than victory possible. They had things to worry about. Really, I could hardly wonder that I was forgotten in the face of the recent news.

As for my friends in Batavia, and my lover, I shouldn't find it strange or frightening that I'd had no word from them since the early weeks, but I did. For a minute I was engulfed in a wave of terror and loneliness. I felt like a child lost in those mountains along the horizon, and I said aloud, "What am I going to do?"

A puff of air came from the sea and stroked my cheeks. It was soft, warm air, fragrant with some flowering bush, and somehow it changed the aspect of things. I looked at the mountain range again: the great rock pile was not threatening, but reassuring. As I remembered Captain Saito's words they too had a different effect: I really thought of their significance. *We couldn't possibly last out,* he had said. I put aside the rest of it, the discussion of how many years it might be: what remained was still the astonishing fact that we were some day coming to the end of the war. Saito himself had said it. How could I have ignored that? I stopped short in my tracks to give full attention to this staggering truth. *There was to be an end.*

A goat bleated, and her kid came frisking up toward me. The place seemed crowded. I turned and started downhill toward the Li house and privacy, smiling because I had just thought of a beautifully simple way to get back to Batavia, where Ahmet was. Saito, of course—Saito would send me if I asked him to.

Coming down the staircase by the reservoir that hung over a sparsely settled road, I noticed a car that I recognized parked on the road below, and wondered as I came closer to its level what Yamashita could be doing out here, when the light was waning and he couldn't be taking the photographs he loved to make. No matter: I didn't want to meet him and talk to him, for our last interview had not been pleasant. Fortunately, the steps led to a spot behind the car, and when I got down into the road I could walk off in the opposite direction without being deflected very much from my way. But even as I turned downhill, I felt compelled, as one does, to take a swift look at the car's occupants through the rear window. There were two of them in the front seat, Yamashita and a woman, facing each other and talking earnestly. I knew the woman. Her presence there was so surprising that I hesitated and took another look before walking off with my back safely turned. There could be no mistake: I had even recognized the padded coat of plum-colored silk. It was certainly Yi, the mistress of Captain Saito.

CHAPTER ELEVEN

The captain's office windows looked out on the water, dancing and juggling its lozenges of blue and green under the clear sky. I'd often seen him taking pleasure in the view, though he criticized the landscape for not having enough halftones. Once, in the middle of a busy morning, he gave me a disquisition on the beauty of nature's subtleties and argued that the mists of rain on the mountains were far lovelier than mere sunshine, and for illustration of his point painted a picture on a bit of office paper, using an ordinary writing brush and black ink. I still have it.

But that afternoon the captain was not interested in the sea, or in anything else around him. He scarcely paid attention to what I was saying. This was disturbing because the request I made was so important to me. Too late I remembered that he'd been unlike himself for several days, so pale and unhappy that the Japanese girls talked wisely of malaria, from which, they said, he frequently suffered. Yet, though it wasn't a good time to ask a favor, I was already embarked. I made the speech I'd planned anyway—an unnerving performance, like orating to a statue. I ended:

"So please, Captain Saito, unless it's very inconvenient, let me go back to Batavia."

He stirred at this and smiled a little. "Surely you mean—Jakarta?"

"I'm sorry. I make that mistake over and over again," I said, gaining confidence because he hadn't turned me down immediately. "I would appreciate your permission more than I can say. For some weeks I haven't had any duties that couldn't be performed just as well by someone who lives here: for instance, there's an overseas Chinese boy in Supplies whose Dutch is good. Do you think I could possibly . . . ?"

The veil had fallen over his eyes again, but he said, "Yes, I can at least do that. Presumably you want to go as soon as you can?"

"Oh yes, please, Captain. And if you'd be good enough to recommend me for a place in the plane as well? Otherwise I might have to wait for weeks."

It was better than I'd dared to hope for, because he wrote the necessary form there and then. I thanked him several times, though it was like talking to the monument up on the Peak. I was absorbed in my relief and delight, but I did sense something very wrong with Captain Saito, and even spared an uneasy thought to Yi with Yamashita, out on the reservoir road. It was only for a moment—my own affairs pushed everything else aside.

On the way home I stopped to inquire about passage and was told that the usual plane would be leaving within the next week, on official business. After reading Saito's message they promised to notify me later just when it would be. So far so good, but the worst hurdle had still to be crossed. It was no use telling myself, as I did through a sleepless night, that I didn't have to notify Yamashita of all this: it was at best a forlorn hope that he would accept the *fait accompli* without making trouble. The services were very jealous of each other, I knew. Surprisingly, when after making a long trip to his office I broke the news, it didn't elicit more than a flicker of interest in Yamashita. He was not angry at all, that I could see.

"I call that enterprising of you," he said genially, "especially as you've already got all the arrangements made, thanks to your kind captain. Well, well! I may have an envelope or two for you to take back to Jakarta." He made a note on his pad and added, "And again, perhaps I won't. If no message shows up, you needn't worry."

Though this sounded like dismissal I hardly dared seize my luck, and I lingered. "I'm sorry not to have been of more use on this project, Mr. Yamashita. I really couldn't do more, and I do hope you believe me."

"That's all right." Yamashita made a careless gesture, as if scattering largesse. His face creased with private mirth as he added, "It happens I've found other channels. Don't think about it any more, Miss de Jong; your responsibility has ceased." He turned away.

I continued to visit the office every morning, waiting for word of the plane. At last the notice arrived. The time had come to say goodbye to everyone, so I made the rounds of the assistants, stopping for a few polite words with the office manager. Nodding toward Saito's closed door, I asked, "Is the captain free? I'd like to say goodbye."

He said, "Nobody's in there with him, but he hasn't felt well lately, and I don't know if we ought to disturb—"

He stopped talking to listen. Together we turned toward the outer corridor, from which came a new sound, of marching feet. Both of us realized it was no ordinary visitor coming in, even before the door swung open to admit three officers in army uniform. They marched toward us, long swords swaying like stiff tails in their wake, to pause at the manager's desk, where their leader barked,

"Captain Saito." Meticulously he added his name and those of his companions. The manager had already drawn himself to attention. He said,

"Yes, sir. I'll tell him you are here."

I backed slowly toward my desk. Menace hung in the air, and everyone in the office felt it and watched the manager as he knocked on Saito's door and pronounced the names of the visitors in a high voice. We heard Saito reply, the words coming through distinctly, that he would not keep the gentlemen waiting. He didn't. Almost immediately, we heard the shot.

214

We found him in the middle of the room crumpled on the floor, quite dead.

"But if they didn't hurt you, what's the matter?" asked Ahmet. He had been asking the same question for hours, and he showed no impatience or fatigue though his efforts got no response. Ever since arriving I had lain on the bed, shivering and crying.

"They did maltreat you," he said at last. I raised my head to say,

"No, they didn't. It has nothing to do with me at all. I told you that. It's just that I can't bear it any more, Ahmet, I can't work for those people ever again, ever again. I—" My voice was cracking and I nearly gave way to another storm of tears, when Yvonne pushed Ahmet aside and took over.

"Julie, stop this immediately," she commanded me. "You're frightening all of us. You've had quite enough time to be foolish. Now sit up and be sensible."

I obeyed, and struggled to a sitting position, muttering that I was sorry. Yvonne sat on the edge of the bed and took my hand. "Now tell us just what happened up there in Hongkong, and control yourself."

Meekly I obeyed, and they both listened without interruption to the story of Saito, Yamashita, and the suicide.

"I wanted to stay on," I said at the end, "because it seemed heartless to rush off before he'd been buried or anything. It was only my luck that I wasn't responsible, you know, instead of Yi. I could have done just as much harm." My voice threatened to give out again, and I looked at Ahmet with puffed, tear-stained eyes. "I might easily have done that dirty work; you know I meant to do it if I could, before I went away. They must have got Yi to report things he sometimes said—how the Japanese might not win the war, all that. Any little thing would have been enough to condemn him, once they'd made up their minds to get him. Anything at all . . . And they wouldn't let me stay; they said I had to go right away— It was just a few hours ago, do you realize that? Less than a day ago he was alive. He shot himself only a little while ago. Oh, Yvonne, he was such a good man." Tears rolled down my cheeks.

"Were you lovers?" asked Ahmet.

Yvonne sighed and said, "Oh, really, Ahmet!" I stared at him. Ahmet repeated, as if Yvonne had not spoken, "Were you lovers?"

"No." My voice was crisp and angry. We were so taken up with glaring at each other that we didn't notice Yvonne slipping out of the room. I was furious with Ahmet, but for the first time since my return I also felt warmth and reassurance. This was what I'd been needing. I was at home again.

Trying to pick up the threads of the old Jakarta life, I found a few missing. Most important, my work with the secret police was indefinitely suspended: at least I hoped so, as I heard nothing from them. But something new had been added. Ahmet was teaching again, and now his work was not a mere cover, as it had been when I met him. He was really busy and enthusiastic about the school. He told me that it was one among several establishments set up under the encouragement of a few Japanese naval officers, who must have been unusual in that they had strong communist sympathies. The students were young men who were taught certain principles of government during intensive courses that lasted only two months. According to Ahmet, batch after batch of these youths were instructed not with the usual Japanese pap, but with strong stuff; the teachers urged them to fight for an international brotherhood, against wicked capitalistic imperialism . . . Ahmet rolled out the words with relish. I could hardly believe it.

"You mean you teach all this openly, with Japanese approval?" I asked. "But surely, Ahmet, you'll get into trouble. It's communism."

"I know, and I admit it's unexpected," he said, "but those were my orders—and I'm not the only one in it. Many far more important men are teaching in the schools. We're allowed to talk as much as we like about independence, too, and Indonesia's rights in the future. Things have changed a lot since you left."

"They must have done," I said, shaking my head. Ahmet's eyes sparkled as he hurried on:

"We think it's time to ask for the whole thing—independence now, with a constitution. The signs are good. The Japanese have given in in several small ways—some Indonesians are getting places in local government councils, but that's not nearly enough, of course: we want our constitution working before the Dutch come back."

He had never before talked with so much assurance about the return of the Dutch, but as I'd already observed, the thinking in Jakarta had kept pace with Hongkong's.

"You've made friends with some Japanese. Won't you be a little sorry when they've got to go?" I asked, though I knew the answer.

"Julie, if I were given the choice, I'd side with the Allies today," he said. "But I thank Allah that I won't have to choose. Indonesia is going to stand alone. We'll have to push out the Japanese, by force if necessary, but Indonesia can and will stand alone."

"And that heaven you're always talking about, when all men are brothers and everything is international?"

"The international heaven will come later," said Ahmet, and smiled at my teasing.

It sounded very pretty, but I saw holes in the picture, and said so, apologetically. "I don't quite understand what good your independence will be if you get it from the Japanese. When they've been beaten, surely the Dutch won't recognize its legality. Anything you get from a nation that's defeated—"

"Of course the Dutch would try it ignore it, but a thing that's been accomplished isn't easily set aside, no matter what the law might be. We'll fight. We're eager to fight. Remember, the Dutch will be tired after all these years, and we aren't. We're prepared as we've never been before. People are going to fight hard to keep what they've just won. And not all the

Allies will feel like the Netherlanders about this. America might well line up on our side, and the British have promised to set India free. Oh, it's going to be all right."

I couldn't help sounding sad as I replied, "You're always hopeful, Ahmet." I saw myself stagnating in the middle of all this activity. Ahmet was happy and busy. Yvonne, though no doubt from the kindest of motives, had said she didn't need my help.

She complained that trade was falling off and she didn't have enough work to keep her assistants busy.

"The Japanese just aren't interested in shopping any more," she said. "A lot of them are going away. I've lost some of my best customers."

"But you've still got Ito hanging around?"

"Oh, Ito! He'll be around until doomsday," she said.

At least I could do one useful job—I could go back on the old prison-camp routine. Yvonne reported that as far as her inexpert eye could detect, there had been no changes at either place. It happened that Agatha's camp was the first one with a parcel day, and I went there. Riding past in the old way, I saw Agatha almost immediately and she saw me at the same time. There was no mistaking it; I was a sensation. Agatha smiled broadly as if in relief; indeed, for a second I was afraid she would forget herself and wave. A general ripple ran through the line, and though I couldn't hear it I imagined the outcry as one after another noticed that I was back. It was a great relief: I hadn't felt such satisfaction for a long time. Whatever was the matter with Agatha, I reflected, must have been forgotten. I was halfway home before I wondered if in the excitement of seeing Agatha I'd missed any other faces. Marge? Mina? I couldn't recall them, but it didn't matter. Agatha was the important one.

I wasn't happy as I set out on Phil's errand, for there had been time to listen to neighborhood gossip about the military camps, and it was gloomy. Some prisoners had disappeared, the woman next door told me. It was presumed that they'd gone to Japan, but nobody of course was sure. I was immediately convinced that Phil was among the missing. I even had a premonitory dream in which I went to camp and looked for him in vain, and asked the guard, who refused to answer. In the morning when I reported on this to the household, Mrs. Dutoit began to cry in sympathy. She believed in premonitions. She promised to consult her latest seer that very day about Phil's fate.

"Mother, it's nonsense!" protested Yvonne, and Ahmet muttered something unflattering about Europeans in general. After so much of this, it was a wonderful surprise to see Phil alive and evidently well behind the barbed wire. He made a V sign that I saw though the guards did not, and I came home in good spirits, to find Mrs. Dutoit triumphantly full of news. Before I could head her off she told me that Mr. Brewer had been taken to Japan and was only just alive. I was grateful to her and sorry for her too, and braced myself to defend her against Yvonne's jeers when the truth came out. For some reason, however, Yvonne did not seize the chance to pester her mother, but sat through dinner silent and absent-minded. Later she came to see me alone.

"The war's going to end soon," she said abruptly. "Have you thought about that, Julie?"

"I haven't dared," I confessed. "It would mean bad luck, like tempting God to postpone events."

Yvonne shook her head. "You're as bad as Mother. Still, anyone can see that it's coming to an end, so what do you think you're going to do afterwards? Stick to Ahmet, or what?"

I was surprised. "Why should peace make any difference to Ahmet and me? What a strange thing to ask! Of course I'll stick to Ahmet, as you put it. You know all our plans: he's going to get divorced and—"

"You're sure about that? Sometimes I can't help wondering when I watch you rushing off to see your friend Brewer. Ahmet doesn't like it one little bit, I can tell you, and I don't wonder." She paused, then said impulsively, "It would serve me right if you told me it was none of my business, my dear. I know that, but I wanted to remind you that you'll have to decide one of these days. It won't always be easy as it is now, carrying food to an abstract idea there in the camp, as if Brewer was the Goddess of Mercy in a temple. There's a real man there, Julie, behind the barbed wire, don't forget that. . . . And Ahmet, he's a real man, too." Astonishingly, for Yvonne was not a sentimental girl, she leaned over and kissed my cheek. "Goodnight, Julie," she said.

Though Saito remained in my memory as an unresolved sorrow, I had nearly forgotten the *kempeitai* of Jakarta before I got the summons to report to Shiga. It came as an unpleasant shock.

"I don't want to work for them again. I won't. Can they make me do it?" I asked Ahmet. He looked uncertain and puzzled.

"Of course if they want to make a point of it . . . but I hardly think you'd be any good to them at this stage of the game. One would think they'd had enough of you. Surely, now they know your heart isn't in it, you wouldn't be dependable," he said. "They might turn nasty about me, but—"

"Oh, Ahmet, what can I do if they try to make me talk about you?"

He came to a decision. "They won't. If they wanted to get me, they wouldn't try anyone as prejudiced as you. It's most unlikely."

Still, I was afraid. I quaked as I turned in at the familiar house, and my heart fell as I saw that Shiga was not alone. Sitting behind the desk next to him was another Japanese, whose face was somehow not strange to me, though I couldn't recall where I had seen him before, and he stared at me as if I were a new and unpleasantly interesting insect. So did Shiga, for that matter. What could be the trouble? I bowed respectfully and waited, but for some time nobody spoke. Was Shiga angry because I hadn't turned up unbidden to make a report? Or had Yamashita, perhaps, talked against me? I couldn't think of any crime heinous enough to account for this hostility.

Shiga broke the silence in the approved *kempeitai* manner, as if he were addressing a criminal—hectoring and icy. "Miss de Jong, you have not been truthful with us."

His companion lowered his head and grunted in affirmation.

"I'm sorry you think that, sir." My voice quavered. Though I couldn't think what I had done, I had all the symptoms of deep guilt. Still, after I'd waited a while and he vouchsafed no explanation, but merely continued to look like a deeply affronted goblin, I gathered my strength to say, "In what way have I been dishonest?"

"Don't play innocent," he shouted. "You know as well as I do. When you joined the service, you were supposed to tell us all about your background, weren't you? Wasn't it made perfectly clear that this was expected?"

"Yes, sir." Frantically I wondered what could have been wrong with my credentials. As I remembered, Kiyama had asked ordinary questions, and I hadn't deviated in any respect in my answers from the facts already on the colony's record sheets. "I replied truthfully," I said.

"Did you? Be careful now, be very careful. I have here your documents: I see that you gave the name of Margrethe de Jong as your mother. Miss de Jong, who *was* your mother? This time we want the truth."

Death must be something like that moment, when everything I could see or sense tottered wildly, and nearly went black. I was ripped open. My heart was being snatched out of my breast. All that had been warm and secret was taken from me and scattered in the cold. They might as well have blown me up with a grenade. I swayed where I stood, eyes closed. I could hear Shiga's voice roaring dimly, like wind from some high, snow-filled ravine in the mountains. Then I felt my arms held tightly, and opened my eyes, and saw that the other Japanese was gripping me. The roaring subsided.

"Tell me her name," Shiga said, in a human voice.

I pushed angrily at the other man's hands. "I can stand. Leave me alone," I told him, before facing Shiga. "I was a foundling, an orphan. You know that. How can I tell you my mother's name, if she didn't tell the truth herself? What does it matter? She's gone, and I don't know who she was. Nobody knows."

"I see. You thought you were safe. Just a minute, Miss de Jong." Shiga nodded to the other man, who walked out through the door behind the desk. He was back immediately, pushing ahead of him a woman—a European woman, burned to a dark tan by days in the sun. She was unkempt and almost unrecognizably thin, but I would have known Mina anywhere. I had never forgotten that spiteful gaze, though it was a long time since I'd seen her at close quarters.

Because I was taken by surprise, I spoke. "Hello, Mina," I said, as if we were meeting in some hotel lobby. Mina, more sensible, did not try to reply, but drew herself up like a tragedy queen, pursing her lips. Lieutenant Shiga said to her,

"This is the girl?" Mina nodded. Shiga said, "Tell us in front of her who her mother was."

"Her mother was Mata Hari, the spy. Her mother was executed, and serve her right," said Mina shrilly. "Julie's never admitted it, but I know all about it. I found out—I found out before the war, long ago." She turned to me. "You thought nobody would ever guess, didn't you? You thought you'd be safe out here in Java. Well, I want you to know that I made it my business to look you up, Julie de Jong. My friends at home uncovered the whole dirty thing and wrote to me, just before the mails stopped. It wasn't easy, you've been so careful. You forgot to be careful *only* once, when you told a friend about it. You remember Ellie? At first I wasn't going to say anything, even to Jan. I thought nobody could help what her mother was. But then you started going the same way, parading past the camp with a Japanese arm band, flaunting new clothes when we didn't even have enough to eat . . . You're just like her, as dirty as she was."

"And so of course you told," I said. My head was spinning. Ellie! Ellie, all those years ago.

"Why shouldn't I tell? Why shouldn't I warn decent people against you?" cried Mina.

The Japanese waited and listened as she went on and on, raving like a lunatic. She said that Jan was wounded and might be dead, because of me: that Marge's baby had dwindled away and died, and that I had killed that baby. She spoke of many people whose names I did not know, who had come to grief in the war. All of them had suffered through me—it was time I was exposed. God had told her to do it.

The Japanese listened while she ranted, and I stood with my head bent, letting her abuse wash over me. I didn't try to answer or defend myself. No matter what Mina said, I deserved it. Mina knew nothing of Saito and couldn't mention his name, but I supplied it for her, in my mind, as I waited silently. This was the hour of reckoning, when I must take the blame for my mother and myself. I must pay for all the crooked reasoning I was guilty of; I must let Mina and the Japanese between them tear away my dreams, expose my mother as they had exposed me, and trample on both of us. We had earned it.

Mina fell silent at last, when her voice gave out. The camp Japanese led her away, and I was alone with Shiga. When he spoke, he sounded tired.

"So, you will admit you lied to us," he said. "What do you think we are going to do to you?"

"It doesn't matter. Do whatever you think right."

He bit his lip. "That woman," he said in a low voice. Then, a man who has acted a play all the way through and now faces an empty house, he threw up his hands and said, "There is no use going on. You are finished and disgraced with us. You may go."

If it had not been impossible, I would have believed that the tears in his eyes were real.

CHAPTER TWELVE

———

What I begin to remember with normal clarity is a series of days when I was recovering from a high fever. I am vague about what went on beforehand. They say I came home from Shiga's house shivering and with chattering teeth, and that I looked like an old woman who had long been ailing. The family was much alarmed and supposed I'd been flogged and tortured, but when I was undressed—something the Dutoit women had to do for me—they couldn't find any marks. Then my jaws unlocked and I talked, quite a lot. I don't recall any of this, but the others do.

"It was something about your mother," Yvonne said. "Those Japanese found out she was notorious a long time ago—and who cares?—and they threw it in your face. Of course you were upset, to have your mother insulted, but really, Julie, it was all over and done with many years ago. You needn't have taken it so hard." Her perplexity was the most comforting thing I'd seen for days.

The older Dutoits, too, were gently mystified, but Ahmet helped the most. We talked for long periods about my mother, and me, and the whole affair.

"The Japanese are clever," said Ahmet, "but it was bad luck that they should have understood you so well. Shiga knew you were ill. You were, you know. A healthy girl wouldn't have been bothered about what they dug up—they couldn't have got at you if you hadn't been going around all these years

224

hiding an unhealed wound. Or do you know what I'm trying to say?"

"I think I do."

"Now you must get well," said Ahmet.

In spite of all my gratitude I felt slightly impatient with him for talking as if I needed building up with rest and nourishing food. I told myself that I was not a dysentery patient but a woman whose core had been removed by surgery. I was hollow. My mother couldn't help me any more: my mother was gone, because she had been dragged out into daylight and had vanished. Ahmet scolded me for saying this. He said I was like a superstitious Javanese, "believing" in my mother as if she were a ghost.

"Perhaps, perhaps," I said at last, tired of talk. "I'll be all right now, I promise. It's all finished."

Poor Ahmet; it was no time to distract him with family troubles, when everything was happening to the Japanese campaign at once. It was clear that the Americans would soon be on top of us, and he spent much of his time in our room, from which I was excluded while he talked in private with colleagues, planning and replanning the next move. Sukarno made a speech in which he outlined the aims of the soon-to-be Indonesian nation, but in spite of repeated urging from younger members of the group, he would not let them rise up yet in revolt. I gathered from Ahmet's angry complaints that his leader stubbornly refused to be convinced that the young Nationalists were strong enough to carry the operation through.

"And in the meantime the end comes nearer and nearer," fretted Ahmet. "He will make us miss our chance through being too cautious."

Suddenly a rumor spread all over town that the Americans had dealt a killing blow to Japan, dropping on the home country a giant bomb that did not merely explode but pulverized a complete city, and had ghastly effects on people miles away. Some believed it because they always believed the latest story; others were skeptical because that was their habit. As might be expected, Mrs. Dutoit swallowed every word and lived in terror that the Americans might next bestow a bomb on us. But I was one of the skeptics. I spent much time trying to laugh Mrs. Dutoit out of her worries, scoffing at the terrible tales, which sounded like a child's wildest nightmares. Mrs. Dutoit kept me so distracted I scarcely noticed that Ahmet did not come to my support. He couldn't. He knew that the rumor for once was correct, and even feared that Japan had already surrendered. That night, after Sukarno failed to keep his promise and declare a republic then and there, he and his cronies took the desperate step of kidnaping Sukarno and Mohammed Hatta. They took the leaders to a meeting place outside town, where the affair was talked out.

"Sukarno wanted to arrange it without fighting, if possible," Ahmet told me afterwards. "He was hoping until the end that the Japanese would let us have what we wanted, but it was as I said—he waited too long. By the time we let him try it his way and ask them, they'd surrendered. The Emperor told his people by proclamation on the radio. So now, they can't do anything. It's up to us, and Sukarno's proclaiming the Republic tomorrow. At last!"

Nothing worked out as simply as he expected. Instead of a clean-cut end to the war, we were suddenly plunged into a revolution. The fighting spread like explosions along an old-fashioned string of firecrackers—there would be a pop and crackle at one point, answered by fire from the Japanese, and then all would be quiet there. Then, along the road at a distance of a mile or more, another set of pops broke out. One reason for this bewildering pattern was that the Japanese didn't have their hearts in it. Stunned and grief-stricken by the surrender, they were not anxious to serve as the tools of the Allies in keeping down our rebels, but those were their orders and they were well-disciplined. To add to their troubles, a rash of suicides affected their higher ranks. Honor demanded that officers die rather than lay down their arms, and many of them, Japanese medieval warriors that they were, did just that. Ahmet's particular friends, who had sponsored the schools and encouraged rebellion, were thrown into prison.

Allied victory, for which we'd waited nearly four years, crept almost unnoticed into Jakarta, now preoccupied with the revolution. My vision of a splendid breakout from the camps had to go the way of most visions, as did the hope of meeting my friends at the very gates. I did try to get close to Agatha's camp, but it was more heavily guarded than ever, and I saw familiar faces among the soldiers who warned me off before I'd approached nearer than a quarter of a mile. Their orders were different now, since they'd been told to protect their European charges from the presumably maddened rebels, but the effect was the same. The prisoners stayed behind the wire, and I remained outside. It was a crazier world than I'd ever imagined.

As for the military camp that held Phil, knowing Yvonne's sardonic eye was on me, I hardly liked to make the most tentative effort. I told myself that it would have been useless at any rate, until the situation became clearer. As far as we in the Dutoit house were concerned the war was not much with us. Sometimes, though not frequently, a rifle cracked out once or twice, or a military car full of Japanese bounced along the road. Soon after the proclamation Ahmet told us he was going away for a few days, to Surabaya, and said I was not to worry. Though this is as good a way as any to start up anxiety in nervous women, I found it easy to obey his directions. It all seemed unreal somehow, probably because it had happened to us once too often. I couldn't believe Ahmet was in danger, or that we were either. I was startled, therefore, when I rushed into Yvonne's room one morning and found her in tears, and she confessed that she was afraid. This had never happened before.

"Whatever are *you* afraid of?" I asked. I put my arms around her. "Don't cry, Yvonne, or you'll scare me too. You never cry. Don't you feel well? Is that it?"

Her head on my shoulder shook vigorously, and she said into my sleeve, "I'm all right." The muffled tone sounded impatient. Then she jerked upright and dabbed with vigorous jabs at her traitor eyes. "It's not that I'm afraid for me," she said, "but for Ito. It's going to be so awful for the Japanese. No matter how this new war turns out—"

"Ito? What do you care about that little crook?" I wondered if Yvonne had gone crazy. The ones that bend the least, I reflected, break the fastest. She flared at me:

"He's not, and you're not to say things like that. I know he's not pretty, and we've made fun of him all along, but . . . You might as well know right now that he's my—my fiancé." I might have stood there, frozen by amazement, for longer than I did if she hadn't put her head on my shoulder again in a desperate swoop, wailing, "Oh Julie, what's going to happen to us? It's all so hopeless."

Ineptly, I comforted her as well as I could. Ito was a civilian, I pointed out, and would no doubt be let alone. By resolutely forgetting his image I must have managed to sound serious and even convincing, since Yvonne soon cheered up and chattered at length about her love affair. Oh well, I thought, why not Ito? It was the same old thing: if I hadn't been so wrapped in myself I might have guessed earlier. After all, Yvonne and Ito did have business interests in common. Her parents might not like it, but for years they'd been concerned over their daughter's stubborn spinsterhood. Japanese were generally disliked in Jakarta, but that dislike would die down in time. After a few years everything might be comfortable again. . . . I said all this to Yvonne, and her tears dried.

She stayed at home that morning, but as nothing frightening took place within our hearing, she went out that afternoon, leaving me to mope in the house. I was trying to read on the veranda when I heard one of the noisy Japanese trucks and looked up to see it slow down in front of our house. As it came to a halt a tall figure stepped down and turned toward me. It took me a few seconds to realize that it was

Phil, white-haired and emaciated in his torn shirt and badly worn army shorts. Irrelevantly, I noticed that as he came up the path he walked as easily as a Javanese on his bare feet. And then, heedless of Mrs. Dutoit as a possible witness behind the window, I threw myself on his neck.

"Phil! Phil!"

He held me tight.

"Completely wild, these last three days," he told me over a celebration tea. The Dutoits had been kind, but firmly refused to join us, though Mrs. Dutoit brought out her best cake. "For a while it looked as if they'd made up their minds to shoot us all, but then I guess they got their orders to act for the Allies, and that made us friends. All in a minute, Julie. The guy who'd knocked out teeth was now our brave champion against their former little brown brothers, now their bitter enemies. It makes you wonder what we had to go through all this for, doesn't it?"

"But you've still got to stay in camp," I said resentfully.

Phil didn't seem to mind that as much as I did. "Where else would we all go, all of a sudden like that? We aren't prisoners any more, not officially. I got a permit to come out today—they're nuts about permits, of course—to help start off reconstruction, whatever that means, and when the Allied troops get here things should settle down." I must have looked as doubtful as I felt, for he went on, "You don't think all this nonsense about independence is going to be serious, do you, Julie?"

"Oh, it's serious," I assured him. "They aren't going to forget it, if that's what you're hoping. They've got their republic and they mean to keep it."

"And you think they ought to," he said, watching me.

"Well, of course I do. They won it."

Phil waited a minute before he spoke. "I've got a lot of reorienting to do," he said apologetically. "Living the way I've been doing, a fellow gets into habits of thought. Everything looks cut and dried in there. You wouldn't pull through if you didn't simplify things. And maybe it's the same with you, Julie. You've been with these people the whole time, identifying, I guess you'd call it. It's going to take a while for both of us to shake down."

I did not reply, and we sat in silence, drinking tea, thinking our own thoughts. Phil had to leave soon afterwards because the truck was coming to pick him up. "I'll come in tomorrow if you'll be here," he said. "Sorry if I talked your head off—it's the relief. The trouble is, I didn't get around to saying anything important, but I guess you know how I feel without my saying it. Goodbye for now, darling."

That night I slept badly. But in the following fortnight, seeing Phil almost every day and getting used to his face again, I recovered balance. Life slipped into a new routine. Every day he had something to report about the outside world. Everything was in turmoil after the surrender, but the victorious Allies were doing their best to rush aid and support to the many liberated areas that had been caught, like us, by sudden peace. What made the difference in Java was that the peace had already given way to new war, though Phil refused to think that this couldn't be settled easily enough when the first Allies arrived.

"I wish they could get here before October," he said. "Some of the Dutch boys are in a nasty mood, which you can't wonder at. A term of four years in prison doesn't turn people into saints. But I wish they had more sense."

He was referring to incidents all over town that were having a bad effect on the locals. Ex-prisoners, who now found it easy to come in and out of the city, flooded the place, determined to flout what restraining rules remained and snatch back their long lost property and privilege. It was to be expected that they would treat the Japanese badly; presumably the Japanese themselves expected it. But some of the Dutch seemed to vent most spite and contempt on the Javanese. This aroused old resentments that even the Javanese had half forgotten. We had all simply smoldered over such things: now, surprisingly, I felt an urge to explain and thus excuse them.

"I suppose it's been especially hard on them inside there, feeling humiliated in front of the Javanese. They've always known the Javanese, you see. The others are foreigners, but when these people turned against them and kicked them while they were down—" My voice trailed away in surprise at what I was saying. It was as if seeing Phil had opened for me the long closed shutter of a lens that looked on the West. There was stimulation in this open view; I looked questioningly at him to see if he was sharing my excitement, but he said only,

"Never mind all that just now, Julie." Phil, who was smoking a pipe, took it out of his mouth and put it on the table where the coffee cups stood. "It's time we got our affairs sorted out, don't you think?" he asked.

My heart jumped. Yes, I did think so. I'd made up my mind about Phil; for several days I had waited serenely for this moment to tell him so. But he didn't wait; he went on:

"I've had word at last from Lily, you see, and I'm free. She's through with the marriage, with me, with all that. She's found somebody else, and of course that's fine as far as I'm concerned. Julie, everything's all right, isn't it? I haven't rushed you, because I was waiting for Lily's letter—not that I'd have let her spoil it, mind you—and besides, I thought, well, I want it to be solid this time." He put his hand on mine. I wanted to respond. I wanted to turn my head and kiss him, and lean on his shoulder, but I didn't. I don't know why. I suppose I didn't want to quite enough. All sorts of thoughts held me back.

Phil's grasp tightened on my hand as if willing it to become less flaccid. "Just tell me," he said. "Give the word and I'll start making all the arrangements. As soon as we can be married—well, what about it, Julie? You're very quiet." Again he waited. My tongue wouldn't move. He said urgently, "If you only knew how I hope this is just a formality. I hope you've been expecting and waiting for it as I have . . . ."

"Phil," I burst out desperately. "Of course I—well, I'm awfully fond of you, you know that. But I've been living with another man. That Indonesian I told you about—Ahmet. You must have guessed it."

"Of course, you little idiot. Why, I took it for granted that there must have been someone. In fact I wouldn't have been surprised if you'd found a Japanese protector these past years, and certainly I wouldn't have blamed you if you had. For God's sake, Julie, you don't think *that* would make any difference to us, after everything we've been through? No girl can help what happens when a country is occupied. The men talked about this a lot in camp."

For the first time since Phil had come back, I was irritated by him. He was more obtuse than I remembered. Couldn't he see that I wasn't asking for forgiveness? No, he couldn't, but the subject must have been near to his heart —this question of fidelity and wartime affairs—because he continued talking about it, being broad-minded and kindly and annoying, until I stopped listening. I consoled myself with the reflection that there would be all the time in the world to set him right. And now, I thought, I must decide what I was going to say to Ahmet. I felt a pang at the idea of breaking the news, yet surely, I thought, Ahmet would not really be surprised. Surely he had known, all along, that it wasn't forever. It couldn't be. Our love affair had been born in an ephemeral time, it was artificially nourished, and doomed from the beginning. Jakarta had changed, Ahmet had changed, and I too—

"You can't blame me for reverting to type," I argued with the absent Ahmet, silently. "I'm not of this country. I know that. Never mind who my father was; I'm a Dutch girl. I'm a European. One can't eradicate the past, darling. I used to think I could, but there it is; my childhood and youth, going to school in the snow, riding in trams, living a Northern life—how can I wipe it all out, even with love? This is not my country. Indonesia's sorrow is not mine. Not mine. Not mine."

"Darling." Phil's voice broke in on my excited monologue. "Why are you crying? Don't cry." When he put his arm around me I leaned against him at last, and felt grateful for that strong body. I wiped my eyes and blew my nose.

"Phil, we aren't out of the woods here, you know—not yet. Aren't you the slightest bit worried about what's going to happen? I think these people are heading for a terrible crash before things are settled with the Netherlands, can't you see?"

He patted my shoulder and said, "Sure. That's true, but what do we care? We'll be out of it. We can forget the whole damned mess. From now on, whatever happens here is no skin off *your* pretty little nose. Try to get that into your head."

"Well . . . yes. I suppose that's so."

"Sure it's so. Before you know it we'll be in America."

America. It sounded new, like a name I'd never heard before. "Sounds funny," I admitted.

"Does it? Not to me. You'll get used to it. You won't even think it sounds funny when you're called Mrs. Brewer of California, do you realize that? Mrs. Brewer of California, U.S.A., sweetie. You'll love it."

There on the Dutoit veranda Phil described a vision of America. He didn't talk about the national capital city with its monuments, or the Statue of Liberty. He talked about families living in houses like little palaces, and I saw them, like the advertisements in the magazines—bathrooms of clean, clean tile, with pretty towels of pastel colors, and I saw shops made all of glass, and shining motorcars, and endless fields of grain, and great heaping plates of food, and two children with chubby legs and pink faces, playing on a swing outside our door. Phil talked of peace, safety, wealth—the things Ming had always said I would not have unless I should mend my ways. Ming was wrong. I was going to have them. I laughed aloud with pleasure.

"It is all true?" I asked Phil.

"All true. And then there are the neighbors, nicest people in the world, Julie. You'll love them."

"But will they love me?"

I asked the question carelessly, coquettishly, hardly expecting a reply. But Phil gave one—an answer that changed everything. He said,

"They'll be crazy about you. Don't you worry, darling. Nobody in California could possibly guess."

For a split second I was going to ask him what he meant, then understanding flooded in and I knew. He meant my father, my mixed blood, the old business I'd forgotten. My father, my blood, had kept me out of prison camp, and I'd long since come to terms with the fact and forgotten, but Phil had not. Phil was just the same—part of the old, hateful world that I'd fled from. For another second I was furious; then that, too, dropped away, like my hope and joy.

He didn't realize what he had done. It was hardly fair even to say he had done it; he had only called up a lot of forgotten truths and reminded me of them, innocently and crudely. How could I have considered living with Phil in California? How could I have been so stupid? It is easy to talk and say things about forgetting the past and starting out new; what is hopeless is to believe that one can actually do this.

"Marge knows," I said absently, to give myself time to think. "You'll have to do something about Marge."

I don't know how he managed to reassure himself about that, because I didn't hear what he was saying. Poor Phil: couldn't he see for himself how impossible it was? He would never be able to stop feeling self-conscious on my behalf. For the rest of our life together he would have worried for fear the truth about me might get out. Some day he might even turn on me in revenge for years of nagging, niggling worry.

No. I realized besides that I didn't even want the life he had promised so enthusiastically, the existence I was giving up before I'd had a taste of it. How could I put all this, Java, behind me and forget it? My ears were attuned to the speech, the music; my eyes might be blind if I couldn't see my friends and my lover with whom I'd suffered and been happy. I would be homesick. I would be bored.

All this time Phil was unaware of the way my thoughts

were going. He talked happily, fluently, as he'd done before. He didn't notice that I had drawn away from him and was sitting straight in my place, without contact.

"This is over for you," he said, indicating the hot, hushed afternoon, and the motionless tree growing beyond the veranda, that threw no shade on the street under the sun's vertical rays. "This—it isn't our world. We don't belong here. What have their troubles to do with us?"

"What indeed?" I heard from the doorway in a third voice. There stood Ahmet. His face was grim, and I thought it no wonder. My heart was heavy as I introduced the two men: so was the silence. Then Phil spoke easily, pleasantly, the triumphant male to his defeated rival:

"Well, it's time I was running along. I may not see much of you in the next few days, Julie—they're organizing the boys into a corps to help the Japanese knock some sense into these rebels, and I'm one of the commanding officers." I winced at his words, but after all, a person must be on one side or the other. Phil went on, grimacing in self-deprecation, "So now you know the sort of caliber we're depending on. Don't expect big things of us, will you?"

"No."

"So long, darling." He leaned over and kissed my cheek. He nodded smilingly to Ahmet and strode down the path. He was better dressed nowadays, and wore shoes.

I turned to Ahmet, but he was staring out as if he could still see Phil, though the American had swung around the corner. His face was stony.

"How are things going?" I asked at last. "Were you in danger?"

Now he looked at me, and I was frightened for his sake. His eyes were those of an animal in deep pain, and I knew that it wasn't because of Phil. I knew Ahmet. No person, even his beloved, could hurt him that much.

"Julie, it's over," he said.

"What's over? The rebellion?"

"No. I—come into our room."

There he turned and faced me, drawing a deep breath. "I've just come from a committee meeting," he said.

"You mean the Party? A Party committee?"

"Yes, of course. They—they talked about you."

It was so mystifying that I didn't try to comment, but waited while he selected further words.

"They talked about you and—I hate to say it; promise you aren't going to let it hurt you, Julie. Promise you'll hold on to yourself. They'd heard about your mother, and they were angry." He compressed his lips, and I imagined that the anger had not been all on one side. It was strange, but I did hold on to myself. The mention of my mother seemed to affect me very little: I was concentrated on Ahmet's distress. I said calmly;

"Was it like Shiga? They were angry because they'd been fooled, was that it?"

"That was it. They behaved as if we'd gone into conspiracy against them, somehow. It was ridiculous." Ahmet scowled at the memory. "Fools! They said I'd have to give you up—for the good of the Party. They said I wasn't trustworthy, or I'd have kept them informed about you. We had a scene. I hadn't realized how much some of those people hate me."

"It does sound—"

"We lost our tempers," Ahmet went on, "and it boiled down to a matter of choice. If I didn't give you up, they said, I'd be put out of the Party. So here I am, out of the Party."

"Oh darling, darling. After all these years."

His arms were around me, holding me tight. "Of course it doesn't mean I'm finished with the rest of it," he added more brightly. "The revolution goes on, and we go on with it."

I closed my eyes. I don't know if that moment meant that I was making up my mind, or if it was already made up for me. It must have been settled all the time. Yet through the morning I'd been dreaming of a very different life, I'd seen myself married to Phil and living in America, safe and contented. I almost felt as if I'd been there—standing in that kitchen, my children just outside the door, where everything was clean and quiet and safe, safe, safe . . .

Instead it was to be Ahmet.

A girl could still have broken away. A girl could have gone straight away that minute, and nobody would have stopped her, least of all Ahmet. What I could not do was think of him without me. I don't mean that he would not have survived: I am sure he would. He had something urgent to live for, with or without me, but I preferred not to think of him doing it.

He was talking softly into my ear of our life together. We would have to spend weeks in flight through the countryside, he said, and I thought of what it would be like, sleeping in flimsy shelters or out in the open on the mountainside. Hunger, heat, insects, and leeches; rain and grueling sun—but, always, Ahmet, with me to take care of him.

There had never been any other possibility. I opened my eyes and smiled.